THE SCION OF STATIC

BOOK ONE OF THE CHAINED HORIZON SERIES

Elowen Kage

First published in 2025 by MK Storyworks.

ISBN: 978-1-80700-042-4

TABLE OF CONTENTS

DEDICATION

To the misfits, the strategists, and every fragile soul who learned to turn stillness into a weapon.

THE CREED OF THE SPIRES

The Spires' motto is defiance. The ground is where history sleeps. Only the Ascended defy the fall. Only the Bonded survive the Zenith.

Fear is a momentum. Stillness is power.

PROLOGUE

THE MAGMA'S VERDICT

I watched the cadet named Torian die.

The scent of burnt ozone and iron rolled off the Convergence Circle, so thick I could taste his end. He was eighteen, built like a brick parapet, and arrogant enough to stalk directly toward the hulking elemental spirit shimmering above the stone. He hadn't even bothered to wipe the smear of mud from his cheek after the brutal Descent.

He carried the single greatest trait required of an Aetherian Conduit: unquestioning, brute strength.

He needed it. Because the creature hovering over him was not flesh, but the embodiment of raw power.

It was a Magma Aetherial, a churning, obsidian thing laced with fissures of molten orange light. It pulsed with the heat of a captured sun, and its presence alone made the air crackle. The stone platform under my boots felt soft. The air hummed with the energy the Aetherial commanded, and every soul watching—myself included—felt the crushing weight of its sheer existence.

"I am Torian," the cadet roared, his voice thick with desperate ambition, his knuckles white where he gripped his sword hilt. "Bind me! I have the strength for your fire!"

The Magma Aetherial, eyeless, seemed to consider him with the infinite, glacial patience of time itself. Torian dropped to one knee, offering his hand, palm up, in the traditional pose of submission. He was pleading for power, offering his life force for a taste of the fire that could save the world—or end him.

Suddenly, the molten core of the Aetherial surged. The entire Citadel seemed to gasp, the ancient magnetic field holding the Spires aloft protesting the strain.

Wrong, a colossal, silent thought echoed in my mind, a mental broadcast meant for every observer. *Too much noise. Not enough depth. You offer only a hammer when I require a furnace.*

The Magma Aetherial did not incinerate him. That would have been too kind. It rejected him with pure, indifferent kinetic force.

A single, thick coil of obsidian tendril slammed down. It didn't burn Torian—it struck him with the impact of a falling siege hammer, a force channeled from the magma core of the planet itself. The sound was a horrifying crack, and I felt the ground shudder under the blow.

Torian was not simply broken; he was instantly flattened, hurled across the platform like a discarded training dummy, his armor crumpling inward like dried paper. His body hit the protective magnetic railing with a sickening thump and bounced, rolling toward the edge of the Citadel.

He was still breathing. Still trying to crawl. A thin line of crimson tracked the dust as he dragged himself forward, his eyes wide and vacant. The effort was agonizingly slow, a last, desperate protest against a fate already sealed.

Below us, a thousand meters down, the Miasma waited.

I knew it wasn't a fog. It was a shifting, deep purple void—a sentient cloud of toxic energy that was slowly eating the world. Anything organic that touched it simply dissolved, silently and instantly. The sight of it alone could make a grown man tremble, knowing that centuries of lost civilizations lay dissolving in that toxic haze. The Miasma emitted a low, continuous psychic hum, a vibration that promised oblivion.

I watched Torian desperately scrabble for purchase on the slick, warm stone, his shattered fingers finding nothing but smooth air and the terrifying, empty drop. A Wing Leader shouted something—a command to help, perhaps, or a curse—but it was drowned out by the metallic grinding of the Citadel rotating on its pivot, a constant, menacing reminder of the danger. The rotation of the Spires was never truly silent, a mechanical heartbeat keeping them aloft.

Torian's momentum, too great to overcome, carried him over the edge.

He did not scream. He did not cry. He simply fell. I watched his body disappear, a rapidly shrinking speck, before the Miasma swallowed him whole, absorbed without a sound or trace. It was the quickest, most silent death in Aeris, a perfect erasure.

The Magma Aetherial merely pulsed, contracting its vast, glowing form. The obsidian cooled, the orange light receding slightly, as if bored by the entire event. The air immediately felt clearer, the overwhelming heat receding, leaving behind a cold, hard finality.

The Ascended defy the fall, the creature's silent thought whispered across my mind-link. *But only the worthy may attempt the climb.*

The message was clear: In the Spires of the Zenith, there were no second chances. You bonded, or you became nothing but a whisper in the toxic purple haze.

And they were calling my name next.

CHAPTER 1

THE ASCENT OF BONE AND IRON

Ihad trained my entire life for the quiet, for the safety of silence, but my mother had decided that silence was not what Aeris needed. It needed a weapon.

My name, Lyssa Varen, was called. It resonated over the roar of a thousand desperate, terrified candidates, amplified by the same brass megaphones used to broadcast the daily casualty counts. The sound felt like a physical blow against my ears, a cruel mockery of the quiet life I'd been robbed of.

The ground was a mess of churned mud and adrenaline. Below the towering, impossibly complex architecture of the Spires of the Zenith, the staging field felt like a slaughterhouse disguised as a boot camp. Cadets—all of them trained since childhood for this exact moment—stood shoulder-to-shoulder, their heavy wool uniforms already stained with the fear-sweat of the morning. Most of them were hard, wide, and steady.

I was not one of them. I was a ghost among giants.

I was meant to be across the field, in the small, organized line for the Archivist Quadrant. I should have been receiving my inkwell and my charter to begin my life cataloging the secrets of the Miasma, precisely as my late father had intended. I was good with numbers, with history, with the quiet power of preserved knowledge.

Instead, I was being shoved toward the queue marked *Aetherian Conduit.*

The Riders. The quadrant with a fifty-percent mortality rate within the first month.

"Move it, Varen!" A drill sergeant, all brawn and gravel voice, clipped my shoulder with an elbow, forcing me into line behind a behemoth of a man whose neck was thicker than my waist. The scent of unwashed wool, fear, and damp earth choked the air, a physical manifestation of the crushing pressure.

Every step was an exercise in calculated endurance. The movement sent a familiar, dull ache radiating from my hips to my knees. My condition—a rare, degenerative weakness in the connective tissues—meant that physical exertion cost me double. My muscles demanded more oxygen, more energy, just to manage the weight of my simple pack and uniform. I was small, slight, and brittle. The General of the Spires, my mother, was a woman carved from granite and fueled by reputation. She knew this, yet she had condemned me anyway.

"Your intellect is wasted on dusty scrolls, Lyssa," she had said two days ago, her eyes cold as winter ice, not seeing her daughter but a flawed component of her military machine. "Your heritage demands you defend Aeris. The Archival Quadrant is for the cowards who cannot fight. You will be a Conduit. Survive or fail, your name serves the Spires."

It was a punishment cloaked as duty, designed to either break me or forge me, and I resented her equally for both possibilities. Her indifference was more damning than any death sentence; it was the abandonment of a mother in favor of a legacy.

I adjusted the heavy pack on my back, the leather biting into my shoulders. It held nothing necessary for the trek—only regulations demanded we carry provisions. All I truly carried was the weight of my mother's reputation and the targets it painted on my back.

The cadets here weren't just terrified; they were vicious. They had fought for years for this chance, sacrificing comfort, family, and sometimes limbs, for a shot at ascension. Me? I was a General's daughter who had stolen a spot from someone stronger, someone more deserving. I felt their resentment like the static charge before a storm. I was a lightning rod in a crowd of desperate conductors.

My eyes lifted, past the mud and the chaos, to the Spires of the Zenith themselves.

They didn't look like a school. They looked like a challenge thrown down by the gods. They were a network of colossal, spiraling stone structures that pierced the perpetual clouds, held in place by massive, humming magnetic fields—the only defense against the Miasma below. They were built on a core of condensed, raw Aetheric energy. I knew from the Archival scrolls that the Spires were slowly dying, the magnetic defenses weakening, and that the Dragon-equivalent Aetherials were the only things powerful enough to recharge them. The fate of Aeris rested entirely on the survival of these brutal towers.

The line began to move. We were being directed toward the first test. It wasn't the Convergence—that came later, where the Aetherials chose their human batteries. This was simply The Crossing.

I watched the first ten cadets reach the base of the canyon. A loud, sharp whistle split the air, and the next sequence of the day began.

The canyon, carved eons ago by a geothermal river, was a jagged gap about thirty meters wide and several hundred meters deep. Spanning it was the Parapet, not a solid bridge, but a series of worn, heavy chains anchored to iron spikes on either side. It was a gauntlet of loose stone and frayed strands, designed to test footing and nerve, demanding precise weight distribution and minimal horizontal movement.

The rule was simple: cross the chains, reach the vertical platform on the other side, and board the Ascension Elevator up to the Spires.

The unspoken reality was simpler: Fall, and you die. And the Aetherian Cadets weren't always killed by the fall. Sometimes, a disgruntled rival gave them a gentle, lethal shove.

I watched two more cadets fall—one due to a misstep, one due to a deliberate clip from a woman in the group ahead. Both fell in silence, the air pressure stealing their screams before they were swallowed by the Miasma. Just another statistic, already forgotten.

I flinched, biting the inside of my cheek until I tasted blood. The taste of salt and iron brought my focus back. My hands were shaking, and it wasn't fear, not exactly. It was the physical response to adrenaline and the exhaustion already setting in.

Panic is momentum, I repeated the core principle of my personal philosophy, a philosophy born not from Archival scrolls, but from managing my own body's constant betrayal. *Stillness is power.* The more controlled my movements, the less energy I wasted, the longer my body would hold out.

I watched the movement of the chains. The sway. The momentum. The cadets who tried to rush, who relied on raw power, were losing their balance due to the uneven shifts of weight from their peers. The chains were constantly in motion, a pendulum waiting for the perfect moment to throw someone off balance. I identified the rhythm: a six-second primary sway, followed by two seconds of near-stillness. That was my window.

My turn was approaching, and I knew exactly what I could not do. I could not rely on grip strength, which would fail me quickly. I could not rely on speed. I had to rely on observation.

As the next group was cleared to proceed, I pushed myself forward, stepping onto the first chain during the two-second equilibrium window. The rough iron bit through the thin soles of my mandated boots. The chain immediately swayed, and a wave of nausea hit me, but I used the small movement to gently settle my weight, maintaining my center mass.

I ignored it. I planted my feet and calculated my next step, not based on the distance to the next anchor, but on the vibration of the chains. Every step was a strategic placement, a decision to neutralize the momentum of the previous cadet and maintain my own center of gravity, a quiet, almost meditative dance. I was a counterbalance, moving with the rhythmic energy of the bridge, turning the motion against itself.

I was three-quarters of the way across when a voice, deep and laced with malice, spoke from behind me.

"Look at the General's pathetic fawn. She can barely manage a walk."

I didn't turn. I didn't acknowledge the massive figure approaching—a third-year cadet, easily a meter taller than me, whose face I vaguely recognized from my brief stint at the Archival Library. His name was Roric—failed out of the Riders Quadrant last year for arrogance and forced to retake the Descent. He had nothing to lose and everything to prove by eliminating a General's daughter.

"Watch your footing, fawn," he sneered, and then he deliberately jumped down onto the chains, landing with a jarring impact that felt like a localized earthquake.

The chains bucked violently, swinging in a chaotic arc. The movement was instant and brutal, intended to snap my small grip. My arms screamed in protest, and my knees nearly gave way. The metal screeched a frantic protest.

But I had anticipated the disruption. At the moment the chains hit the peak of their swing, I didn't try to pull myself toward the anchor. Instead, I released my upper-hand grip and threw my weight down and out, using the momentum of the swing itself to stabilize my lower body against the chains. I let the motion pass through me, focusing on the sheer stillness of my core, absorbing the kinetic shock through controlled tension.

I was the point of rest in a storm of kinetic energy.

I didn't fall. The cadet behind me, Roric, relying on brute strength, was thrown off balance by his own aggressive motion, cursing loudly as he wrestled to regain his purchase.

I used his brief moment of chaos. I darted the last five steps, ignoring the burning ache in my muscles—my tendons felt like taut bowstrings ready to snap—and lunged onto the solid rock of the receiving platform.

I leaned against the stone, gasping, my whole body trembling, not from fear, but from the physical toll. I had survived the Parapet, the first deliberate attempt on my life.

Roric reached the platform seconds later, his face purple with anger, his massive hands clenched. He loomed over me, blocking the faint daylight. "That was lucky, Varen. The Spires are a long climb. You won't be able to dodge every push." He kept his voice a low, gravelly whisper, preventing the drill sergeant from hearing the overt threat. "We don't need deadweight from your mother's bedchamber."

Before he could advance, a hand clamped down on my arm, not a gentle touch, but a firm, anchoring pull.

"The rules state you must maintain a forward pace," a low, measured voice stated.

I looked up at a girl whose face was covered in a lattice of fine, dark scars—scars I recognized from the brutal, unchanneled Aetheric energy burns that often occurred during practice. Her name was Eysa, and she had the quiet, haunted look of someone who has already seen too much of the Spires' cruelty. She gave Roric a curt, cold look that held no fear.

"Walk, Varen," Eysa ordered, pulling me firmly toward a narrow, winding path that led higher up the cliff face. "Don't give him an excuse to finish the job." She didn't offer sympathy, only a mutual understanding of survival.

We moved quickly. The path wound around the precipice, forcing us to keep our focus on the rough, unpolished stone. The air here was thinner, cooler, and tasted of the metal in the Ascension Elevator cables. The terrifying purple sheen of the Miasma was closer now, swirling below the cliff edge like a vast, hungry ocean. It made the small hairs on my arms stand up—a physical echo of the raw, deadly Aetheric energy it contained. I could feel the residual heat from the Magma Aetherial's rejection still radiating from the cliff face.

The elevator platform awaited, a wide, open plate of iron large enough to hold about forty cadets. Already, thirty or so cadets—the survivors of the Parapet—stood in tight, nervous clusters, their adrenaline levels visibly dropping into exhaustion.

As Eysa and I stepped onto the iron, she murmured, her eyes flicking across the crowd, "Stay on the edges. The middle is reserved for those who think they matter. And try not to look terrified. They feed on it."

I nodded, grateful for the curt advice. We found a spot near the heavy, rust-colored cable that hoisted the platform, placing the immense bulk of the machinery between us and the center of the crowd.

It was then I saw him.

He wasn't standing in the crowded center of the platform. He was leaning against the far railing, utterly alone, radiating a silent, compressed intensity that drew the eye and chilled the blood.

Teron Draken.

Wing Leader. The most lethal third-year cadet in the Spires. And the son of the rebel leader whose execution my mother, General Varen, had commanded five years ago. He was a symbol of resistance to some, and a constant, living threat to the General's regime. He wore the black uniform of the highest-ranking cadets, and his Signet—Void Energy—was notorious for its raw, crushing power.

He was tall, built with lean, economical muscle, and possessed a severe, angular handsomeness. His black hair was slicked back from a sharp widow's peak, and his eyes—the startling, bright silver typical of those bonded to the most dangerous Aetherials—were fixed on the Miasma, as if counting the dead. He was an embodiment of controlled fury.

Our eyes met for a fraction of a second. His silver gaze was not accusatory or angry; it was worse. It was pure, freezing indifference, the kind a predator reserves for prey too small to warrant a chase. He knew exactly who I was, and the look in his eyes promised that my death was inevitable, whether by his hand or the Spires' trials.

I quickly turned away, my heart pounding a panicked rhythm against my ribs. He was the single most dangerous creature in the Spires.

The drill sergeant from before stepped onto the platform, clapping his hands. "Forty up! Ascension begins! The weak are culled. The worthy rise! Congratulations, maggots. Now, look up, and greet your new home!"

The ancient machinery of the Spires groaned to life. The iron platform shuddered, and with a metallic, screaming whine, we began our climb. The world below—the ground, the crowds, the corpses—shrank instantly. We rose into the perpetual gloom and the cold, thin air that surrounded the floating Citadel. The magnetic hum surrounding the platform grew louder, a deep, resonant chord that felt like it was vibrating the very bones in my chest. Below us, the Miasma looked like a waiting, velvet cloak of death.

I didn't dare look at Teron Draken again, but I could feel the invisible, kinetic field between us. He was a master of stillness, of contained destructive power. I was an acolyte of strategic balance.

Fear is a momentum, I reminded myself, forcing a slow, steady breath into my burning lungs as the elevator cable stretched higher and higher, pulling us toward the unknown danger of the Zenith. *Stillness is power.* And I desperately needed every ounce of it to survive the next five minutes, let alone the next five years.

The true test had just begun.

CHAPTER 2

THE FOURTH BARRACKS AND
THE CHILL OF COMMAND

The ascent had been a silent, agonizing twenty minutes, a dizzying crawl up the sheer, crystalline flank of the Spires. When the heavy brass doors of the elevator finally hissed open, I stumbled out onto a landing chilled by mountain wind and the oppressive weight of history.

The air here was thin, sharp, and biting, carrying the sterile, metallic tang of the Aetherium, the raw magic that was said to course through the very stone of the Spires, holding them aloft against the forces of gravity and the creeping Miasma below. I braced my palms on the icy granite archway, fighting the dizzying effects of the altitude and the violent tremors still shaking me from the death-defying Crossing. I forced my analytical mind to take control: *Stabilize the core. Slow the heart. Survival is a siege—treat every breath as a resource.* My body was a brittle cage of fragile joints and over-stretched sinew, but my mind was the most powerful weapon I possessed, and I would wield it with ruthless efficiency.

The corridor was a monolithic nightmare of polished obsidian and dark granite, lined with colossal, judging statues of legendary Zenith riders and their massive, armored Aetherials. Every face was grim, unyielding. Here, the weak didn't just fail; they were incinerated, their names instantly scrubbed from existence. The silence, broken only by the whistling wind outside the narrow arrow slits, felt like a judgment in itself.

A stern-faced Quartermaster, silver-haired and clad in heavy, unadorned leather, waited for the group of twenty-two surviving cadets. He didn't bother with a roster; he pointed a rigid, unforgiving finger at a section of wall where massive, metal plaques were already embossed with names and assignments.

"Find your Barracks. Training begins at dawn, and it will not wait for the injured," the Quartermaster stated, his voice a dry rasp that echoed too loudly in the chilling space. "If you fail to report, the Spire guards will ensure you meet the Miasma before noon. There are only two ways out of the Zenith: graduation or the drop."

I pushed through the exhausted, defeated crowd. Dread, cold and familiar, settled deep in my stomach when my eyes finally fixed on my name.

Varen, Lyssa: Fourth Barracks.

The Fourth Barracks. The name was notorious. It was the furthest barracks from the primary training wards, located in the oldest, draftiest wing. It was reserved for the "least promising" cadets, the ones Command—specifically my mother, General Varen—fully expected to be eliminated in the first, brutal waves of attrition. It was where potential fatalities were stored out of sight, maximizing the illusion of order elsewhere. I saw the assignment for what it was: a death warrant concealed as an administrative act.

I located Eysa's name next to mine—a small, much-needed comfort—and then scanned further down the list. Roric was there, his name practically radiating malice from the metal. But the final name on the plaque sent a chill that permeated my bones:

Draken, Teron: Fourth Barracks. Wingleader.

Teron Draken. The son of the executed rebel leader. The man who saw me only as the embodiment of my mother's unforgivable crimes. The problem was compounded: he was assigned as the Wingleader for the entire Fourth Barracks. This wasn't just a storage unit for failures; it was a strategically placed den of wolves, and I was the fresh, vulnerable bait placed deliberately in the center.

As if summoned by my rising terror, a shadow, impossibly dense, fell over me.

"Well, well. The General's prized little Scion of Static gets the Fourth Barracks." The voice was low, resonant, and utterly devoid of warmth.

Teron Draken was leaning against the stone archway, arms crossed over the brutal efficiency of his black tunic. The fabric stretched across the immense width of his shoulders and chest, a testament to a strength I knew I could never match. His eyes—a startling, glacial grey, like frozen water—were fixed on me. The omnipresent press of the Void Energy of his bonded Aetherial, Morgal, seemed to warp the very air around him, making the fine hairs on my arms stand on end.

I straightened my spine until I felt a faint protest in my fragile joints, forcing the violent tremors down. *Do not flinch. Do not look away. He feeds on fear.*

"The sorting is administrative, Wingleader Draken," I replied, my voice steady, an iron sheath around my rising panic.

"No, Varen," he corrected, pushing off the cold wall. The sound of his boots on the granite was soft, predatory. "The sorting is a formality. The placement is a death sentence."

He took a deliberate, menacing step closer, his gaze raking over my slender frame, cataloging my inherent weakness. "Everyone in the Fourth knows why you're here. You're a liability, a symbol, and a piece of bait. Survive, or don't. Either way, it brings me closer to the day I see your mother pay for her crimes. But be warned: if your incompetence endangers my squad during training, I will not wait for the Miasma to claim you."

He walked away, leaving me with the heavy weight of his vow.

Eysa and I followed the winding, cold corridors to the Fourth Barracks. The room was immense, a large, rectangular space dominated by forty simple, steel-framed bunks. The bunks were tiered, stacked three high, offering no privacy and little comfort. The air was stale, already thick with the scent of damp wool and fear.

We claimed two bottom bunks near a window that offered a terrifying view of the sheer drop to the clouds below. As I unpacked, carefully folding my civilian clothes and arranging my leather-bound scribe journals under the mattress, a new face approached.

"That's the General's girl, right? Lyssa Varen?"

The voice was sharp, laced with undisguised contempt. The speaker was a tall, athletic woman with closely cropped auburn hair and the muscular frame of someone who had trained relentlessly for this moment. This was Vera Silo, a fifth-year Cadet held back for an injury, now repeating the first year and notorious for her brutal efficiency.

"I am Lyssa Varen," I confirmed, keeping my tone measured, non-aggressive.

Vera sneered, gesturing toward the journals I had set aside. "Look at that. Bringing books to a death match. Listen, Scion. This barracks is a chain. One weak link drags us all down, and you're a paper-thin thread. You get one chance to keep up. After that, Roric won't be the only one hoping you misstep during formation." She tapped a finger sharply on my bunk frame. "Don't waste the good air we breathe."

Vera walked away, joining a cluster of other physically dominant cadets who watched me with cold, judging eyes.

Eysa leaned in conspiratorially. "Vera is a Blazer—Magma Aetherial potential. They're the physical beasts of the Spires. She truly believes being the General's daughter means you've taken a spot from someone more deserving."

"In a way, she's right," I admitted, but I didn't let my gaze drop. I was an intruder here, and I had to survive the internal warfare before the external one. "But if they want me gone, they'll to have to out-think me, not just out-muscle me."

At the sound of a distant, ringing bell, the cadets began shuffling out for the mandatory evening meal. The Mess Hall was a cavernous space where the entire student body—the Infantry, the Healers, the Scribes, and the elite Riders Quadrant—congregated. It was a visual representation of the Zenith hierarchy.

The Riders Quadrant tables were elevated on a small dais, giving them an air of almost god-like status. As a first-year Rider Cadet, my peers and I were seated on the lowest, longest tables, closest to the serving line and furthest from the light.

Eysa and I sat, with Roric and his sullen group just a few seats away. The silence around us was a heavy blanket, thicker than the stew we were served. Every gaze in the room seemed to drift toward the tables occupied by the Wingleaders—the powerful, often cruel, upper-year students who oversaw the first-year groups.

I was peeling a tough piece of bread when my eyes, almost involuntarily, lifted to the Wingleader's table. Teron Draken was seated at the head, surrounded by other Wingleaders. They were not talking or laughing; they were simply eating with quiet, devastating efficiency. Teron, in particular, moved with the stark economy of a killing machine.

Then, his gaze lifted. It cut through the hazy steam and the noise of cutlery, locking onto mine.

It wasn't a glare of pure hatred, but something colder, more analytical—like a seasoned General measuring a siege target. He didn't move a muscle, but the message was clear: *I see you. You are in my sight lines. I am waiting for you to make a mistake.*

I knew I should break contact, look down, and hide my fear. But doing so would confirm my weakness. Instead, I performed a meticulous, psychological maneuver: I held his gaze for a second longer than was comfortable, allowed the faintest flicker of challenge to cross my features, and then turned my attention back to my plate, resuming the slow, rhythmic process of eating. I gave him no quarter, no visible panic, only the calculated indifference of a mind already five moves ahead.

The brief, intense connection broke, but the electricity remained, humming in the air between the tables. Teron Draken hadn't won a confrontation; he had simply been reminded that I, fragile as I was, possessed an unusual, steely nerve.

I am not just bait, Wingleader Draken, I thought, my teeth grinding on the tough bread. *I am a strategist, and I am already observing your movements.*

The challenge had been officially accepted. Now all I needed was the power to back it up.

CHAPTER 3

FIRST CLASSES AND THE WHISPER OF STATIC

The training schedule at the Zenith Spires was designed not to build strength, but to burn away all possibility of failure in a slow, agonizing fire. If the Miasma didn't get me, exhaustion or my fellow cadets would. The first classes were dedicated to basic combat conditioning, sparring, and aerial theory—all brutal reminders of my inherent disadvantage.

The Saber Ward was a cavernous dome carved into the heart of the main Spire, its floor a mosaic of hardened, ancient leather. The air was loud, thick with grunts, the clang of steel, and the heavy, humid smell of sweat and polished metal. The atmosphere was one of calculated, aggressive noise, a stark contrast to the chilling silence of the corridors.

I stood stiffly in the back row, clad in simple, padded training leathers that felt more like a costume than protection. I wasn't weak, I was fragile. My joints were prone to painful misalignment, and my slender build meant I lacked the muscle mass to absorb a significant blow. My defense was not strength; it was anticipation.

Wingleader Draken commanded the entire training floor, a black monolith of effortless power. He moved among the first-year cadets, his voice a low, carrying command that required no shouting. When he spoke, the noise in the massive hall seemed to dim, a testament to the primal deference his Void Energy commanded. He was conducting the drill—a relentless, timed sequence of defensive blocks and counter-strikes using dulled, wooden sabers.

"Movement is power. Hesitation is death," Draken's voice sliced through the din. "If you spend a single second reacting, your Aetherial will incinerate your corpse."

I knew the sequences perfectly. I had memorized the Scribe texts, visualized the maneuvers, and calculated the necessary footwork for maximum stability. But applying theory to my body felt like trying to force a river to flow uphill. My left ankle, still bruised from the Crossing, screamed with every pivot.

Eysa, positioned beside me, was faring only slightly better. Eysa was stronger but lacked my theoretical knowledge, her movements frantic and inefficient. "I'm going to pass out," Eysa muttered, wiping sweat from her brow.

"Don't," I whispered back, my own breathing tight. "Focus on your opponent's center of gravity, not the blade. Anticipate the shift in mass."

Draken was now moving down our line. I saw his eyes, those piercing glacial gray irises, track me with cold scrutiny. He wasn't looking for failure; he was looking for justification for my elimination.

"Varen. Your pivot is lazy. You lean into the strike, confirming your weakness." His words were low, for my ears only, a cutting personal judgment. "If you rely on your body, you're dead before Threshing. Find another path, or fail swiftly."

Find another path. The words burrowed into my mind. I had another path: the Kinetic Resonance that lay dormant within me. But it wasn't a physical power; it was a theoretical one, a phantom of pure motion. How could I access something that felt like a quiet hum beneath the violent chaos of combat?

Draken called the next drill: Free Sparring.

"Pairs. First to disarm or incapacitate. No Signets. No exceptions."

My heart hammered against my ribs. I was paired with Roric, the hulking cadet whose animosity ran deeper than training rivalry. He grinned, a nasty, predatory flash of teeth.

"Looks like the Miasma doesn't get to you first, Scion," Roric growled, raising his wooden saber. "I promised you'd pay for your mother's arrogance."

My mind instantly began calculating. Roric was a brute. His attacks would be powerful but predictable, relying on vertical force and sweeping arcs. I needed to rely on footwork and minimal contact defense, absorbing his brute strength through deflection, not frontal blocking.

The signal horn blared.

Roric charged.

He moved with the heavy momentum of a falling tree, a massive, overhead strike designed to shatter my guard. I barely managed to bring my saber up, catching the blow high. The impact was still enormous; a blinding shockwave ripped up my arms, stinging my elbows and sending a searing spike of pain into my shoulder socket. I stumbled backward, the saber rattling in my numb fingers.

"Too slow, General's girl!" Roric roared, pressing the advantage.

He began a relentless assault, swinging with the goal of inflicting pain, not just winning the match. I moved on pure instinct, weaving and retreating. I blocked a hard low thrust, forcing a wince. I deflected a cross-body strike, feeling the jarring vibration in my fragile wrist. I was a leaf against a gale, my energy draining with terrifying speed. *I can't last another five strikes. My stamina is collapsing.*

Then, Roric wound up for a final, catastrophic blow—a massive, side-sweeping arc aimed at my temple, intended to knock me unconscious or, worse, break my neck.

In that micro-second before impact, everything slowed.

I didn't think about blocking; I thought about stillness. I thought about zero.

A cold, silent clarity descended upon my mind, eliminating the panic, the pain, and the noise. I wasn't focusing on my saber; I was focusing on the kinetic energy Roric's entire body was generating—the pure, raw motion pouring from his swing, intended to transfer lethal force into my head.

Stop it.

It was a whisper in the deepest, most quiet corner of my consciousness. And something answered.

A faint, ice-cold ripple spread from my solar plexus, washing outward like a wave of silent, crystalline light. It didn't feel like fire or electricity; it felt like a deep vacuum absorbing all ambient motion.

The tip of Roric's wooden saber made contact with my

guard, but the expected, catastrophic force was not there.

The massive kinetic energy of his swing—the vector, the momentum, the destructive motion—had been subtly, surgically neutralized. His saber rebounded off mine not with a shattering impact, but with a dull, anti-climactic thud.

Roric, relying on the momentum to carry him through the block, was left dramatically over-extended, his center of gravity completely compromised. The sheer force of his own motion, suddenly unrestrained by the collision, pulled him off balance. He stumbled, his huge frame staggering two steps to the side, ending in a wide-legged, clumsy stagger.

I, still in that moment of stillness, saw my opening. With a swift, mechanical movement that surprised even me, I side-stepped his momentum and, instead of striking, I simply lowered my own saber and tapped the inside of Roric's wrist. The touch, insignificant in terms of strength, was enough to complete the disarming.

Roric's massive, wooden saber clattered loudly onto the leather floor.

The Saber Ward went silent.

Roric stared, his jaw slack, not in pain, but in sheer, bewildered shock. He hadn't been hit; he had simply stopped. It was as if the laws of physics had paused their service to him alone.

I stood motionless, breathing hard but whole, my heart now racing, not from fear, but from the terrifying, exhilarating shock of the power I had just accessed.

Draken's voice, colder than the Spire granite, cut through the silence. "Saber down. Varen wins. Roric, retrieve your weapon."

Roric scowled, his face twisting into a silent, venomous vow, but he obeyed. I had won the match, but I knew I had just lost all cover. The sheer improbability of my victory would not go unnoticed.

The rest of the morning dissolved into a blur of numb fatigue. I performed the remaining drills by relying on my razor-sharp focus, attempting to recreate that moment of absolute stillness, but the power remained dormant—a closed door I couldn't remember how I'd opened.

At the mid-day meal, Eysa grabbed my arm. "What did you do to Roric? He looked like a puppet whose strings were cut. No one beats Roric in sparring, especially not a Scribe-in-training."

"I utilized his momentum against him," I explained, choosing my words carefully, a practiced habit from a lifetime of concealing my fragile health. "He overcommitted to the swing. I simply minimized the resistance at the point of impact."

"Minimized the resistance?" Eysa stared. "Lyssa, he hit you with the force of a battering ram! The shockwave alone should have sent you through the wall. I saw your guard wobble. Then… it didn't. That wasn't physics, that was something else."

I knew Eysa was right. The sensation had been utterly alien—not force, but the absence of force. I had tapped into the fundamental principle of the Kinetic Resonance: the manipulation of motion itself. It was the whisper of pure kinetic flow.

I changed the subject instantly. "Forget Roric. Look at the

Wingleaders' table." Draken was there, his gaze fixed on his plate. His presence, though, felt like a directed, heavy silence. I felt a creeping certainty that he hadn't missed the anomaly in my sparring match.

The afternoon consisted of Aetherial Theory, conducted in a vast, tiered lecture hall. The lecturer, a wizened, ancient man named Master Eldrin, had a voice like grinding stones and treated the cadets with barely concealed disdain.

"The Aetherial Bond is not a partnership; it is a servitude," Eldrin droned. "Your purpose is to channel your Aetherial's power—their Signet—to protect the Spires and their wards. You are merely the key to the lock. The power belongs to them. The Signet determines your value."

Eldrin proceeded to detail the primary Aetherials: the Magma (Blazers), who manipulate heat and earth; the Torrent (Sleekers), who command water and ice; and the rarest and most feared, the Void (Draken's type), who wield the gravity of density, the power of suppression.

I hung on every word, furiously taking notes in my scribe's script, focusing on the mechanics. When Eldrin reached the category of Light Aetherials—the class to which my nascent power belonged—my muscles tensed.

"The Light Aetherials are the most unpredictable. They bond with conduits who possess extreme internal control and focus. Their Signets typically involve manipulation of light, sound, or kinetics—pure motion." Eldrin sneered. "They are small, rare, and considered less valuable in the field due to their limited raw destructive power. Their abilities are often defensive, strategic, or simply strange. The only recorded Kinetic Conduit in the last fifty years was executed for treachery."

Treason. The Spires truly did specialize in placing me among the unwanted and the disgraced.

After the lecture, exhausted but energized by the information, I made a beeline for the Scribe Archive. The vast library was a sanctuary of quiet, the one place my training gave me an advantage. I bypassed the open reading rooms and headed for the restricted section, using my father's old, familiar Scribe access codes.

I needed to find every available text on Kinetic Signets and Resonance Absorption.

In the flickering gaslight of the deep stacks, I found a single, thin, and brittle text: *The Doctrine of the Still Point: Principles of Kinetic Displacement.*

The text was dry and academic, but the content was a revelation. It confirmed my theory: the Kinetic Signet wasn't about creation, but precision.

"The Kinetic Conduit does not generate force; they sense the vector and magnitude of an existing motion and, through absolute stillness of the self, can create a momentary vacuum, disrupting the flow of energy at the point of impact. They are a fulcrum of zero resistance."

This explained Roric's stumble. I hadn't stopped the blow; I had redirected its entire force into nothingness, leaving him only with the inertia of his own body.

"The danger is twofold: First, the Conduit must achieve absolute internal silence, a focus that exceeds human capability under stress. Second, attempting to absorb energy greater than the Conduit's own physical limit will result in the fracturing of the self, transferring the residual, unabsorbed kinetic force back into the body with catastrophic results."

This was my limitation. I couldn't absorb a powerful punch from a Magma Aetherial rider, or a Void blast from Draken, without my fragile body collapsing inward. My power was for strategy, not brute force. I had to fight smart, always using the minimum possible force for the maximum strategic effect.

As I finished transcribing the most critical passages, a deep, unsettling sense of being watched prickled the hairs on my neck. I slammed the brittle book shut and turned slowly.

Standing silently between the tall stacks, his shadow falling across me like a crushing weight, was Teron Draken. He wasn't in uniform; he was wearing simple black trousers and a close-fitting linen shirt that barely contained his muscular build. He looked less like a soldier and more like a warrior taking a brief, dangerous pause.

"You're supposed to be in your Barracks, Cadet Varen," he said, his voice quiet, dangerously intimate in the silence of the archives.

"I am studying the history of the Spires, Wingleader Draken. A legitimate academic pursuit. As a Scribe's daughter, I'm uniquely qualified for it."

He ignored my retort, his eyes narrowing on the stack of brittle, classified texts beside me. "You weren't looking at history. You were looking at power. Tell me, Varen. What exactly did you do to Roric in the Ward?"

I forced myself to remain calm. I knew he had detected the anomaly. Lying now would only confirm my guilt.

"I was faster," I said simply.

Teron took a slow, deliberate step closer, making my entire

body tense. The space between us felt electrified. "You were not faster. Roric is twice your mass, three times your speed. I saw your eyes, Varen. They went… still. They went silent right before the impact. You are capable of something beyond simple deflection."

He stepped right into my personal space, the sheer physical force of him overwhelming the cold air. "My father died because your mother was arrogant enough to believe she could judge his motives. I am not arrogant. I am methodical. And I do not tolerate threats."

He reached out a large, calloused hand, not to touch me, but to block my path, forcing me to confront him. I inhaled sharply, my senses screaming. The ambient energy—the kinetic hum of the Spires themselves—felt closer, waiting.

"If you are the anomaly I suspect you are—a rare Light Aetherial Signet—you will be targeted. By your enemies, and perhaps by your allies. You are a threat to my plan, Varen. If you're going to survive, you need to understand the fundamental laws of the Zenith Spires."

"And what is that, Wingleader?" I managed to ask, my voice barely a thread.

He leaned in, the raw heat of his body a jarring contrast to the ice in his eyes. "That in this college, the only thing more deadly than the Miasma, is loyalty. And I am loyal to only one thing: vengeance."

He straightened, the moment of tension shattering, and then, with a casual disregard that was more menacing than any threat, he stepped away, leaving me trembling in the silent archive. I knew then that the danger was no longer just the Spires—it was the intense, volatile proximity to Teron Draken, a man who would watch my every move until I either failed or became powerful enough to stop him. And for a Scion of a powerful General, becoming powerful was perhaps the fastest way to fail.

CHAPTER 4

THE VOID AND THE VOW

I couldn't sleep. The silence of the Fourth Barracks was thick with unspoken threats and the collective exhaustion of the day's brutal training. The air remained perpetually frigid, a cold reminder that we were miles above the warm, breathable lower lands, clinging to a crystalline peak in the grip of the wind. Even my thin, standard-issue blanket provided little comfort.

I had spent hours mentally replaying the duel with Roric, analyzing the moment of Kinetic Resonance. It was still an anomaly—a fleeting, perfect moment of stillness I could not consciously recreate. The theoretical texts in the Archives had confirmed the potential power, but also the lethal risk: the fracturing of the self if I absorbed more force than my body could handle. It was a power requiring meditative control and discipline, not brute strength, making it an entirely mental Signet.

I glanced at the bunk directly across the aisle. Teron Draken slept on the lowest tier, his presence a dark, gravitational anchor in the room. Even asleep, he exuded a sense of latent, immense power, the Void Energy humming low around him like the deepest bass note of a vast, unseen organ. I realized he was the central problem. His hostility was not random; it was political, personal, and meticulously planned. I couldn't fight an enemy whose motives I didn't fully grasp.

Slipping silently from my bunk, I pulled on my dark leathers. I needed to know the truth behind the Execution of the Marked Ones, the rebellion that had claimed Teron's father, Lord Karsus Draken.

The Scribe Archives were deserted late at night. The gaslights were dimmed to mere pinpricks, casting long, menacing shadows that danced with the currents of air. I navigated the winding stacks by memory, feeling the familiar comfort of the parchment and ink, a world far less brutal than the training grounds.

I sought the highly restricted *Navarre Civil Doctrine, Volume III*—the official record of the rebellion and the subsequent trial. The digital files were too easy to alter. True history lay in the sealed physical texts.

Using my father's old access card and a sequence of calculated override commands, the heavy, iron gate to the Cursed Documents section hissed open. I slid inside, the air immediately turning colder, weighted down by centuries of recorded tragedy.

I found the volume, a massive, lead-bound book, on the highest shelf. Dusting it off, I carried it to a reading table, the weight of the book feeling ominous in my hands. I flipped past endless, dry pages of military protocols and judicial findings until I reached the section dated 'The Karsus Rebellion: Trial and Verdict.'

The text began clinically, describing the Draken Family as the leaders of the Northern Province's revolt against the Spires' rigid control over Aetherial resources. The standard narrative taught in the academies painted Lord Karsus Draken as a greedy, reckless traitor who sought to dismantle the protective Wards of Navarre for personal gain. His execution, and the forced service of his surviving children—the 'Marked Ones'—were portrayed as necessary, brutal justice delivered by General Lilith Varen.

I skimmed the official verdict, but my eyes snagged on a single, frayed piece of parchment tucked into the gutter of the page, sealed only with a thin layer of hardened wax, not the General's official seal. It was an unofficial, handwritten Communique from Field Commander A. Sorre (Anya Sorre, my mother's maiden name). It was dated the day before the official execution.

I broke the brittle seal with trembling fingers and unfolded the document. The elegant, familiar script of my mother swam before my eyes:

Communique: Subject Karsus – Status RED

To the Supreme Council:

The traitor Karsus is apprehended. He offered no significant resistance, believing his capture would force a dialogue. His core claim is that the Northern Wards are failing due to a rapid environmental decay that the Spires are ignoring, not from enemy attack. He has presented undeniable evidence, including crystalline decay patterns, that suggest the current threat is not from the external enemy, but from internal systemic failure.

I find his evidence compelling and his motivation genuine: a preemptive, desperate action to save the Northern Province from collapse, not treason. He is not seeking to dissolve the wards, but to force the Zenith to acknowledge the decay and implement systemic change, a change the Council has continuously rejected.

However, my duty to the Council and the necessity of immediate, visible political control overrides any potential truth to his claims. To admit systemic failure is to invite panic and mass rebellion. Karsus and his followers must therefore be executed under the charge of treason to solidify the narrative of external threat.

Recommendation: Execution to proceed at dawn. The truth regarding the systemic failure must be permanently suppressed. The threat of the Miasma must be publicly amplified as external.

—Field Commander A. Sorre.

I gasped, a small, choked sound that died instantly in the silent archive. My hands began to shake uncontrollably, not with physical weakness, but with sheer moral shock.

It wasn't a righteous conviction; it was a lie.

Teron Draken's father hadn't been a traitor driven by greed; he had been a whistle-blower driven by desperate truth. The reason for his execution was not justice, but political necessity—the cover-up of a catastrophic, looming environmental disaster. The "external enemy" was a fabrication, a narrative my mother had deliberately created and enforced with the blood of innocents, all to prevent the Spires from falling into panic.

I sank onto the cold stone bench, the full weight of the truth crushing me. My mother, the revered General Lilith Varen, was not a hero; she was a master architect of deception. And Teron Draken was not a vengeful brat; he was the son of a martyr who died for the truth.

This realization fundamentally shifted my reality and our conflict. My position was clear: I was not just the General's daughter; I was the Scion of Lies. My status, my comfort, my very existence within the Zenith Spires was built on the deliberate execution of Teron's family. His hatred was perfectly justified. He wasn't plotting against a rival; he was plotting against a lie embodied by the Varen name. His life had been ripped apart to hide this very note.

The faint, crystalline hum of my dormant Kinetic Resonance flared under the stress, a quiet, protective force field against the shock. *Stillness. Control the chaos. This truth is a weapon.*

A single tear traced a hot path down my cold cheek, not for myself, but for the profound injustice that had defined Teron's entire existence. He wasn't the monster; my mother was the enforcer of monstrous policy.

I carefully memorized the exact phrasing of the document, the date, and the signature, knowing that taking the physical paper was a death sentence. I gently folded the fragile parchment and slipped it back into the binding of the heavy volume, pushing the book back into its original place. I then meticulously removed the dust motes and smoothed the carpet of dirt, erasing all evidence of my visit.

I left the Cursed Documents section, the truth now burning like acid in my memory.

I returned to the Barracks just before dawn, my heart still thrumming with residual shock. I sank into my bunk, pulling the thin wool blanket over my head, desperately trying to process the enormity of the secret.

When the horn blared for the morning formation, I was the first out, my exhaustion overshadowed by a new, cold clarity. I was no longer fighting for my life alone; I was fighting for a truth that could collapse the entire kingdom.

The morning schedule was brutal: an hour of sparring drills, followed by the Aetherial Riding Theory lecture—the true core of the Zenith training. I endured the sparring, my movements quicker and more precise today, spurred by a desperate energy. I avoided Roric, focusing on the subtle movement of my own center of gravity, trying to coax the Kinetic Resonance into a controlled state. The power remained stubbornly elusive, only a faint shiver behind my sternum, but the mental focus gave me a vital edge.

Eysa and I entered the grand, tiered lecture hall for the riding theory, taking seats far to the front. Master Eldrin was at the podium, his expression as dry and unforgiving as ever.

"Today, we discuss the Aetherial Bond—the connection that separates the living from the Miasma-fodder you were yesterday," Eldrin began, his voice gravelly and devoid of emotion. "The bond grants you two things: the power of the Aetherial's Signet, and the ability to ride them safely across the void. Both are useless without absolute, unwavering loyalty to the Spires and their mission."

He projected a holographic schematic onto the wall: a cross-section of the massive, crystalline Spires and the faint, glowing web of the Wards that protected Navarre from the external Miasma.

"The Wards are sustained by the communal Aetherium channeled through the bonded Aetherials. Every flight, every strike, every Signet use replenishes the shield. Your sole purpose is to maintain this equilibrium."

As Eldrin spoke of the wards, my mind superimposed the memory of my mother's note onto the holographic image.

Systemic failure... must be permanently suppressed.

I realized the catastrophic implications. If the Wards were truly failing internally, the whole structure of Navarre's defense was a sham. Every cadet risking their life was doing so to prop up a political lie, not a functional defense.

A large shadow fell across the projector, eclipsing a section of the shimmering ward diagram. Teron Draken, along with his cohort of Wingleaders, entered the lecture hall, their entrance immediately drawing every eye. They didn't sit with the other students; they stood in a commanding semi-circle along the rear wall, radiating an oppressive authority.

Draken's eyes, glacial and sharp, found me immediately, holding me in a prolonged, deliberate gaze that lasted far too long. He wasn't just establishing dominance; he was establishing ownership of the conflict between them. He had challenged me in the Barracks; now he watched me in the classroom.

Master Eldrin, unfazed, continued his lecture, detailing the dangers of the Threshing—the event where cadets either successfully bond with an Aetherial or are incinerated.

"The greatest danger in the bond is the mental intrusion," Eldrin stated. "A full bond requires the Aetherial to fully breach the walls of your mind. They see your memories, your fears, your loyalties. A bond will not form with a mind harboring disloyalty or internal deceit. If the Aetherial finds you wanting, you will be reduced to ash."

My blood ran cold. *Disloyalty or internal deceit.*

I was sitting on the greatest deceit in the kingdom's history, a secret that implicated my own blood and justified my enemy's existence. If a Light Aetherial—who valued precision and stillness—breached my mind, it would instantly detect the massive, burning secret of the Karsus execution and the failing Wards.

My potential Aetherial wouldn't necessarily incinerate me for being a traitor, but for being a liar.

Teron Draken's gaze remained locked on me. It wasn't just hostility; it was a silent, smug confidence. He seemed to know, instinctively, that the closer I got to the power that could save me, the closer I got to the truth that would destroy me.

The challenge was no longer physical survival; it was mental loyalty. I had to master the Kinetic Resonance without letting the truth of the General's corruption compromise my mind during the crucial bond.

Master Eldrin wrapped up the session, assigning a dense reading from *The Scrolls of the Great Bonds*. I knew I needed the quiet of the Scribe Archives to continue my research, but the risk was too high—Teron Draken clearly used the night for his own purposes, and I could not risk another confrontation while I was still processing the truth.

As the class began to disperse, Teron Draken strode past my desk. He paused for the briefest of moments, his shoulder brushing my chair, a purely physical act of intrusion.

He didn't look at me, but his voice was a low, heavy chord that resonated only for me. "I hear you were doing some... research last night, Varen. Be careful what history you disturb. Sometimes, the dust you kick up settles on your own neck."

He continued walking, leaving me paralyzed. He knew. He had been there, or he had seen me. The Wingleader of the Marked Ones was not just my rival; he was actively tracking my every move, waiting for me to make the mistake that would allow him to eliminate the Scion of Lies and bring justice to his father.

I picked up my scroll, my hands shaking again. The realization was stark: Teron hadn't just sworn vengeance on the Varen name; he was waiting for me to expose the truth for him, setting me up to be destroyed by the very lie my mother created.

CHAPTER 5

COVERT TRAINING AND CALCULATED RISKS

The days at the Zenith Spires bled together into a monotonous cycle of fear, pain, and exhaustion. Every morning began with grueling sparring sessions designed to expose physical weakness, and every afternoon was devoted to Aetherial theory and military tactics that painted the Miasma as the sole, existential threat. I operated on two levels: the visible, fragile cadet who struggled to lift my practice saber, and the invisible strategist who knew the foundation of my entire world was a political lie engineered by my mother.

My immediate goal was to gain control over the Kinetic Resonance. I couldn't risk the Threshing—the event where cadets either bonded or were incinerated—while harboring the truth of the failing Wards and the Karsus execution. The Aetherial's bond was a mental probe, and my mind was now a vault containing treasonous information. I needed the Still Point to lock that vault, to control the chaos of my own thoughts, lest Zephyr, or any potential Aetherial, see the truth and burn me on the spot.

My training had to be secret, and it had to be precise.

The Midnight Scribe and the Silent Practice

I chose the late-night hours in the deserted Scribe Archive

for my covert practice. I couldn't spar, but I could practice stillness—the absolute prerequisite for my Signet.

Eysa, now my steadfast if quiet ally, acted as my lookout. The bond between us had deepened past barracks-mate convenience; it was a pact built on mutual survival. Eysa was physically capable but lacked the academic depth. I was frail but possessed the tactical mind. We complemented each other perfectly.

"I'll take the junction near the Great Scroll alcove," Eysa whispered one night, clutching a small, iron-banded book she pretended to be reading. "Ten minutes. If anyone comes, I cough twice. If Draken comes, I scream."

I nodded, stepping into the empty, high-ceilinged room used for preserving ancient texts. I positioned myself in the center of the cold, polished granite floor. My method was unconventional, derived from my father's forgotten Scribe texts on meditative focus.

I began by emptying my mind, striving for the internal silence required to sense the ambient kinetic energy. It was harder than any physical endurance test. My mind was a torrent of anxiety: The lie. The execution. Roric's hatred. Draken's eyes.

I tried to focus on the rhythmic, nearly silent, mechanical pulse of the Spires' internal systems. The vibration was always there, a low, crystalline hum traveling through the granite. I had to merge my awareness with that hum.

Focus on the vibration. It is pure motion. You are not motion. You are stillness.

I stood for minutes, my muscles trembling from the effort of maintaining absolute, unmoving rigidity. It was during these sessions that I began to realize my frailty was paradoxically my strength. Because my body was so naturally weak, even the slightest energy redirection felt immense.

On the third night of practice, I achieved it.

For a single, breathless second, the ambient noise of the Spires—the creaking of the metal, the distant wind, the thrum of my own blood—vanished. I hit the Still Point.

In that instantaneous, silent moment, I didn't just hear the motion around me; I saw it, or rather, felt it. Every molecule of air, every particle of dust, possessed a unique kinetic signature—a tiny, measurable vector of movement. It was a dizzying, beautiful mathematical chaos that only my mind, in its state of absolute focus, could resolve into order.

I extended my hand toward a small, frayed ribbon attached to a tapestry on the wall. *Pull.*

The ribbon did not move.

Redirect.

I poured my nascent focus, the quiet, ice-cold energy, into the air near the ribbon. I wasn't blowing on it; I was subtly shifting the kinetic vector of the air molecules directly behind the ribbon, reducing the resistance in front of it and increasing the push from behind.

With excruciating slowness, the ribbon gently lifted from the tapestry and drifted silently, exactly three inches to the left.

The effort shattered the Still Point. I collapsed onto the floor, gasping, a searing headache splitting my skull. The backlash was immense, the energy rebound feeling like tiny, burning jolts in my joints.

Eysa rushed over, alerted by the sharp sound of me hitting the stone. "Lyssa! What happened? Are you hurt?"

"I found it," I whispered, clutching my head. "The stillness. It's not strength, Eysa, it's calculation. I can't move anything big, but I can manipulate motion itself."

Eysa looked at the ribbon, now lying flat against the tapestry, and back at me. "You... you moved it with your mind?"

"I moved the air around it," I corrected, grinning weakly. "I can remove the resistance of friction. I can shift momentum. It's defensive, tactical. It's perfect for me."

From that night forward, our secret training intensified. Eysa would throw small objects—a stone, a wadded piece of parchment—and I would attempt to hit the Still Point and subtly shift the object's trajectory mid-air. I failed ninety-nine times out of a hundred, but that single successful redirection was enough to prove the potential of my Signet.

The First Flight: Terror in the Void

The next major hurdle was the First Flight Lesson—a non-negotiable rite of passage that separated the true candidates from the Miasma-fodder. It involved climbing onto the back of a practice Aetherial—a massive, wind-bonded creature named Aethon—and navigating a predetermined course above the clouds. This was where cadets traditionally lost control, were thrown, and met their end in the Miasma.

The flight ward was a massive, open crystalline cavern, the ceiling a transparent dome revealing the cold, endless blue of the high altitude. The air inside vibrated with the raw, untamed power of the Air Aetherials.

I was gripped by a deep, physical fear. I was not afraid of the height; I was afraid of the loss of control, the turbulence, the violent, chaotic motion that my fragile body could not withstand.

Aethon, the practice Aetherial, was gigantic, its scales shifting from ice-blue to wind-grey. The saddle was a rudimentary leather strap, meant only to prevent falling, not to ensure comfort.

Teron Draken was overseeing this lesson, positioned high on a cantilevered platform, his dark figure framed against the light. His presence was not reassuring; it was an expectation of failure.

"Listen, Varen," Draken's voice boomed across the cavern, amplified by his Void Signet. "Aetherial riding is not about force. It is about trust. Trust in your Aetherial, and trust in the Spires. If you hesitate, you endanger us all."

Eysa and I were placed in the last wave. Roric, in the second wave, flew with a terrifying, reckless abandon, enjoying the sheer force of the Aetherial's flight. Other cadets were less fortunate; several returned to the dock pale and vomiting, barely clinging to the straps. One cadet, a muscular Blazer named Corvin, lost control, and Aethon, sensing the lack of competence, deliberately jettisoned him mid-flight. The poor boy fell screaming into the void. The lesson was complete: The Aetherials will not carry the weak.

When it was my turn, I climbed onto Aethon's back, my hands slick with sweat. Eysa squeezed my shoulder, a silent prayer in her eyes.

"Remember the ribbon," Eysa whispered. "Find the

stillness."

I nodded, taking a deep, shuddering breath. Aethon's scales were cold and hard beneath my legs.

"Go!" commanded Draken.

Aethon launched with the force of an avalanche. The roar of the wind and the sheer kinetic force of the ascent slammed me back against the saddle, stealing my breath. I clung to the strap, my vision tunneling, every one of my fragile joints protesting the violent transfer of momentum.

Too fast. Too much motion. I can't stabilize.

I tried to find the Still Point, but the chaos of the wind and the Aetherial's powerful movements were overwhelming. The attempt was a disaster; I only managed to blur my own vision as the power lashed out uncontrolled, destabilizing me further.

Aethon was flying a wide, sweeping arc over the canyon, heading for the marker Spire. The turbulence hit—a sudden, violent cross-wind that slammed Aethon sideways. I was thrown violently to the left, my grip tearing.

This is it. The Miasma.

I dangled precariously, only my right hand desperately gripping the strap. My legs flailed, useless against the whipping wind. Aethon, sensing the loss of control, began to shake its massive head, intending to shake me loose.

My mind, under the immediate, primal threat of death, shut down everything but pure, desperate calculation. *Vector. Force. Motion.*

I felt the violent kinetic energy surging through my arm and down the strap. I didn't try to block it; I tried to redirect it.

A cold, silent force—the Kinetic Resonance—finally surged to my aid, instinctual and desperate. I didn't stop the motion, but I shifted the vector of Aethon's head movement by an infinitesimal amount. The Aetherial's shake, intended to be a vicious, outward jerk, became a gentler, more lateral motion.

It was enough. I, using the minimal shift in the Aetherial's neck movement, swung my body in, managing to hook my left foot under the saddle strap. I was safe, but barely.

I had channeled my Signet not into my body, but into the Aetherial itself, subtly manipulating its own motion to save my life.

I returned to the dock half-conscious, my body protesting with every fiber. I was hauled off Aethon's back, my vision still dotted with stars.

"Pathetic attempt, Varen. You almost lost your grip," Draken's voice was right above me, laced with cold fury.

"But I did not fall, Wingleader," I managed, forcing the words out through clenched teeth. I was exhausted, but my mind was now fully aware. I needed to know if he had seen the subtle shift.

Draken stared down at me, his glacial eyes boring into mine. "Aethon lost its footing for a second. An inexperienced rider would have plummeted. You were lucky." He paused, his gaze dropping to my trembling hand. "Or you are much, much more dangerous than you appear."

He did not wait for my response, leaving me collapsed on the dock.

The Midnight Encounter on the Spires

Later that night, unable to sleep and needing to analyze my near-death experience, I ventured out onto one of the ancient, unguarded balconies that jutted out over the cliff face. It was freezing, but the sheer expanse of the night sky, dotted with a billion cold, hard stars, was a welcome relief from the suffocating stone of the barracks.

I was tracing the path of my fall in the air, trying to analyze the fraction of a second when my Signet had activated, when I sensed the Void presence.

Teron Draken was standing on the neighboring balcony, a black silhouette against the starlight, staring out over the edge. He was shirtless, the immense musculature of his back and shoulders a landscape of disciplined power, scarred by the branding of the Marked Ones. He held a small, unmarked flask, taking a slow sip.

I froze, intending to retreat.

"Don't run, Varen," his voice came, surprisingly soft, a low rumble that barely carried on the wind. "You survive the Crossing, you survive the First Flight. You do not die easy. I've noticed."

I stepped out fully onto my balcony, the cold biting my skin. "Is that a compliment, Wingleader? Or a grievance?"

He turned his head slightly, his profile sharp and unforgiving in the starlight. "It's a complication. Your mother sentenced my father to death for treason. If you die accidentally, I win. If you graduate, I also win, as I kill you myself. But if you die before Threshing, it makes your mother a martyr and strengthens the regime she built on lies."

My heart pounded. He had just confirmed his knowledge of the political stakes, moving beyond personal animosity into grand strategy.

"And if I expose the lie?" I challenged, forcing the words out. "If I reveal that Lord Draken was executed for telling the truth about the failing WWards?"

Teron slammed his fist onto the stone railing. The granite did not crack, but the sound was a devastating thud. His whole body radiated controlled violence.

"You won't," he ground out, his voice thick with raw hatred. "Because you're the only one who can't. You are the General's blood. To tell that truth is to commit treason yourself, forcing the General to execute her own daughter, or admit the original lie. Either way, you validate my father. But it means you will die a traitor."

He raised his flask, taking a long drink. "Which brings us to my problem. If you die now, before your Aetherial bond, your death is pointless. If you survive, you become too politically important to touch until the moment you challenge the system. You have to live long enough to become a credible threat to the General, Varen. And right now, you are too fragile to survive the training long enough to become that threat."

I took a calculated risk, stepping closer to the edge, the wind threatening to pull my balance. "Then help me, Wingleader."

His gaze snapped to me, sharp and disbelieving. "Help you?"

"You need me alive long enough to serve your purpose," I said, my voice dropping to a low, persuasive pitch. "I know the truth of the Wards. I can access the records. But I can barely hold a saber. I need training in the one thing that truly matters: Signet control. You saw it on the dock. Aethon's movement—it wasn't luck. I manipulated the vector of its head. I have the Kinetic Signet that Eldrin called an anomaly."

I felt the thrill of the gamble. This was a treaty, not a surrender.

"You need a threat to expose your mother. I need survival. If you teach me how to control the Signet, I survive long enough to become the threat you need to avenge your father. We have the same ultimate objective, Teron. Vengeance against Lilith Varen."

Teron Draken stared at me for a long, silent moment, his glacial eyes calculating the risk. The air between us was thick with distrust, but also with the sharp, undeniable energy of a shared, deadly purpose.

He finally lowered his flask. "You want training. Fine. But not here. Too many eyes. You will meet me at the Ruin of the First Spire tomorrow, after the mid-day meal. Don't be late, Varen. And don't bring anyone, especially not your Healer friend. If you betray this arrangement, I won't just let the Miasma claim you. I'll make sure your death is painful, prolonged, and politically embarrassing for your mother."

He turned and walked back inside, disappearing into the darkness of the barracks.

I stood alone on the precipice, the wind whipping my hair, the Void energy of Teron Draken receding but leaving behind a profound chill. I had just committed to a secret alliance with the one man sworn to destroy my lineage, a move that carried more political peril than anything my mother had designed. The stakes had been raised again: the training was no longer about physical survival, but about a deadly, covert partnership with the enemy.

CHAPTER 6

THE SECRET WARD AND THE FIRST TOUCH

The Ruin of the First Spire was a graveyard.

It was located in the highest, oldest, and most structurally compromised section of the Zenith Spires, a crystalline cathedral of shattered granite that had been sealed off fifty years ago after an unexplained Aetherial incident. Command claimed it was unstable, but the cadets whispered it was cursed. It was the last place anyone would risk going, making it the perfect training ground for treason.

I arrived precisely at the appointed time after the mid-day meal, my training leathers damp with nervous sweat despite the biting cold. I found the entrance—a barely visible fissure in the stone wall behind the unused North Supply Depot—and slipped inside. The air was dead, thick with dust and the unmistakable smell of ancient, scorched magic.

The chamber beyond was vast, a dizzying vertical space illuminated only by fractured slits in the ceiling where the sky bled through like broken glass. Below lay a massive, unstable floor of crystalline shards and jagged pillars. The silence here was louder than any noise, making me feel acutely exposed.

Teron Draken was waiting for me in the center, leaning against a broken archway. He was still wearing the fitted black tunic from the day before, accentuating the taut power of his physique. His eyes, fixed on me, were assessing, devoid of the aggressive hostility he displayed in the barracks, replaced by a cold, analytical focus. He had shifted from predator to harsh tutor.

"You're on time," he stated, his voice quiet, his Void presence barely perceptible but still heavy. "Rule number one of our arrangement: Punctuality—because if you get caught, I'm not waiting for your execution to begin my vengeance."

I crossed the unstable floor carefully. "Understood. And rule number two: Secrecy. If this alliance is discovered, we both face treason charges. I risk exposure of the General's lie; you risk losing your chance for justice."

A flicker of something—approval, perhaps—crossed Teron's face. "You learn fast. Good. We don't have long. Tell me, Varen, what is the single greatest weakness of a Kinetic Conduit?"

I immediately recited the principle from the hidden archive text. "The power output is proportional to the energy absorbed, and attempting to absorb energy greater than the Conduit's own physical limit will result in the fracturing of the self."

"Correct. It's a subtle power of precision, not brute force. You can redirect a blade, but you can't stop a charging Magma Aetherial. It would splinter every bone in your body," Teron confirmed, pushing off the archway. He retrieved a heavy, obsidian training dagger from a hidden sheath on his belt and tossed it in the air.

"Now, forget the theory. Your Signet, Kinetic Resonance, requires the Still Point—the absolute cessation of internal and external chaos. Your entire body is chaos. You tremble, you breathe too fast, your mind races with political worry. That noise prevents the Signal from activating in a life-or-death scenario."

He walked toward me, slowly, deliberately. The cold, heavy presence of his Void Energy began to build, a low, unnerving pressure in the air. I felt the familiar urge to retreat, to curl inward and protect my fragile core.

"Your task now is simple," Teron commanded. "I am going to attack you. Your only objective is not to defend, but to reach the Still Point before my blade touches your skin. You fail, you get cut. Understand?"

I swallowed hard, nodding. "Understood."

"Good. Now, focus."

He charged.

It wasn't a sparring charge; it was a deadly, lightning-fast sprint. The speed was terrifying, but what was worse was the Void Energy he commanded. As he closed the distance, the ambient sound in the vast cavern seemed to dampen, the air growing thick and heavy. His approach felt like being caught in the vacuum created by a collapsing star—a crushing, physical negation of motion and sound.

He was upon me instantly, the obsidian dagger a black blur aimed straight at my abdomen.

I froze, not from fear, but from being utterly overwhelmed. My mind raced—*Too fast! Too much force!* I tried to focus on the hum of the Spires, but the thunder of my own heart drowned it out. My internal chaos was a shriek.

I felt a sharp, searing pain as the dull obsidian point slashed across my ribs. The blow wasn't intended to kill, but to shock. I gasped, stumbling back two steps, clutching my side.

Teron immediately pulled back, his face devoid of emotion. He showed me the dagger, already stained a thin red. "Chaos. Failure. You reacted. Your mind searched for a plan, and in that second of searching, I won. Again."

He didn't wait for me to recover. "Again."

The next five minutes were a relentless sequence of failure. Teron was merciless, his movements precise and perfectly controlled. He used his superior speed and the oppressive weight of his Signet to flood my senses. He hit my wrist (a searing ache), my shoulder (a dull throb), and my thigh (a stinging reminder). Each blow was designed not to permanently harm, but to shatter my focus, confirming his earlier assessment of my fragility.

On the seventh attempt, battered and breathing heavily, I felt a cold, desperate exhaustion. I knew I was only seconds from collapse. Teron was already winding up for the final charge, his eyes gleaming with a mixture of professional distaste and mounting frustration.

He needs me to survive. He needs me to be a weapon. I cannot fail him now.

The thought wasn't about my mother or the lie; it was about Teron. A sudden, fierce, protective loyalty to the shared objective—Vengeance against Lilith Varen—burned through the panic.

As Teron launched his final, massive charge, I didn't focus on the chaos of his speed; I focused on the purpose of his motion. I ignored the fear, ignored the pain, and focused only on the clear, geometric line of his advance.

Vector. Stillness. Now.

In that instant, the noise of the world receded again. The Still Point snapped into place. It felt like standing at the center of a perfectly formed, silent sphere. I felt the vast, cold consciousness of Zephyr—my dormant Aetherial—stirring deep in my core, approving of the control.

Teron was moving at maximum velocity, the obsidian dagger aimed at my neck. But to me, he was now moving in agonizing slow motion. I could trace every particle of dust he displaced, every minute shift of muscle.

I didn't move. I held the Still Point, allowing the sheer, enormous kinetic energy of his charge to wash over me. At the precise moment before contact, I subtly, surgically, directed a sliver of the Kinetic Resonance to the air directly in front of his forward-leading foot.

It wasn't a push; it was the removal of resistance. Teron's foot suddenly met a pocket of unnaturally slippery, frictionless air.

His entire mass, moving at full speed, instantly shifted its center of gravity. He did not fall, but his balance was compromised. His obsidian dagger, instead of striking my neck, grazed past my ear by a fraction of an inch. He pulled the blow instantly, knowing the training had to stop short of decapitation.

Teron skidded to a stop five feet beyond me, his breathing heavy, his powerful body vibrating with the effort of fighting his own momentum.

He turned slowly, his expression no longer one of

professional indifference, but of raw, stunned recognition. He stared at the spot where his foot had slipped, then back at me, I was still trembling, but fundamentally whole.

"You didn't deflect the blade, Varen," he stated, his voice a low growl of grudging respect. "You manipulated the friction beneath my boot. You stole my balance before I could commit the strike. You hit the Still Point."

I nodded, tears of pain and exertion blurring my vision. "I did. But I can't hold it. The backlash…"

Teron stepped closer, his demeanor changing entirely. The threat evaporated, replaced by the intensity of a shared professional secret. He reached out a hand, and for the first time, I saw the scars of the Marked Ones—intricate, dark, jagged lines that covered his forearms and shoulders, a permanent record of his family's execution.

He didn't offer the hand as comfort, but as an instruction. "Show me where it hurts."

I hesitated, unused to any form of physical gentleness, especially from him. I pulled back the padded collar of my leathers, revealing the thin, bleeding gash across my ribs.

Teron's fingers—large, calloused, and surprisingly warm—gently traced the line of the wound. The touch was agonizingly tender, a stark contrast to the violence of his previous actions.

"The backlash is the energy you failed to neutralize. It recoils into the weakest parts of your body, Varen. Your joints, your ribs, your core," he explained, his thumb now resting just beneath the wound, his gaze fixed on my skin. His proximity was overwhelming; I could smell the clean, cold scent of his sweat and the underlying metallic tang of his Void Signet.

"You need a secondary anchor. Something outside yourself to absorb the excess vibration." He looked up, his eyes meeting mine, and the intensity of the contact made my breath hitch. "For your Signet to work at full capacity, you need a conduit—a non-living extension of your power that can handle the raw force. You are too fragile to be the only container."

I stared at the obsidian dagger lying on the floor. "The dagger."

"Precisely," Teron confirmed, releasing my ribs. "Your Signet can channel through a physical medium that shares a deep, personal connection with you. We start tomorrow. Bring your most treasured physical possession—something you and only you can channel through."

He paused, sweeping his eyes over the ruined space. "This ruins is our secret. No one sees us. No one knows our purpose. You and I, Varen, we are now bound by the truth of your mother's treason. I hate your lineage, but I need your survival. Don't make me regret this arrangement."

I nodded, stepping back, the phantom heat of his touch lingering on my skin. "I won't. Wingleader Draken. I need my vengeance just as much as you need yours."

"Good. Now go. And clean that cut. I need you healthy tomorrow."

I turned and hurried out of the ruins, my mind reeling. The physical pain was overshadowed by the profound, volatile reality of their alliance. Teron Draken hadn't just become my trainer; he had become the only person in the Spires who knew the extent of my weakness and the measure of my strength. Their shared secret was a weapon that could destroy them both, or, terrifyingly, bond them together.

The Barracks and the Quiet Threat

Back in the Fourth Barracks, Eysa was waiting up, feigning sleep in her bunk. She sat up immediately when I entered, her eyes falling on the blood seeping through my tunic.

"Lyssa! What happened? You were gone too long."

"Sparring with a fifth-year," I lied smoothly, retrieving my first-aid kit. "He insisted I learn a lesson about speed. I learned it."

"That fifth-year has a name, Lyssa."

"It doesn't matter," I insisted, carefully applying an antiseptic salve to the shallow cut. "What matters is I found something that works. I found a way to fight outside of brute strength."

I spoke only in generalities, protecting my greatest secret—the alliance with Teron Draken—even from Eysa. I couldn't risk anything that might compromise the plan, especially since the Aetherial Bond would eventually probe Eysa's loyalty too.

I then pulled my most treasured possession from beneath my mattress: a slender, silver stylus used by my late father, the Chief Scribe. It was delicate but solid, cool to the touch, and imbued with the profound memory of his quiet strength and love of truth.

"This is my anchor," I murmured, running my thumb over the stylized, bird-wing crest of the Scribe Quadrant engraved on the silver. This would be the non-living extension I would channel my Kinetic Resonance through. It felt right—the physical tool of the Scribe, now weaponized by the Rider.

I spent the remaining hours until dawn carefully reviewing my father's history texts, trying to find any obscure reference to the Karsus execution that might corroborate my mother's hidden note. Nothing. The official record was impenetrable, a seamless tapestry of lies.

When the horn blared for the morning formation, I was already dressed, the silver stylus strapped discreetly beneath my leathers.

As I stepped out, I passed Roric, who was leaning against the doorway with a sneering look. "The General's girl looks pale today. Did the fifth-years finally teach you what weakness feels like?"

"I learned exactly what I needed to learn, Roric," I replied, my voice low. "I learned that relying on sheer brute force is predictable. And predictability, in the Zenith Spires, is the fastest route to the Miasma." I walked past him, my head held high. I was battered, bleeding, and exhausted, but I was no longer just a target. I was a secret apprentice, trained by the very man sworn to be my nemesis.

At the edge of the training ward, I saw Teron Draken. He didn't acknowledge me with his eyes, but I felt his Void Energy reach out, a cold, silent probe checking my presence.

"She came back. She is whole."

The signal was sent and received. The alliance was holding. The perilous journey of the Scion of Static had just become infinitely more dangerous—and more intimate.

CHAPTER 7

THE GAUNTLET AND THE GAMBIT

The War College Gauntlet was an institution of brutality designed to filter out the weak before the Aetherials even had a chance to choose. It was a timed obstacle course combining combat, agility, and pure nerve, set over a massive, open chasm in the Second Spire. Every cadet had to run it blind, knowing that a miscalculated step, a clumsy block, or a moment of hesitation meant a quick, unrecoverable descent into the Miasma.

I stood at the starting line, my entire body rigid with cold focus. This was my first public test since the sparring match, and the stakes were exponentially higher. My mother, General Lilith Varen, was scheduled to observe from the viewing box—a clear sign that my unexpected survival was now an object of official scrutiny.

Underneath my training leathers, I had meticulously strapped my silver stylus—my kinetic anchor—to my dominant forearm, the cool metal a grounding presence.

The Anchor and the Target

I had spent the last three nights practicing with Teron Draken in the ruins. Our training was merciless. Teron would use his Void Signet not to attack, but to flood my senses with crushing pressure, forcing me to find the Still Point amidst chaos.

"The Void is a field of absolute density. When I use it, you feel the lack of air, the weight of the Spires, the sheer pressure of your impending demise," Teron had explained, his face inches from mine in the darkness. "You must learn to ignore the gravity of my presence and focus only on the smallest available vector of movement. Find the hum, Varen, and use the stylus to absorb the tremor before it reaches your core."

The stylus became my secret lifeline. By concentrating my focus through the silver point, I could externalize the initial, violent kinetic feedback of the Resonance, preventing my body from fracturing. It allowed me to neutralize small, sharp motions—like the snap of a tripwire or the quick thrust of a blade—with greater reliability.

I took my place, ignoring the loud, contemptuous snicker from Roric nearby. I looked up briefly at the tiered viewing box. There, framed by the dark granite, stood my mother, General Varen, a figure of daunting command, her expression unreadable. Beside her was a council of stern, high-ranking Wingleaders. They were watching me, analyzing me like a dangerous variable.

The Gauntlet Master, a hardened, scarred man named Captain Korvin, raised his hand. "The objective is speed, precision, and survival. No Signets are authorized, but survival is paramount. Begin!"

I heard my name called. My time had begun.

Into the Gauntlet

I sprinted forward, my training with Eysa—drills focused on maximizing speed with minimal motion—paying off immediately. The course began with the Saber Block Cascade—a line of automated, heavy wooden blades swinging down in complex, overlapping patterns designed to force cadets to use brute strength to ward them off.

I did not block. As the first saber swung, I felt its immense kinetic signature rushing towards me. I aimed my mental focus, sharp as the stylus point, at the saber's axis of rotation.

Target the joint. Shift the vector.

I unleashed a tiny surge of Kinetic Resonance. It didn't stop the blade, but it subtly offset its center of momentum. The saber grazed my shoulder, but the force of the blow was neutralized, turning a bone-shattering hit into a mere shove. I flowed past, my muscles burning, conserving energy where others were exhausting themselves with violent, unnecessary blocks.

The crowd gasped—a faint ripple of shock. My movement was too effortless, too smooth for my known frailty.

The next section was the Rope and Blade Crossing—a series of thin, slippery ropes stretched over the Miasma, guarded by rapidly moving, razor-sharp blades that swung randomly, controlled by wind shifts. A false step meant a cut, which meant a slip, which meant death.

I pulled the silver stylus from my arm. It was not a weapon, but a focus. I gripped it tightly.

Stillness.

I stepped onto the rope. The rope swayed violently. I felt the chaotic, kinetic motion of the rope threatening to throw me off balance. I channeled my Signet through the stylus and focused on the motion of the rope beneath my feet.

I created a thin, localized field of Kinetic Absorption around my boots. It didn't stop the motion, but it dramatically minimized the recoil and vibration from the rope itself, granting me a near-miraculous stability. I moved with a fluid, terrifying grace, appearing to defy the natural laws of balance.

The blades whipped toward me, the sound slicing the air. I didn't dodge the blades; I focused on the wind they displaced. I targeted the high-velocity air molecules pushing against me.

I achieved the Still Point for nearly two full seconds—an eternity in combat. I stepped through the chaotic web of blades, my movements so precise and calculated that I might as well have been walking across a still floor.

I reached the solid granite on the other side, dropping the stylus back into its sheath. I hadn't been touched. I had beaten the ropes by manipulating the very air and motion that governed them.

Confrontation at the Core

The final challenge was the Timed Wall Climb, a sheer face of unpolished granite that required raw upper-body strength. This was the point of guaranteed failure for me.

Roric had finished his run minutes ago, setting a new, brutal time, and he was now standing near the finish line, sneering, waiting for me to fail. The crowd was silent, waiting for the expected collapse.

I began the climb. My arms burned instantly. My delicate grip slipped on the abrasive granite. I was already fatigued from the exertion of maintaining the Kinetic Absorption across the ropes. I made it a third of the way up, my muscles screaming in agony. I knew I couldn't reach the top; my body would give out.

Not yet. Not here. I need to live long enough to become the General's undoing.

I looked down, catching sight of Roric's smug, hateful grin. And then, I saw Teron Draken.

Teron was no longer on the viewing platform. He had moved to the edge of the chasm, standing directly beneath the wall climb. He was looking at me, and his eyes weren't challenging—they were commanding.

He performed a subtle, single movement: he lifted his hand and pressed his thumb and forefinger together, a silent signal we had practiced in the Ruins. *Pinch the chaos. Find the center.*

I understood immediately. I didn't need to be strong enough to pull my full weight; I needed to reduce the gravity of my own body.

I closed my eyes for a split second, reaching for the Kinetic Resonance. I didn't manipulate the external environment; I manipulated the force vector of my own mass. I aimed the Signet inward, channeling it through my silver anchor.

I didn't stop gravity, but I created a small, focused field of Reduced Kinetic Resistance around my own body. The effect was marginal—I was still heavy—but I suddenly felt one-tenth lighter.

That marginal difference was the difference between impossible failure and agonizing success.

With a final, desperate surge fueled by pure adrenaline

and the borrowed lightness of the Signet, I hauled my body up the wall. My hands bled, my muscles screamed, but I reached the top, slamming my palm onto the granite ledge with seconds to spare.

I was alive. I had completed the Gauntlet, not with strength, but with cunning.

The General's Gaze

I collapsed at the top, gasping for air, my mind already racing through the potential fallout. I looked down and saw Roric's face, a mask of baffled fury.

And then I saw Teron Draken. He was still standing there, his head tilted slightly, an unnervingly calm expression on his face. He offered no overt recognition, but his eyes communicated a fierce, volatile pride. *You survived. You are now the weapon I need.*

The sense of victory was cut short by a cold, commanding voice that reverberated through the Gauntlet Ward.

"Report to my office, Cadet Varen. Immediately."

I looked up at the viewing box. General Varen had descended, now standing at the edge of the chasm, her eyes radiating a cold, penetrating suspicion. She had seen the impossible smoothness of the saber dodge and the supernatural lightness of the wall climb.

I picked myself up, my legs wobbly but my posture rigid. As I walked toward the General, I passed Teron Draken. He spoke without moving his lips, his voice reaching my mind through the terrifying intimacy of his Signet:

"You were too efficient, Varen. Too perfect. She knows. Your next move must be a calculated lie. Do not break."

I entered my mother's office moments later. The room was Spartan, dominated by a massive, polished map of Navarre and the surrounding Miasma. My eyes swept the spartan room, landing on a single anomaly on the corner of the polished map table: a small, tarnished silver compass, an old gift from my father, a reminder of the quiet, safe life I was supposed to have had.

General Varen stood at her desk, her hands clasped behind her back. "Your performance was… illogical, Cadet."

"I compensated for my physical deficits with advanced tactical planning, General," I stated, using the very jargon my mother respected.

"Tactical planning does not account for the frictionless pivot I witnessed on the rope crossing. And cadets do not complete the wall climb with that level of fatigue. You manifested a Signet." It wasn't a question; it was an accusation.

I maintained eye contact, remembering Teron's command: *Do not break.* I knew the General was fishing—she couldn't know the exact nature of the Kinetic Resonance, only that it was anomalous.

"With respect, General, I am a Scribe's daughter. I understand physics. I leveraged the principle of minimal resistance to conserve momentum. As for the wall, I was driven by the sheer terror of disappointing my General—a motivation stronger than my physical limits." I played the dutiful daughter, a sickening, necessary performance.

General Varen studied me, her gaze peeling away layers of defense. "The Signet of a Conduit is revealed upon a successful

Aetherial Bond at the Threshing. If you possessed a Signet before bonding, it would be unprecedented—a sign of immense latent power, or an anomaly that could compromise the Wards.”

The threat was clear. If I admitted to an unbonded Signet, I risked being immediately designated an unstable threat and neutralized.

“I have no Signet, General. But I am highly motivated to survive,” I insisted.

General Varen moved around her desk, standing uncomfortably close. “You are the last of my blood. I need you to survive the Threshing. But I need you to do so cleanly. No anomalies. No deviations from the norm. Do you understand, Lyssa? The Zenith does not tolerate unknowns.”

I understood: Survival meant conformity. To reveal my subtle, intellectual Signet now would be political suicide.

“I understand, General,” I replied, a perfect blend of respect and fear in my voice.

General Varen dismissed me with a wave of her hand. As I reached the door, the General spoke one last, cutting sentence: “The only reason you are still alive, Cadet, is because I need you to prove that the Varen line is superior. Do not disappoint me, or your fate will be worse than the Miasma.”

I stumbled out, the interview having drained me more than the Gauntlet. My mother hadn't been watching me for pride; she had been watching me for weakness, ready to eliminate the failure.

I found Eysa waiting anxiously outside the ward entrance. “She saw it, didn’t she?” Eysa whispered, pulling me toward the safety of the barracks.

"She saw an anomaly and suspected a Signet," I confirmed, my voice hoarse. "I deflected the accusation, but it won't hold. I have bought us time, Eysa, but now we have to move faster. The Threshing is next. We need to find our Aetherials."

And we needed to find them before the General or the vengeful Wingleader Draken decided my time was up. I ran my finger over the silver stylus beneath my tunic. The silver felt warm, charged with the stolen kinetic energy of the Gauntlet. I had survived the test, but only by partnering with the enemy and deceiving the one person who supposedly wanted me to live.

CHAPTER 8

THE SHADOW PACT AND THE GROWING INTIMACY

The alliance between me and Teron Draken was a delicate, serrated blade—lethal to wield, but the only defense I possessed. After the Gauntlet, our secret meetings in the Ruin of the First Spire became a daily ritual, a sanctuary carved out of the terror of the Zenith Spires. It was a space defined by absolute silence, profound treason, and the rising, dangerous temperature of our shared purpose.

Our training was no longer about simple defense; it was about integration. Teron needed me to be able to hit the Still Point instantly, reliably, and powerfully enough to deflect a significant threat. I needed Teron's Void Signet to create the extreme pressure necessary for my power to stabilize.

The Null Field and the Stillness

In our early sessions, Teron would simply attack me with dull blades, forcing me to find the Still Point to minimize his kinetic vector. Now, he used his Void Energy.

The moment we began, Teron would activate his Signet, a crushing wave of energy that felt like the atmosphere itself had doubled its weight. He created a Null Field around us—a bubble of oppressive, dampening force designed to simulate the terror of facing an enemy Void Aetherial in combat.

"Don't fight the density, Varen! Don't struggle against the weight!" Teron's voice was strained as he maintained the field, the effort making the thick veins stand out on his neck. "A Void attack is the cessation of motion. It will crush your body and your mind if you resist. You must flow through the zero point."

My muscles burned and trembled under the enormous pressure. The weight of the Null Field pressed me down, trying to force me onto the sharp granite shards of the floor. My mind screamed for release, for panic, but I had to override the physical reaction.

Stillness. I am a vacuum. I am zero.

I channeled my will through my silver stylus anchor, trying to find the quiet space where the Kinetic Resonance could activate. The first few attempts ended in disaster. The backlash from resisting the Void's pressure was agonizing, sending sharp, internal tremors through my fragile frame.

"It's too much, Draken!" I gasped once, collapsing onto the stone floor, my chest heaving. "The residual force is fracturing my ribs!"

Teron immediately deactivated the Null Field. The sudden release of pressure was almost as dizzying as the pressure itself. He knelt beside me, his expression tight with controlled worry that betrayed his harsh exterior.

"It's too much for your internal structure. You need a physical buffer," he decided, his eyes scanning the ruin. "You need to understand the Void's motion, not just fight it."

He then did the unthinkable. He positioned himself

directly behind me, his hard, powerful body shielding me from the imaginary forces of the room.

"Stand up. Now, put your back to me."

I hesitated, every alarm bell in my strategic mind screeching a warning. This was far too close, too intimate for an alliance built on mutual destruction. His physical proximity was already a weapon against my carefully maintained emotional guard.

"This is unnecessary, Wingleader," I managed, my voice suddenly breathless.

"It is necessary," he countered, his voice flat. "The Void Aetherial, Morgal, channels through my core, but the power radiates outward. If I can anchor that void against my own body, you only have to fight the recoil, not the source. It acts as a shield."

I slowly turned, placing my small, slender back directly against the broad, powerful expanse of his chest.

The contact was a shock. He was solid rock, radiating immense, controlled heat that immediately contrasted with the cold of the Spires. I felt the powerful, rhythmic beat of his heart against my spine, a profound counterpoint to the chaotic flutter of my own. The air around us changed—it was no longer purely cold. It was charged, a volatile mix of our opposing Signets.

"Ready, Scion?" Teron murmured against the crown of my head, his breath warm and dangerous.

"Ready," I whispered, closing my eyes.

Teron reactivated the Null Field.

This time, the pressure was immediate and crushing, but

the result was completely different. The weight of the Void Energy slammed into Teron's massive frame, but I, protected by his body, only felt the subtle, external wave of the recoil. I was shielded from the direct force.

The Spark of Resonance

In that instant of protected pressure, the Kinetic Resonance surged to life effortlessly. The Still Point was easy to find; I was shielded from the external chaos, and the primal heat of Teron's body and the rhythmic thud of his heart provided a constant, calming anchor against my own internal turmoil.

I focused on a tiny shard of granite on the floor thirty feet away. *Shift.*

The shard, held fast by the Null Field's weight, suddenly skittered sideways two inches, its path perfectly, momentarily frictionless.

"Yes! That's it, Varen!" Teron's voice was a low growl of triumph that resonated through my spine. "You're not fighting. You're finding the leak. The Void is absolute, but motion can always escape, always find a path of zero resistance. You are that path."

We continued the practice for what felt like hours. Teron would increase the Void pressure, and I would strain to hold the Still Point. The physical contact was unavoidable and deeply sensual. His hands often moved to stabilize me, gripping my waist, his thumbs pressing into the sensitive skin just above my hipbones, guiding my center of balance.

The purpose was technical—maintaining my center of

gravity against the crushing pressure—but the effect was erotic. I could no longer separate the Signet training from the physical intoxication of his power.

I realized with a terrifying clarity that I was addicted to the safety and the feeling of being protected by the very man who should be my enemy. His presence, his immense power, was my only solace in the Spires.

During one particularly intense session, Teron was using his free hand to create rapid, shifting kinetic threats in the Void Field—simulated blade strikes and snapping wires—forcing me to use my Signet for both defense and subtle offense.

He was pressed close, his cheek resting momentarily against the top of my head as he maintained the draining Signet. "You're perfect, Scion. You are the perfect counter to the Void. Morgal finds you… intriguing."

My breath hitched. I hadn't expected the Void Aetherial to have an opinion on me.

"And what do you find, Wingleader?" I dared to ask, my voice low.

Teron's body tensed against mine. He released the Void Field instantly, the shift so abrupt it left me momentarily dizzy. He stepped away from me, turning quickly.

"I find a means to an end, Varen," he stated, his voice now cold, devoid of the earlier warmth. He pulled the hard, professional shield back over his emotions. "A weapon trained to dismantle the General's lies. Nothing more."

The denial was too swift, too rigid. I knew he was lying. The physical, electric charge between us was too potent to be ignored, even by his hardened heart. He was afraid of the very intimacy that was training me.

The Forbidden Truth and the First Kiss

I was not easily deterred. I had exposed my mother's lie; I would expose Teron Draken's emotional truth.

The next night, Teron was waiting for me with a dark, brooding mood. The training began immediately, with a punishing level of Void pressure. I endured the session, achieving the Still Point faster than before, successfully deflecting all his simulated attacks. But the emotional distance between us was back.

When the training concluded, Teron simply stepped away and began cleaning his obsidian dagger. "That's enough. Go back to the barracks."

I did not move. I watched him, seeing the deliberate effort he put into avoiding my eyes.

"You're avoiding the truth, Wingleader," I challenged quietly.

Teron stopped, his grip tightening on the dagger. "I avoid nothing but failure, Varen. And you are a distraction that could lead to it."

"I am a threat to your revenge because I am the Scion of Lies. You want me to survive to expose her. But you are afraid that surviving with me will expose you," I pressed, walking toward him, closing the distance he had deliberately created.

I stopped inches from him, so close I had to crane my neck to meet his gaze. I could see the conflict raging in his glacial eyes—the desire for vengeance battling against the profound, unwanted connection.

"The Void Signet senses density and suppression. It requires truth, absolute honesty, to function at its peak," I stated, using the technical language of the Scribe to pierce his emotional armor. "And right now, Wingleader, you are suppressing a truth so massive it's compromising your own Signet."

He didn't move, a massive statue of coiled violence. "Watch your words, Varen. You cross a line."

"I am across it," I confirmed, taking the final, fatal step. I lifted my hand and pressed my cold, trembling fingers against the harsh, scarred skin of his cheek, right near the dark branding of the Marked Ones. The warmth of his skin was overwhelming.

"Tell me you don't feel the truth of this connection," I whispered, my voice barely a breath. "Tell me the rage is all you feel, and that the only thing you want from me is a political execution."

Teron's control shattered. His eyes closed, a muscle twitching violently in his jaw. His hands, still gripping the dagger, trembled.

"Don't push me, Lyssa," he ground out, the use of my first name, stripped of rank and formality, a profound breach of their contract.

"I am pushing you, Teron," I insisted, my thumb tracing the line of his scar. "Because I know the truth of my mother, and you need to know the truth of us."

With a sound that was a low, desperate mix of rage and hunger, Teron Draken dropped his dagger. He grasped my face, his calloused hands surprisingly gentle, and kissed me.

The kiss was devastating. It was not tender; it was a violent collision of two forces that had been fighting gravity for weeks. His mouth was hard, demanding, tasting of metal and cold night air. The raw, immense energy of his Void Signet surged around us, pressing against me, demanding a response.

I didn't pull away. I responded with every ounce of the silent, fierce energy of my Kinetic Resonance. I didn't fight the Void pressure; I absorbed it, channeling the excess energy of his passion into my core, stabilizing the moment, creating a perfect, intimate stillness at the center of the storm.

The contact was a catastrophic, beautiful transfer of power and emotion. The hatred was real, the treason was real, but the magnetic, undeniable attraction was a force even stronger than the Void.

When Teron finally pulled away, his chest was heaving, his eyes wide, glazed with shock and self-loathing. He looked at me, not with hostility, but with utter devastation.

"That was a mistake," he stated, his voice hoarse, raw.

"That was the truth, Wingleader," I countered, trembling from the power surge. My lips were numb, but the rest of me felt gloriously, dangerously alive. "And now that the truth is out, you can't put it back in the bottle. We are bound by more than vengeance, Teron. We are bound by necessity."

He didn't argue. He simply turned and sprinted out of the ruins, leaving his dagger lying on the floor. He ran from the truth I had forced him to confront.

I stood alone in the ruins, touching my lips, the taste of him lingering. I had won the psychological battle, securing the dangerous intimacy I needed to survive. I picked up his dagger. It was heavy, cold, and a perfect extension of his power.

His dagger. His Signet. His secret.

I was holding his Signet anchor, and he had fled without it. I knew this was the ultimate sign of his capitulation. He had left me with a physical piece of his power, sealing their shadow pact.

I had to ensure that the romantic entanglement didn't derail their primary objective. The Threshing was rapidly approaching, and now, with my mind compromised by both treason and forbidden love, I had to achieve the Still Point like never before. My life, and Teron Draken's revenge, depended on it.

CHAPTER 9

THE TRIAL BY FIRE

The air in the Zenith Spires had changed. It was no longer merely cold and thin; it was electric, thick with the scent of fear and the raw, untamed energy of thousands of Aetherials gathered for the Threshing. This was the great reckoning, the moment where the training ceased, and the natural order of the world asserted itself: an Aetherial would either choose you, or burn you alive.

The event was scheduled for the coming dawn. The entire day leading up to it was a blur of ritualistic preparation designed to amplify the terror. All cadets were scrubbed clean, stripped of their uniforms, and clad in simple, thin linen tunics that offered no protection from fire or judgment. The loss of the heavy leather felt like the loss of a second skin, leaving me feeling painfully exposed.

In the Fourth Barracks, the silence was suffocating. The sheer number of empty bunks was a stark reminder of the fifty-three cadets who had been culled by the Gauntlet, the Crossing, and the daily skirmishes. Roric sat polishing his blade, his focus predatory. Eysa, pale and shivering, clutched a stone talisman she had kept hidden.

I sat on my bunk, legs crossed in a modified meditative position. My silver stylus—my kinetic anchor—lay on my palm, the only object I was permitted to bring into the chamber.

I closed my eyes, trying to find the Still Point.

Stillness. Stillness. Stillness.

My mind, however, was a roaring torrent. It was chaotic with the memory of Teron Draken's harsh kiss, the warmth of his body against mine, and the heavy secret of my mother's treason. The Signet of the Aetherial was a probe for disloyalty. I had to bury the truth so deep that even the ancient, probing consciousness of Zephyr could not find it.

The secret is not mine. It is the General's. I am merely the vault.

I worked the logic, treating my mind like a complex Scribe archive: I couldn't erase the file, but I could bury it under layers of professional duty and rehearsed loyalty. I recited the Zenith Code, the official doctrine of the Spires, over and over, trying to superimpose the lie over the raw, terrifying truth.

The Midnight Pact

The sound of soft, precise footsteps broke my concentration. I opened my eyes. Teron Draken stood at the foot of my bunk, his towering figure a silhouette in the dim gaslight. He was dressed in his simple linen tunic, his formidable physique barely contained by the light fabric, and he looked dangerous, restless, and consumed by purpose.

Eysa, alerted by the subtle shift in the room's energy, pretended to be deeply asleep.

Teron knelt, his face on level with mine. His glacial eyes searched mine with a desperate intensity. He did not touch me, but his Void presence was an undeniable, heavy blanket wrapping around us both.

"We have no more time for games, Varen," he whispered, his voice low and strained. "The Threshing is a pure test of allegiance. If you succeed, you become a powerful political weapon against your mother. If you fail, you become ash, and my vengeance dies with you."

"The lie is buried," I replied, my voice steady despite the flutter in my chest. "I have practiced the Still Point until my mind is numb. The Signet will see loyalty, not treason."

Teron shook his head, his dark hair falling over his forehead. "You don't understand the Aetherials, Lyssa. They are not satisfied with mere performance. They see the truth of the self. You are hiding the execution of my father—a profound, devastating injustice. If your Aetherial sees that trauma in your core, it will interpret your loyalty to justice as disloyalty to the Spires. You will be incinerated."

I felt a jolt of panic. He was right. My commitment to truth was my most dangerous weakness in this system.

"Then what do I do?" I asked, the cold, steel edge of my composure finally faltering.

Teron reached out and covered my hand, his massive palm engulfing mine. The contact was a violent surge of heat and cold—the opposing forces of Void and Kinetic energy merging.

"You need an absolute truth to anchor your soul," Teron commanded, his eyes burning with fierce conviction. "Something that supersedes the lie of your mother and the execution of my father. Something true that your Aetherial can recognize as a worthy purpose."

I stared at him, suddenly understanding. The true purpose

was not the Spires, and it was no longer solely vengeance.

"My anchor is not the stylus," I whispered, looking down at the cool silver in my palm. "It's the fact that I will survive this to expose the corruption that killed your father. That is the truth I commit to."

Teron brought our joined hands to his lips, pressing a hard, cold kiss to the back of my fingers—a vow sealed in the presence of his enemies. "Then find an Aetherial who values cunning and justice over brute force, Lyssa. Find one who can accept the truth of your commitment."

He released my hand, the sudden loss of his heat leaving me cold and alone. He backed away, disappearing into the darkness of the barracks.

I sat alone, my hands trembling, the silver stylus now warm with the residual energy of our shared vow. I no longer feared the Miasma; I feared the truth of my own heart.

The Hall of Judgment

At dawn, the remaining cadets were marched in grim silence to the Hall of Judgment—the largest, most ancient cavern in the main Spire. The sheer magnitude of the space was designed to humble and terrify. The walls were unpolished, jagged granite, and the ceiling was so high it was lost in perpetual shadow.

The Hall was lined with massive, silent Spires Guards, their faces hidden behind dark helmets. But the true occupants were the Aetherials.

They were gathered on a colossal, tiered platform at the

far end of the hall: the Threshing Ground. They were magnificent and terrifying. Magma Aetherials, gleaming with volcanic heat; Torrent Aetherials, crystalline and shimmering; and the rare, ancient Void Aetherials, their scales the color of deep space, their presence a palpable pressure on the air.

I scanned the creatures, my heart sinking. They were all gargantuan, instruments of war built for strength, heat, and crushing gravity. There was no room here for the subtle power of Kinetic Resonance. No space for Zephyr, the crystalline wind Aetherial I needed.

Captain Korvin stood at the head of the hall, his voice ringing with cold ceremony. "Cadets of the Zenith Spires! Today, you face the Aetherial Court. Walk the line. Present your soul. The weak will be purged. The chosen will rise."

The Threshing began.

It was a systematic, terrifying culling. Cadets were required to walk the long line of Aetherials. The creatures did not speak with words; they communicated through pure, elemental energy. They would sense the cadet's core loyalty, their strength, and their potential.

The first ten cadets were strong, eager Blazers. Most were rejected instantly. The Magma Aetherials would simply turn their enormous heads away, their eyes glowing with contempt. Three were not so lucky. One, a boy named Farris, approached a massive, fiery red Aetherial, his face radiating desperate loyalty. The Aetherial paused, then emitted a low, contemptuous hiss of superheated steam. Farris's linen tunic burst into flames, and he collapsed, screaming, reduced to charred ash before the Guards even moved.

The lesson was brutal: Aetherials do not tolerate

weakness, or misdirected purpose.

The line moved quickly, each step I took a calculated, agonizing effort of mental control. I saw Eysa approach a mid-sized Torrent Aetherial. The creature looked at Eysa, its crystal scales shimmering. Eysa, radiating pure, desperate survival, managed to pass. The Aetherial simply nudged her forward with a massive, cold head. She was safe, for now.

I knew my turn was approaching. Roric, the Blazer brute, was just ahead of me. He walked the line with arrogant confidence, his muscles flexing. A Magma Aetherial—a colossal beast named Vulcan—stopped him. The creature examined Roric's core, and its eyes glowed with fierce, shared aggression.

Vulcan roared—a sound that shook the very foundation of the Spires. It was a sound of approval. Roric grinned, his face a mask of victory, and he was enveloped by a surge of fiery power. He had bonded. He was a Rider, and now, an even greater threat to me.

The Void Aetherial and the Test of Truth

I was next. I walked the line, my bare feet silent on the stone, my silver stylus a cold comfort in my hand. I felt the oppressive pressure of the Void Aetherials as I passed them—crushing, deafening, heavy.

Then, I reached the section of the line that contained the most dominant Aetherial of all: Morgal, Teron Draken's bonded partner.

Morgal was an absolute leviathan, the largest of the Void Aetherials, scales the color of solidified midnight. Its presence was a physical weight in the Hall, and it was surrounded by

Teron Draken and his inner circle of Void Riders.

As I drew even with Morgal, the massive Aetherial's head turned slowly, its vast, intelligent eye—a swirling vortex of black and grey—fixing on me.

The contact was immediate and devastating. Morgal's Signet didn't use fire or ice; it used mental suppression. It plunged my mind into absolute, terrifying silence. It was the Still Point achieved by external, crushing force, and it sought to flatten my will.

I gasped, collapsing onto one knee, battling the sheer gravity of the Aetherial's mind. *I cannot hide the truth from this one. It feels the lie.*

Teron Draken, standing on Morgal's enormous foreleg, watched me with an expression of cold, agonizing tension. He gave no overt signal, but his entire body was rigid, channeling a silent message of support. *Anchor, Lyssa. The Vow. Find the truth!*

I fought back, not with strength, but with commitment. I didn't try to suppress the truth of the General's lie, or the injustice of the Karsus execution. Instead, I brought forward the absolute, crystalline truth of my new purpose: Vengeance against the General and the exposure of the Wards.

My loyalty is to justice. My purpose is to expose the corruption. I need survival for this mission. I am a weapon aimed at the heart of the lie.

I channelled this fierce, honest commitment through the silver stylus in my hand.

Morgal paused. Its colossal eye studied my core, feeling the powerful, destructive focus. It sensed the truth of the

General's lie, but it also sensed my unwavering, lethal commitment to justice—a loyalty against the Zenith, but pure to myself and to the vow I shared with its rider.

The Void Aetherial rumbled, a sound that shook me to my bones, but the sound was not one of rejection. It was one of calculating curiosity. Morgal sensed the potent, rare Kinetic Resonance humming beneath my frailty, recognizing it as a unique counter-force to the Void, and a necessary strategic asset.

Morgal did not incinerate me. It simply shifted its colossal head away, its massive eye flickering towards the far side of the Threshing Ground, where the line of the small, Light Aetherials waited. Morgal had judged me worthy of a choice.

I pulled myself up, gasping for breath, sweat plastering the linen tunic to my skin. I had survived the Void.

I walked on, passing Teron Draken. He still didn't move, but his mental Signet reached out—not the crushing Void, but a simple, cold, clear word: *Go.*

The Final Chance

The last section of the line was occupied by the Light Aetherials. They were smaller, crystalline, and often overlooked. I focused my entire being on finding the one who valued stillness and precision.

I passed a dazzling, firefly-like creature (Sound Signet). It ignored me. I passed a flickering, water-colored Aetherial (Light Signet). It didn't react.

Then, I saw him.

The Zephyr Aetherial was waiting at the very end of the line. It was small for an Aetherial, scaled like clear quartz and woven with threads of crystallized wind, humming with a low, complex frequency. It was beautiful, intellectual, and looked utterly bored.

As I approached, the Zephyr Aetherial turned its small, elegant head. Its eyes—twin prisms of perfectly focused light—locked onto me.

It did not invade my mind with force, but with a single, intricate question—a complex, silent equation that demanded absolute precision. It sensed my Kinetic Resonance, the potential for perfect stillness, and it offered a choice: *Can you achieve zero in the eye of the storm?*

I didn't fight. I relaxed my body completely, channeling my entire being into the silver stylus anchor. I reached for the Still Point—not the protected one with Teron, but the absolute, independent, internal silence. I presented my soul as a perfect, empty, silent vessel, ready for the bond.

The Zephyr Aetherial's gaze intensified. It registered the latent power, the subtle strength in my weakness, and the cold, unyielding commitment to my truth.

It moved.

It launched itself from the platform not with a roar, but with a silent, blinding flash of crystallized light. It didn't incinerate the ground; it enveloped me in a whirlwind of absolute, perfect motion. The raw kinetic energy poured into me, but it did not shatter me. Instead, the energy flowed into the silver stylus, anchoring the Signet, stabilizing the connection.

The world dissolved into the humming crystalline light. A

voice—ancient, sharp, and utterly without patience—echoed not in my ears, but in the deepest, most silent core of my mind.

"I choose the Scion of Static. You have stillness. Do not waste it, Conduit."

The bond was instantaneous. I felt a profound, chilling connection—the power of pure motion, of precision, of perfect wind—flow into me. I was a Rider. I had survived the trial by fire.

As the light receded, I stood on the Threshing Ground, a single, frail figure surrounded by the massive presence of my new Aetherial, Zephyr. The crowd was silent, stunned by the unorthodox choice of the rare, quiet Signet.

I looked up, my new Aetherial—my bond—now a crystalline, shimmering sentinel beside me. My eyes instinctively found Teron Draken. He stood on Morgal's leg, his face a complex mask of vindication and profound danger. The alliance was cemented, their secret now bound by the elemental power of their dragons. The game had changed.

CHAPTER 10

THE FIRST FLIGHT AND SHARED MINDS

The world I inhabited after the Threshing was no longer one of simple, objective reality. It was a vibrating, high-definition canvas of motion.

As the crystalline light of Zephyr receded, I felt the bond settle, not as a surge of fire or crushing weight, but as a profound, chilling clarity. My Kinetic Resonance was no longer a sporadic whisper; it was a constant, humming undercurrent. I could feel every molecule of air move, sense the subtle tremor of the Spires' engine miles away, and map the trajectory of every cadet walking nearby. It was overwhelming, a flood of kinetic information that threatened to shatter the fragile architecture of my mind.

A voice, sharp, ancient, and utterly devoid of softness, cut through the kinetic chaos directly in my mind.

"Control the intake, Conduit. You are a filter, not a funnel. Focus. Stillness."

I gasped, the voice not auditory, but an undeniable presence in the deepest core of my being. *Zephyr.*

You can hear me? I thought, the panic making my thoughts rapid and disorganized.

"I hear the noise of your entire lineage, Conduit. Focus on the equation of the moment. Your heartbeat is chaotic. Stabilize the vector."

I forced a deep, stabilizing breath, channeling the excess kinetic energy through my silver stylus anchor. The chaotic input stabilized, transforming into a controlled stream of data. The world snapped into terrifying, crystalline clarity.

I was a Rider.

I looked up. Zephyr stood beside me, his quartz scales shimmering, his massive wings—made of woven, crystallized wind—folded patiently. He was the most beautiful thing I had ever seen, and the most demanding.

The Immediate Danger: The Mind Probe

Captain Korvin was barking orders, moving the newly bonded Riders toward the main flight docks. I followed, stumbling slightly, trying to maintain the internal wall of Stillness between the Aetherial and the secret of my mother's treason.

"The suppression is noted, Conduit. You harbor deep political dissent. I am bound to the Zenith Wards. Your internal chaos threatens the integrity of the bond. Justify your purpose."

The mind probe. It was instantaneous and relentless. Zephyr sensed the core lie immediately.

My purpose is survival to uphold the Wards! I projected fiercely, consciously flooding my internal space with the rehearsed mantra of my mother's doctrine. *I will sacrifice all to expose the threat to Navarre!*

"Ambiguity. Calculated. Acceptable. Your personal loyalty is secondary to your commitment to the Zenith's function. Do not compromise the mission, Conduit, or I will initiate the severance. It will be swift."

The threat was terrifying. The Aetherial knew I was a threat to the regime, but its ancient logic accepted me because my rebellion was framed as a higher form of defense. I had justified the treason as a strategic necessity for the greater good.

I felt a second, colder mental intrusion—the Void. Teron Draken was standing on his bonded Aetherial, Morgal, watching me.

"The General's blood is strong. The lie is safe, Scion. For now. Prepare for flight. Do not look at me."

Our secret was now a dangerous current flowing between two powerful Aetherials. I had to hide the fact that my personal anchor—the deep, volatile connection and shared vengeance with Teron—was the true source of my strength.

The First Flight and the Shared Wind

The first flight was not optional. It was a baptism by wind, designed to physically and mentally integrate the Rider with their Aetherial.

I climbed onto Zephyr's smooth, cool back. I felt every movement of his woven muscles, every shift of his crystalline wings. The saddle felt like a natural extension of my spine.

"Focus on the air, Conduit. Become the vector of motion."

"Lyssa Varen, Flight Alpha-4, prepare for immediate ascent!" Captain Korvin shouted.

Zephyr launched with the silent, surgical efficiency of pure wind. There was no roar, no shuddering force. The take-off was a smooth, exhilarating burst of speed—a perfect, frictionless acceleration.

I expected turbulence; I expected to fight the wind. But Zephyr did not fight the wind; he *became* it. He flowed around the currents, his movements guided by my subtle Kinetic Resonance. I didn't pull the reins; I *thought* the redirection of the airflow around Zephyr's wings.

"You sense the path of least resistance. Good. Direct the flow, Conduit. Let us test the turbulence."

Zephyr soared out over the Miasma, plunging instantly into the chaotic, brutal high-altitude air currents. The wind slammed into us with the force of hammers. I felt the raw kinetic energy wash over me, but instead of being overwhelmed, my Signet instantly activated.

I reached out with my mind, channeling the power through my stylus anchor. I found the core of the turbulent wind—the chaotic vector—and shifted the resistance around Zephyr's body. The violence of the wind remained, but the effect on Zephyr was neutralized. We moved through the gale with the impossible stillness of a gyroscope.

I can stabilize us! I realized, exhilarated.

"We do not fight the motion. We command the stillness within it. We are the perfect counter, Conduit. Now, observe the enemy."

Zephyr directed my gaze to a distant, higher sector of the Spires. A black, crushing Void Aetherial was practicing a massive, brutal aerial maneuver, a corkscrew dive designed to maximize destructive force. It was Morgal, carrying Teron

Draken.

As Morgal executed the dive, Teron's Signet activated. The entire air around them seemed to compress, creating a localized field of intense, crushing gravity. It was a pure display of Void power.

"That is the antithesis of our existence, Conduit. That power crushes the unready. Can you evade that force? Can you turn that gravity against itself?"

I didn't answer in words. I projected a silent, shared commitment: *I can survive it. And I will use it.*

Teron, sensing the mental exchange, looked up. He executed a sudden, violent braking maneuver—a raw expression of contempt.

I understood the message: *I see your power. Do not think it will save you from me.*

Our exchange was interrupted by a new, powerful intrusion in my mind—a deep, ancient sense of rage and frustration.

"They are neglecting the South Ward. The crystalline structure is decaying at a rate of 1.4 percent per annum. The humans are deaf to the structural integrity. They prioritize this display of vanity over the necessity of survival."

Zephyr was focused not on the war games, but on the true enemy: the failing Wards. I felt a surge of validation—the Aetherial had corroborated my mother's treasonous note. The secret was now shared by the most powerful, non-human entities in the kingdom.

I spent the rest of the flight mastering the Kinetic Flow

with Zephyr, practicing the near-subtle direction that allowed us to move faster and more efficiently than any other pair. We were not the strongest, but we were the most precise.

The General's Retaliation

Upon landing, the reaction was immediate and absolute. The other cadets—Blazers, Torrents, and even the Void Riders—were impressed by the impossible stillness of my flight, but their awe was tinged with suspicion.

Captain Korvin had me and Zephyr sequestered instantly. "The General requests your presence, Cadet Varen. And your Aetherial's."

I was marched back to the main command center, the full political weight of my bond crashing down on me.

General Lilith Varen was waiting in a large, unadorned chamber overlooking the Spires. She was not alone. Roric, the Blazer I had beaten in the Gauntlet, stood to her left, his arms crossed, a dark scowl on his face.

"So, you bonded," the General stated, her voice cold and flat, offering no praise. "With Zephyr. The Light Aetherial of Crystalline Wind. Predictably unorthodox."

I remained rigid. "Zephyr is a Signet of Kinetic Precision, General. It provides the highest strategic value for reconnaissance and defense against fast-moving targets."

"Flattery is noted, Conduit. Do not waste my time with human politics." Zephyr's mental voice was a low hum of impatience.

The General addressed the Aetherial, a rare act of

submission. "We are grateful for your service, Zephyr. However, Cadet Varen's performance, while surprising, has created a necessary administrative complication. Her unique Signet requires specialized conditioning."

I realized what was coming. *Isolation.*

The General continued, her eyes locked on me. "Effective immediately, Cadet Varen is transferred from the Fourth Barracks to the Farthest North Isolation Annex. You will receive highly customized training for your unusual Signet, effective immediately. This will ensure your specialized strength can be safely controlled and utilized by the Zenith."

The Isolation Annex. The name was synonymous with failure and disciplinary action—a stone cage reserved for unstable Aetherial conduits or political prisoners. This was my mother's retaliation for my surprising success: total control through total isolation. The General couldn't kill me now that I was bonded, so she would neutralize me.

Roric spoke up, his voice heavy with satisfaction. "The Fourth Barracks is better without her, General. We need strength, not frail tacticians."

"Silence, Cadet," the General snapped, but her eyes held a chilling agreement. She looked back at me. "You will be escorted to the Annex before the next formation. There will be no contact with your previous cohort. Your training will be personally overseen by Wingleader Roric and his squad of Blazers."

I felt the cold dread sink its claws in. Roric, the one who hated me most, was now my direct supervisor. I was being delivered to my enemy, gift-wrapped by my own mother.

She's trying to eliminate me using plausible deniability.

"Roric's core is pure aggression. A necessary counter. This is a severe threat, Conduit. Calculate the risk." Zephyr's presence was a demanding echo in my mind.

I forced myself to look directly at my mother. "Understood, General. I will comply with all directives."

As I was escorted away, I caught sight of the main flight deck. Teron Draken was watching me, standing beside Morgal. His expression was a storm of contained fury and dawning realization.

The Isolation Annex. He knew exactly what his new enemy, the General, was doing. She was cutting me off from my only lifeline—him—and handing me over to his biggest rival, Roric.

I met his gaze, and through the charged mental space, I sent a single, clear thought, amplified by my new bond: *She has severed the tactical alliance. Now it is war.*

Teron did not move, but his massive Void Signet flared violently, the pressure briefly overwhelming the air in the command center. He hadn't just received my thought; he had committed to it.

I was escorted out, my silver stylus a cold promise in my hand. I had survived the Threshing, bonded with an impossible Aetherial, and was now placed in the most politically dangerous position yet: isolated, vulnerable, and under the command of my most vicious personal enemy, all thanks to my mother's calculated ruthlessness. My survival now depended entirely on my ability to use the subtle power of Kinetic Resonance to outsmart a physical beast—all while maintaining a dangerous, forbidden mental bond with the one man who needed me to live just long enough to destroy him.

CHAPTER 11

THE NORTH ANNEX AND THE NEW MASTER

The Farthest North Isolation Annex was not a barracks; it was a prison.

It was housed in a detached, crumbling spire, connected to the main Zenith complex only by a narrow, constantly wind-whipped stone bridge. The General's administrative decree had effectively sentenced me to isolation and probable execution under the guise of specialized training.

The chamber assigned to me was a small, circular cell carved directly into the cold granite. It contained a bare, steel bunk, a small writing desk, and nothing else. The only window was a thick, slit of crystal overlooking the sheer, dizzying drop into the Miasma. The wind here was a constant, mournful scream that vibrated through the stone, making the search for the Still Point a near-impossible task.

Zephyr, bound to me now, hated the isolation. *"The stillness here is stagnant, Conduit. This environment inhibits the necessary kinetic flow. Your General seeks to neutralize us through environment."*

"She seeks to neutralize me, Zephyr," I thought back, settling onto the cold bunk. *"You are just collateral damage."*

The immediate peril was Wingleader Roric. He and his two closest Blazer cohorts arrived within the hour. Roric, a man driven by bitter resentment and brute force, now held complete authority over my life and death.

"Welcome to your special training, Scion," Roric sneered, leaning against the cell door frame, his massive frame dwarfing the entrance. His two cohorts—equally massive, equally contemptuous Blazers—stood flanking him, radiating crude, oppressive Magma Signets that made the air feel thick and volatile. "Your mother believes you need conditioning for your 'subtle' Signet. I believe you need to learn what pure force feels like before your Aetherial judges you as weak and burns you. Fortunately for me, the Zenith Code grants Wingleaders absolute discretion in the Isolated Annex."

The First Lesson: Pure Force

Roric wasted no time. The annex included a small, dilapidated, open-air training platform. It was cracked, uneven, and constantly swept by high-velocity wind—the worst possible environment for a Signet requiring stillness.

"Your Signet manipulates motion," Roric announced, standing a safe distance away. "Mine creates it. Today, you learn the difference between precision and power. Your assignment: Survive my momentum."

Roric's Blazer cohorts activated their Signets. A terrifying wave of Magma Energy surged forth—not fire, but raw, blistering heat that instantly super-heated the granite around them, sending plumes of smoke and scalding air into the training space. The goal was to eliminate all possibility of the Still Point through physical agony.

"The heat is destabilizing the bond, Conduit! Find the coldness! Find the zero!" Zephyr's mental cry was sharp with distress.

I drew my silver stylus, my kinetic anchor, the cool metal a momentary refuge from the blistering heat. The pain in my lungs was immediate and crippling. I fought to keep my eyes open, my vision swimming from the heat exhaustion.

Roric charged, not with a blade, but with his full, terrifying mass, channeled by his Magma Signet. He was a human battering ram, a massive, accelerating block of raw, kinetic force aimed directly at my chest.

I knew I couldn't redirect the sheer magnitude of his mass. Attempting to absorb the force would fracture my self. I had to perform a tactical surrender.

I hit the Still Point with desperate, agonizing effort. I ignored the pain, the heat, and the instinct to flee. I focused on the precise, geometric line of Roric's charge—the single, narrow vector of his motion.

At the very last moment, I used my Signet to reduce the friction beneath my own feet, allowing my body to be thrown backward by the force of his approach, instead of absorbing the impact. I didn't block; I flowed.

Roric's massive fist grazed my shoulder, but the force, instead of breaking me, sent me flying backward in a controlled, frictionless slide across the cracked granite floor. I skidded twenty feet before slamming into the far granite wall.

I cried out, the impact stealing my breath and sending a spike of pure, kinetic energy through my core. My ribs protested the brutal deceleration.

Roric stopped, his eyes wide with surprise and anger. "You moved like water, Varen! That's not natural deflection!"

"It's physics, Wingleader," I gasped, pushing myself up with trembling arms, the metallic taste of blood filling my mouth. "When momentum is preserved through reduced friction, the force remains, but the object survives the impact."

Roric, however, was not concerned with physics. He was concerned with obedience. He grinned, a nasty, victorious flash of teeth. "You survived the first one, Scion. But you used your Signet. That is forbidden during conditioning."

He strode over to me, his Blazer cohorts forming a menacing circle. "But since you used the magic, let's see how well you can hold a position."

He reached out, his hand glowing faintly with Magma energy, and pressed his palm directly onto my silver stylus anchor. The silver instantly began to absorb the heat, radiating it back into my hand, a searing jolt of pain.

"Stand still, Scion. Stand perfectly still for the next five minutes, or I'll hold you here until the skin melts to the metal."

The pain was excruciating, testing my Still Point not with chaos, but with sheer, continuous agony. I grit my teeth, my entire body screaming in protest. The heat was overpowering the Kinetic Resonance.

"The heat is overwhelming the silver, Conduit! Release the metal! Sever the anchor!" Zephyr commanded, his fear palpable.

"No! The stylus is the only thing preserving my composure!" I fought back, refusing to let go of my anchor. I stood in the oppressive heat, locked in a brutal, silent battle of will with Roric, my entire being focused on survival.

The Covert Intervention

The second evening brought no relief. Roric's training sessions were relentless, always designed to push me to the point of complete physical and mental collapse. I knew he was trying to break me before the other Riders had a chance to witness my strange, resilient power.

That night, alone in my cell, I collapsed onto my bunk, bruised, aching, and defeated. I was staring blankly at the ceiling when I felt it—a sudden, deep lull in the kinetic flow outside the Annex. The constant, shrieking wind of the high altitude had momentarily been silenced.

Void Energy.

The unmistakable, heavy presence of Morgal and Teron Draken was here.

"Intrusion. Powerful and silent. The Void Aetherial masks its presence from the Zenith sensors. Extreme caution, Conduit."

I got up and walked to the slit window. I could see nothing but the sheer drop and the endless, black night.

Then, a sudden, sharp, metallic sound—a single, distinct tap—came from the stone directly outside my window. I realized the horrifying truth: Teron was standing on the narrow, unstable ledge outside the North Annex, several hundred feet above the Miasma, using his Signet to suppress the wind and the sensor alarms.

I pressed my face to the cold crystal slit. "Teron," I whispered, my voice choked with desperation and fear.

"I can't stay long," Teron's voice was a low, urgent hum that bypassed my ears, resonating directly in my mind, amplified by his Void Signet. His telepathic voice was sharp and clear—the intimacy of the Signet exchange more profound and dangerous than any physical touch. *"The General's orders are absolute. Roric is trying to push you to fail. He wants you dead before you become a political threat."*

"He's using heat," I projected back, sending a wave of my raw kinetic anxiety. *"Magma Signet. It overwhelms my ability to hold the Still Point. The heat drains the flow of the Kinetic*

Resonance."

"I know." Teron's mental response was a cold wave of understanding. *"He's weaponizing your fragility. You need to redirect the heat's kinetic energy. You can't cool the air, but you can neutralize the transmission of the heat molecules through your skin. Focus the Resonance on your nervous system—create a tiny, kinetic shield beneath your skin."*

I was stunned by the genius of the tactical advice. It was a complex, suicidal maneuver requiring absolute precision, but it was the only way to beat the heat.

"Why are you here, Teron?" I asked, the question laced with the desperate ache of our forbidden connection. *"You risk everything for this."*

His mental projection faltered, a momentary break in his stoic composure. *"I made a vow, Scion. And I don't break my word. I need the lie exposed, and you are the only one who can deliver the blow. Survive this, Lyssa. Use the stylus. Use the coldness of the granite. And stop fighting his momentum—steer it."*

A sudden, sharp alarm began to sound far below—a low, rhythmic pulse indicating a sensor disturbance near the Annex bridge.

"I have to go," Teron projected instantly. *"They are detecting the anomaly. Remember the lesson: Steer the motion."*

The Void presence vanished as quickly as it had arrived.

The wind immediately returned, shrieking past the cell window with full, deafening force.

I pulled away from the window, my heart pounding. Teron Draken had just risked his life and his Signet to give me a secret lesson. I had survived the emotional culling and received the exact technical advice I needed to beat Roric's physical brutality.

The Third Lesson: Steer the Motion

The next morning, Roric was waiting, his eyes gleaming with anticipation of my breakdown. He had added a new element to the training: a massive, swinging iron pendulum—an enormous kinetic weapon—that he would swing at me during my timed endurance trials.

"Today, Scion, we introduce chaos," Roric announced. "You will stand here. When the pendulum swings, you will use your Signet to stop its motion. If you fail, it cleans the slate."

I stood in the center of the training platform, my silver stylus tightly gripped. The pendulum was heavy, moving with terrifying, natural inertia.

Roric counted down. "Three. Two. One. Swing!"

The pendulum was released. It moved with crushing, unstoppable kinetic force. I watched it, my mind calm, remembering Teron's words: *Steer the motion.*

I didn't try to stop the iron mass. I focused on the heat

and the motion simultaneously. I achieved the Still Point, my mind a cold, silent fortress against the pain and the noise. I targeted the swing's arc and the heat's molecular transfer beneath my skin.

At the exact moment of contact, I focused my Signet on two simultaneous actions:

1. Internal Defense: I created the minute, kinetic shield beneath my skin, neutralizing the heat transfer from the Blazer energy. The heat pain was still there, but it was bearable.

2. External Offense: I focused the rest of my power on a minute shift in the pendulum's vector. I didn't stop the weight; I simply redirected the trajectory of its swing by two degrees.

The iron mass, guided by my subtle manipulation, swung past my head by a hair's breadth. It didn't miss; it had been *steered*.

Roric stared, his jaw slack, his victory ripped away by an impossible subtlety. I stood whole, breathing hard, the silver stylus hot but manageable in my hand.

"That was not luck, Wingleader," I said, my voice strained but firm. "That was precision. Your momentum is predictable. And I have learned how to steer the predictable."

Roric's face twisted in pure, incandescent fury. He had been defeated not by force, but by my intelligence—an intelligence that had been honed and perfected by the very man sworn to be my greatest enemy. He knew, instinctively, that I had received outside help.

"The session is over, Scion," Roric snarled, his voice low and shaking with contained violence. "Report back to your cell. But know this: I may not be able to incinerate you, but I can break every bone in your body slowly. Your special training has only just begun."

I walked away, my entire body aching, but my mind clear. I had survived the initial, brutal culling of the Isolation Annex. My secret alliance was now a fundamental, deadly necessity. I was the weapon, and Teron Draken was the only person who knew how to load the chamber. My life was now a constant, terrifying dance between survival, treason, and a forbidden, kinetic attraction.

CHAPTER 12

THE SECRET COMMUNICATIONS AND THE STRATEGIC CULLING

The Farthest North Isolation Annex was meant to be my end, but thanks to Teron Draken's covert intervention, it had become my crucible. The daily, brutal sessions with Wingleader Roric were no longer a threat to my life, but a demanding training regimen that forced me to refine my Kinetic Resonance to surgical precision.

The Void-Kinetic Connection

The true miracle of my survival was the Signet-Link I shared with Teron. After our last exchange, we established a system of clandestine communication based on the unique properties of our Aetherials.

The Void Signet was the perfect, massive anchor for long-distance mental contact. Teron would use Morgal's immense power to create a brief, dense wave of silence—a subtle pause in the ambient kinetic noise of the Spires—at predetermined times, usually during the deepest hours of the night.

I, with my honed Kinetic Resonance, would then perceive this moment of absolute stillness and use my mind to ride the receding Void wave back to Teron. It was a perilous, taxing mental journey—a silent, high-stakes conversation conducted entirely in shared sensation and abbreviated, urgent thoughts.

I'd project a burst of kinetic data: *I survived Roric. He used a triple-thrust pattern. Predictable.*

Teron would respond almost instantly, his thoughts a cold, concise strategic command infused with his Void Signet's confidence: *Avoid the pivot. Roric is weak at rotation. Push the counter-motion to his left quad.*

The link was intimate and terrifying. It bypassed all language and all guards, connecting our minds and our Signets at the most primal level. It meant every moment of my pain, every flicker of my resolve, and every surge of my adrenaline was felt by Teron. And every time I achieved the Still Point, Teron felt the profound, chilling rush of my zero-resistance energy—the counter-force to his own power.

"The alliance is symbiotic, Conduit. His density strengthens our clarity. But the human emotion is a variable. Control it." Zephyr's voice, now a constant, demanding presence in my mind, was wary of the emotional danger.

I tried to follow my Aetherial's command, but every successful training maneuver, every moment of survival thanks to Teron's instruction, deepened the unwanted, profound connection. I was bound to him by the truth of his father's martyrdom and the blood on my mother's hands. The boundary between tactical necessity and passionate longing was disintegrating rapidly.

Roric's Escalation and the Water Culling

Roric, furious at my continued, impossible survival,

escalated the training from endurance to outright assassination attempts. The Annex training platform was replaced by the High Pools Ward, a vast, freezing cavern where candidates practiced underwater combat and endurance.

The danger here was two-fold: the crushing pressure of the water and the presence of Torrent Aetherials—creatures that commanded water and ice. For the Kinetic Resonance to work effectively, I needed stable vectors, which were impossibly chaotic and unpredictable in a body of churning water.

The session was designed to be a mass culling. Roric oversaw the exercises from a catwalk, while Torrent Riders patrolled the surface, their Signets churning the water into dangerous whirlpools and frigid currents.

I noticed Eysa struggling immediately. Eysa was strong, but her Signet was a non-combat support class—likely a Healer or Sustainer. She lacked the core elemental power to fight the Torrent Aetherials' manipulation of the water. Eysa was caught in a brutal whirlpool created by a disgruntled Torrent Rider named Bryn, who was clearly enjoying the slow torture.

Eysa is going to drown. She is too strong to die, but not strong enough to fight the chaos.

I had to act. I couldn't use my power to move Eysa—it would be too obvious and too energy-draining. I had to use my Signet to disrupt the Source of the chaos.

I plunged into the freezing water, feeling the immediate sting on my bruised skin. I pushed toward Eysa, concentrating fiercely on Bryn, the Torrent Rider who was generating the whirlpool.

I reached out with my mind, finding the pure, swirling kinetic vector of the whirlpool. I didn't try to stop the motion.

I focused on the point where Bryn's Signet was injecting the kinetic energy into the water—the precise, tiny spot where the elemental force met the physical medium.

Stillness. Zero. Disruption.

I unleashed a subtle, surgical pulse of Kinetic Resonance directly into Bryn's localized output. It was not a violent strike; it was the creation of a brief, momentary point of zero resistance at the Torrent Rider's nexus of power.

The effect was instantaneous and shocking. Bryn's Signet faltered. The massive whirlpool did not vanish, but its core tension collapsed. The water flow immediately became chaotic, disorganized, and harmless.

Bryn gasped, pulling his Signet back, baffled by the sudden, inexplicable failure of his power. Eysa, released from the crush of the whirlpool, managed to kick free and swim toward the side of the pool, exhausted but alive.

I slipped away, merging back into the chaos of the other struggling cadets. I had saved Eysa, but I had used my Signet to influence a hostile Signet's output—a calculated act of war that demanded absolute secrecy.

The Unspoken Verdict

Roric, watching from the catwalk, missed the subtle exchange. He saw only Eysa's unexpected escape. But Bryn, the Torrent Rider, knew something had gone profoundly wrong. His eyes, searching the pool, fixed on me. He didn't see weakness; he saw an unsettling, inexplicable control.

Later that evening, the strategic culling began. Captain

Korvin announced that due to "inefficiency and a lack of Aetherial compatibility," three cadets were being immediately sent to the Scribe Quadrant—the ultimate, humiliating demotion for a Rider. Bryn, the talented Torrent Rider I had subtly sabotaged, was one of them.

I felt a jolt of cold, guilty satisfaction. I had used my power to effectively cull a political opponent, ensuring Eysa's survival and eliminating a potent Signet from the pool of threats.

"The calculation is efficient, Conduit. Your method of neutralization is strategically sound. But the cost of this ruthlessness will be tallied." Zephyr's warning was sharp.

I knew the cost. I was descending into the ruthless, calculated world of my mother. Survival here meant becoming a monster, but a monster aimed at a just cause.

The Confession and the Embrace

That night, Teron Draken initiated the midnight Void-Kinetic Link. I was waiting, sitting rigidly on my cold bunk, my body aching, my mind churning with the moral ambiguity of the day.

Bryn is gone. Eysa is safe. I created the collapse. I projected the facts in cold, concise bursts of kinetic data.

Teron's mental response was a wave of cold, powerful silence, followed by a surge of raw approval. *A bold move, Scion. You used the Signet to break his Signet's output. You eliminated a threat efficiently. You are learning the true cruelty of the Zenith.*

I am learning the cruelty of my mother, I retorted, my

thoughts laced with pain. *I felt no remorse, Teron. I condemned him for Eysa's survival.*

Remorse is weakness. Survival is vengeance, Teron countered, his mental voice hard. *You are becoming the weapon I need, Lyssa. You are embracing the ruthlessness of the Varen bloodline and aiming it at its source. That is true justice.*

I couldn't argue. His approval—the one thing I craved in this isolated hell—was built on my moral compromise.

I need a physical anchor, I projected, the desperate plea breaking the professional boundary. *The cold is relentless. I need stillness I can feel.*

The mental link snapped, replaced by the sound of muffled stone on stone. Teron was using his brute strength to silently open the narrow, sealed service door on the Annex bridge.

Minutes later, a tall, dark shadow filled my cell doorway. Teron Draken, clad only in simple trousers, stood there, his body radiating a mixture of cold air and intense, contained heat.

"This is the last time," he stated, his voice a low, physical growl. "I risk execution if I'm caught here."

"I risk execution every time I breathe," I shot back, not moving from my bunk.

Teron strode across the small cell, his steps silent, and stopped at the foot of my bunk. He reached out and gently took the silver stylus from my hand.

"This is not enough," he decided, the metal feeling ridiculously small and fragile in his massive grip. "It anchors the energy, but it doesn't anchor you."

He then did the unthinkable. He lay down on the narrow bunk beside me, his body pressing against mine. The steel frame groaned softly under his weight.

"Void meets Kinetic," he murmured, pulling me close, his massive arm wrapping around my waist, pulling me back against the solid wall of his chest. "I will be the anchor. You will channel the coldness of Zephyr into my heat. We will stabilize the chaos together."

The physical contact was immediate, profound, and overwhelmingly intimate. The cold, frantic energy of my body and my Kinetic Resonance flowed instantly into the immense, burning heat of Teron's body and his Void Signet. It wasn't just physical comfort; it was an elemental merge. I felt my chaos stabilize instantly, the coldness in my core dissipating into his heat.

Teron buried his face in my hair, his breath warm against my cold skin. "This is not affection, Lyssa," he ground out, his voice thick with suppressed emotion. "This is a tactical maneuver. We are utilizing the opposing forces of our Signets to achieve optimum stability. My heat will contain your chaos. Your coolness will temper my violence."

I didn't argue. I knew he was lying to himself, trying to maintain the professional distance. But I also knew the technical truth: for the first time since the Threshing, my mind was silent. I had achieved the Still Point effortlessly, anchored by the solid, warm core of the man sworn to hate me.

"My silence is your survival, Wingleader," I whispered, closing my eyes, allowing the forbidden, intimate stability to wash over me.

Teron held me tighter, his arm a band of iron around my waist. "Then use it, Scion. Rest. Tomorrow, we plan how to get you out of this prison. You are too valuable to the lie to die here."

I drifted into the deepest, most tranquil sleep I had known since entering the Spires, my body held by the one force that truly understood my power and my pain. The unspoken truth was overwhelming: we were no longer just allies in vengeance; we were two opposing elemental forces bound together by a desperate, volatile necessity. The cost of our shadow pact was becoming exponentially higher, risking not just our lives, but our very souls.

CHAPTER 13

THE ESCAPE VECTOR AND THE GENERAL'S TRAP

The cold, shared intimacy of our midnight rendezvous had solidified my pact with Teron Draken. We had moved past the emotional pretense; we were complementary forces, Void and Kinetic, bound by a singular, dangerous purpose. The Isolation Annex was now just an obstacle, and General Lilith Varen's tactical maneuver—to use Roric as her executioner—was a challenge to be meticulously dismantled.

The plan was devised entirely through our nocturnal Signet-Link. The Void acted as the secure channel, the Kinetic as the data stream. It was the fastest, most secretive exchange of information ever known in the Zenith Spires.

The Impossible Plan: Kinetic Shield, Void Anchor

The problem was simple: Roric was planning a final elimination drill on the North Bridge, the narrow, wind-lashed span connecting the Annex to the main spire. It was a perfect choke point for an "accident." Roric would use his Blazer squad and his Magma Signet to create a sudden, catastrophic blast of kinetic force, simulating a Miasma gust and ensuring I would be thrown into the chasm.

"Roric will use four Blazers. Synchronized kinetic force. Too massive to redirect, Scion," Teron projected the military analysis. *"You must neutralize the momentum before it reaches the core of the bridge."*

"If I neutralize the *blast, I risk self-fracture,"* I argued mentally, sending the warning tremor of my physical limits. *"The energy is too crude, too powerful."*

"Then we neutralize the transfer medium," Teron commanded, the Void presence heavy with absolute certainty. *"I* will anchor the North Bridge with Morgal's Signet, stabilizing the structure against the blast. You will create a Kinetic Shield—a sphere of zero resistance that encapsulates the point *of impact. You don't deflect the force; you vacuum the motion around you, converting the Blazer's attack into absolute stillness for one second."*

It was a suicidal maneuver, requiring a perfectly timed, simultaneous activation of our opposing Signets from miles apart. My life depended on Teron hitting the peak of his Void Anchor at the exact moment I activated my Kinetic Shield. The smallest delay would mean the catastrophic failure of my still-fragile Signet and my disintegration.

The Execution: The North Bridge

The day of the drill arrived, freezing and clear, perfect conditions for a fatal fall. Roric, flanked by his four largest Blazer cohorts and their bonded Aetherials, waited on the main spire side of the North Bridge. I, with Zephyr walking silently beside me—his crystalline scales catching the sunlight—stood alone on the Annex side.

The General was not in attendance, a calculated absence

designed to grant Roric plausible deniability.

"Cadet Varen," Roric shouted across the windy expanse, his voice laced with venomous satisfaction. "Your special training concludes with the Simulated Miasma Gust Drill. Cross the bridge. If you fall, the Annex is cleansed of your weakness."

The North Bridge was fifty feet long, built of slippery, aged stone, and constantly battered by the high-altitude winds. I drew my silver stylus, gripping my anchor tightly.

"The wind is a chorus of chaos, Conduit. The Void presence is distant, but focused. Prepare *the Still Point."* Zephyr's mental voice was a low, urgent warning.

I started across the bridge, my movements slow, meticulous. I didn't have to look to know that Teron Draken and Morgal were positioned on the highest peak of the nearby Sentinel Spire, their Signets already active.

I am crossing. Roric is readying the assault. Mark. I sent the final kinetic burst.

"Understood. Anchor is deploying. Prepare for Zero. Now." Teron's mental command slammed into my mind, clear and absolute.

As I reached the center of the bridge, Roric raised his hand, a malicious grin splitting his face. "Now, Blazers! Give the Scion a proper send-off!"

The four Blazer Aetherials—massive creatures of heat and magma—unleashed a coordinated, synchronized torrent of kinetic force. It was a wave of pure, brutal air pressure and scalding heat, designed to hit me with the momentum of a falling mountain.

The force slammed into the bridge. I felt the enormous kinetic pressure hit the surface, threatening to crack the stone beneath my feet.

In that millisecond, Teron executed his maneuver. Morgal's Void Signet flared. A massive, silent wave of density flowed down the bridge. It didn't stop the Blazer attack, but it anchored the bridge structure to the bedrock with crushing gravity, preventing the stone from shattering and collapsing under the kinetic force.

I felt the stabilizing weight of the Void. *Now.*

I activated my Kinetic Shield. I poured every ounce of my focus, every cell of my body, and every fiber of my bond with Zephyr into the silver stylus. I didn't create a deflector; I created a perfect, spherical Kinetic Vacuum around my body.

The brutal, synchronized blast of the Blazers—the pure, crushing motion—collided with my Shield. The energy did not bounce; it was absorbed into stillness. The air around my body went dead, silent, and completely motionless.

The devastating kinetic force of the four Blazers vanished.

Roric's blast simply continued around the sphere of stillness, the force flowing harmlessly past me and hitting the far wall of the Annex. The only effect on me was the blinding pain of the internal backlash—the sheer, residual energy trying to shatter me. But the Void Anchor had bought me a crucial, fraction-of-a-second delay, and my silver stylus absorbed the remaining kinetic tremor.

I stood untouched, utterly motionless, at the center of the North Bridge.

Roric stared, his jaw slack, his Signet faltering. His two

Blazer cohorts looked equally aghast. Their perfectly executed assassination attempt had been neutralized by an invisible counter-force.

I slowly lowered my stylus, my face pale, my body trembling with exhaustion, but my eyes burning with cold, resolute triumph.

"Insufficient force, Wingleader," I said, my voice shaking but carrying clearly across the bridge. "Your momentum is predictable, and mine is absolute. You failed the drill."

The Political Fallout

Roric roared, a sound of pure, defeated rage. He lunged across the bridge, intending to finish the job with his bare hands.

But before he could cover five feet, a powerful, organized force arrived on the bridge.

"Wingleader Roric! Retreat! The drill is terminated!"

Captain Korvin, the Gauntlet Master, led a troop of Spires Guards onto the bridge. Korvin had been observing the 'drill' from a safe distance, and his face was tight with confusion. He hadn't seen a kinetic shield; he had seen a sudden, impossible failure of the Blazer Signets.

"The Cadet survived the simulation," Korvin announced formally, looking pointedly at Roric. "The Annex conditioning is complete. Cadet Varen is officially transferred back to the main barracks, effective immediately. Wingleader Draken has requested she be placed under the direct command of the Void Quadrant for 'Signet synergy purposes.'"

I knew instantly what Teron had done. He hadn't just anchored the bridge; he had moved quickly to the command center, utilizing his rank and the political turmoil of my escape to pull me out of the General's direct control and into his own sphere of influence.

Roric was physically restrained by his own cohorts. "Draken! He is protecting her! She is a traitor's spawn!"

"That is a political accusation, Wingleader Roric," Korvin said coldly. "Cadet Varen is a bonded Rider and has survived every test. Report to your unit. Cadet Varen, you are released to the Void Barracks."

I walked across the bridge, passing Roric. I didn't look at him, but I sent a single, clear mental flash through the kinetic air currents: *You failed the General's trap.*

I arrived at the main spire and was immediately taken to the Void Quadrant barracks—a newer, cleaner, and far more imposing structure than the Fourth Barracks.

The Void Barracks and the Shared Space

The Void Barracks was the territory of the Marked Ones—the children of the executed Northern rebels. The air inside was heavy, silent, and thick with contained resentment.

I was led to my new bunk. I found my small trunk of belongings already there, and beside it, a large, dark leather journal—a Scribe text on ancient military fortifications. Tucked inside the cover was a small, tightly folded note.

I waited until the escort guard was gone, and I opened the note. It was Teron's sharp, elegant script:

"The move was necessary. Your mother will assume you are now under my control, making you untouchable until a formal political opening is created. But do not mistake this for safety, Scion. You are now a target in my home. The Marked Ones hate your blood, and they are fiercely loyal to my command. You are my greatest tactical risk. Your new bunk is across the aisle from mine. Do not betray my trust. Do not fail me. And do not, under any circumstances, show weakness."

I looked up from the note. My new bunk was on the lowest tier, in a small, private alcove. I looked across the aisle. Teron Draken's bunk was directly opposite mine. He was already there, meticulously arranging his gear, his back to me, an imposing wall of dark, contained power.

He finished his task, turning slowly. His eyes met mine, and the intensity was breathtaking. The hatred was still there, but it was now irrevocably mixed with a fierce, possessive need.

"Welcome to the Void Quadrant, Cadet Varen," he said formally, his voice loud enough for the nearby cadets to hear. "You are now under my command. I expect perfection."

Then, he sent a private, silent message through the Void-Kinetic link: *"You defied my expectations, Lyssa. You are mine now. And the risk is exhilarating."*

CHAPTER 14

THE CODE OF THE MARKED AND THE SCRIBE'S DECEPTION

The Void Barracks was a landscape of deep, contained resentment. My transfer from the crumbling, abandoned North Annex to the pristine, obsidian-laced structure of the Void Quadrant was a promotion in physical comfort but a catastrophic descent into political danger. I was the enemy's blood, now sleeping directly across the aisle from the only man sworn to avenge my mother's crime.

The air in the barracks was heavy, not with the chaos of the Fourth Barracks, but with the palpable Void Signet energy that radiated from every Marked One. It was a perpetual, ambient pressure, a constant reminder of the immense, cold power they collectively wielded—the power of density and suppression. Every cadet here was a child of the executed rebels, their loyalty forged in shared grief and burning hatred for the Varen name.

I sat on my bunk, the silver stylus warm in my hand, listening to the silence. No one spoke to me. No one made eye contact. When I walked through the hall, the Marked Ones simply parted, their faces expressions of chilling, controlled indifference. I was a biological weapon, sequestered by the one force they respected—their Wingleader—and their collective hatred was a physical force I had to endure.

"The containment is absolute, Conduit. This environment is designed for internal cohesion and external rejection. They perceive you as a parasitic element. Your Signet must be equally absolute in its subtlety." Zephyr's mental voice was a low, constant calculation, mapping the kinetic flow of the hostile room.

The Wingleader's Ownership

Teron Draken maintained absolute, visible control over my presence. Our public dynamic was one of cold, unforgiving command, designed to broadcast a simple, lethal message: *This Cadet is under my total authority. Touch her, and you challenge me.*

The first morning formation was the proving ground. I stood in the Void line, the only one without the dark, jagged scars of the Marked Ones. Teron stood before the ranks, his imposing figure a study in controlled dominance.

"Cadets," he stated, his voice ringing with the metallic clarity of his Void Signet. "Cadet Varen is now under Void command. Her Signet, Kinetic Resonance, is a strategic counter-force to our own, and therefore, a necessary asset. You will treat her with the respect due to any bonded Rider."

He then locked eyes with a tall, grim-faced Marked One named Jax, Teron's second-in-command. "You will also remember the Code of the Marked. Our vengeance is not satisfied by petty aggression. Our vengeance is a strategic, patient, and total act. Cadet Varen is necessary to that long-term objective. Any attempt to compromise her integrity will be viewed as an act of treason against my command. Understood?"

The final word was infused with Void power, slamming into the consciousness of every cadet with crushing, undeniable weight.

"Understood, Wingleader," Jax responded, his voice tight with resentment. Jax hated me, but his loyalty to Teron was absolute.

Later that day, Jax found me sitting at my desk, studying the complex military schematics of the training ward. He paused, his massive form filling the aisle. "You are smart, Scion," he muttered, his voice grudgingly low. "That is a kind of strength the General never truly understood." He nodded sharply once and walked away. The respect was cold, but it was earned.

Teron had publicly declared me his property, my tool, and the focal point of their collective, unspoken mission. This did not earn me friendship, but it bought me survival. It elevated our shared secret from a dangerous romance to a political pact.

The Scribe's Deception: Mapping the Chaos

I embraced the isolation. I used the silence of the Void Barracks for intensive mental training. My physical training was now done privately, running the long, empty corridors of the high spire, Zephyr a silent, soaring guide in my mind, helping my Kinetic Resonance to neutralize the friction of my movement, turning my exhausting run into a near-silent glide.

During the mandatory evening study periods, I began the crucial work of penetrating the Void Quadrant's archives—the Scribe work that was my only true expertise. I was looking for any document that shed light on Lord Karsus Draken's actual rebellion and, more importantly, the specific, structural weaknesses of the Zenith Wards.

The Void archive was located in a heavily shielded sub-level. It was protected by advanced kinetic dampeners designed to prevent sabotage. I realized the irony: the dampeners, intended to suppress the kinetic energy of external threats, made the area unnaturally still—the perfect environment for me to achieve the Still Point.

I slipped into the archive late one night, my heart pounding against my ribs. I was looking for 'Project Nightingale', a codename mentioned in my mother's hidden note.

I reached the central server bank, a massive metallic sphere pulsating with energy. It was sealed with a complex, multi-layered lock based on kinetic signature recognition—only a Void Rider's unique energy signature could open it.

I need access, Zephyr. Find the key.

"The lock is kinetic. It requires extreme density, which we

lack. However, the system's kinetic sensor generates a precise, rhythmic frequency. If you eliminate the noise of the ambient air flow, the sensor's tolerance will sharpen."

It was a complex maneuver. I placed my silver stylus against the lock panel. I achieved the Still Point, and then, with surgical precision, I used my Kinetic Resonance to neutralize the kinetic energy of the air molecules directly over the lock sensor.

The effect was subtle but immediate: the sensor's tolerance for disruption vanished. It became acutely sensitive, waiting for the perfect, massive kinetic signature of a Void Signet.

I smiled grimly. I couldn't replicate Teron's Void energy, but I knew the exact kinetic signature of Teron Draken's hand resting on my back—the feeling of his Void energy radiating into my core.

I pressed my palm to the lock and focused, projecting a memory-signature of Teron's crushing kinetic presence, amplified by the vacuum of stillness I had created.

The lock clicked open. The Void Scribe Archive was mine.

Project Nightingale: The Truth of the Miasma

Inside the server, I found what I was looking for: a series of encrypted reports marked Project Nightingale.

The reports confirmed Lord Karsus Draken's fears: the Miasma was not an external threat. It was a symptom. The crystalline Spires were built on a fault line of latent, unstable Aetherium, and the excessive channeling of magic for the Wards was causing the crystalline bedrock to leak raw, unstable magic—the Miasma—upwards. The wards were not failing due to enemy attack; they were failing because the Zenith was structurally unsound.

Lord Karsus had planned a controlled depressurization— a painful but necessary shutdown of the Wards to stabilize the bedrock. General Varen had executed him to prevent the ensuing panic, choosing to maintain the facade of control.

I also found a list of Vulnerability Points—precise, localized sections in the bedrock where the Miasma leakage was most severe. One point, ominously labeled 'The Dreadnought Nexus,' was directly beneath the main training ward. If it failed, the entire center of the Spires would collapse.

"The corruption is structural. The General's betrayal runs deeper than execution. We now possess the architectural map to the entire lie, Conduit." Zephyr's voice was cold with analytical triumph.

I quickly downloaded the key data—location, collapse timeline, and the original depressurization plans—onto a heavily encrypted, tiny data chip stored in my stylus anchor.

I closed the archive, carefully neutralized the air again, and left. I was no longer just a Rider; I was a spy who held the architectural blueprint to the collapse of the Zenith.

The Midnight Demand

I returned to the Void Barracks just as the early dawn light began to filter through the windows. I found Teron Draken waiting for me, sitting on the edge of his bunk, his shirt unbuttoned, his face etched with exhaustion and suspicion.

He hadn't been asleep. He had been monitoring the kinetic energy of the archive's lock.

"You took a risk, Varen," he stated, his voice a low, gravelly warning. "I felt the disturbance—a subtle skip in the lock's rhythm. You used your Signet on the archive."

I walked to my bunk and sat down, meeting his gaze directly. I pulled the silver stylus out and showed him the tiny, integrated data chip.

"I didn't take a risk, Wingleader. I calculated the precise probability of detection and minimized the Signet output. I succeeded. I found Project Nightingale."

Teron's eyes, glacial gray, narrowed with focused intensity. "What did you find?"

I leaned forward, dropping my voice to a conspiratorial whisper, the sound barely audible over the breathing of the sleeping Marked Ones. "Your father was right, Teron. The Miasma is the Spires' own structural failure. The Wards are collapsing from within. And there is a Vulnerability Point beneath the main training ward—the Dreadnought Nexus. If it fails, the entire central Spire collapses into the Miasma."

Teron stared at me, his usual iron control momentarily dissolving into raw, agonizing shock. The vengeance he had sworn was not just political; it was righteous.

"My father died to save this place from its own arrogance," he whispered, the truth cutting through his protective shell. "The General sacrificed him to conceal a ticking clock."

I nodded, placing the stylus and its secret chip on my bunk. "We have the truth, Wingleader. And we have the map to the collapse. Now we need the strategy."

Teron pushed himself off his bunk and strode across the aisle, stopping directly over me. He placed his massive hands on either side of me, trapping me. His face was a mask of dark, desperate determination.

"The time for subtle vengeance is over," he declared, his Signet flaring with contained violence. "The General's trap has failed, but the clock is ticking. You are no longer just bait, Lyssa. You are the only person who knows how to disarm the enemy's bomb, and you are my only key to justice."

He leaned down, his voice thick with a sudden, devastating possessiveness that was both terrifying and intimate.

"The Spires will try to use us. The General will try to eliminate us. But no one will stop us. From this moment on, Cadet Varen, you will be by my side. Every class, every formation, every flight. You are my weapon, my weakness, and my undeniable truth. And I will protect what is mine."

He sealed the pact with a fierce, punishing kiss, a desperate claim of ownership and shared treason. It was a volatile, hungry collision of Void and Kinetic energy, cementing the bond that could either save Navarre or destroy it entirely.

I responded with an equal, desperate surge of kinetic energy, meeting his possessive heat with my cold, perfect stillness. I had navigated the barracks, thwarted my mother, and gained the ultimate tool for revenge. I was a Rider, a spy, and the forbidden lover of the leader of the rebellion. The full battle for the Zenith Spires had just begun.

CHAPTER 15

VOID EXERCISES AND THE PUBLIC LIE

The Void Barracks hummed with tension. I was awake long before the morning horn, sitting in the cold silence, analyzing the architectural data I had stolen—the blueprint of the Zenith's destruction. The Dreadnought Nexus, the weak point beneath the main training ward, was a ticking clock. We had, at most, three weeks before the structural decay reached critical mass.

My focus was broken by the sound of Teron Draken rising from his bunk across the aisle. He moved with a quiet, lethal efficiency, his massive silhouette framed against the dim light filtering through the high window. He caught my eye and sent a sharp, clear message through the Void-Kinetic Link: *Today, we do not survive. We dominate.*

I acknowledged the command with a surge of cold resolve. The time for subtle survival was over. We needed to force the General's hand and expose the lie before the Spires collapsed into the Miasma.

The Psychological Formation

The morning formation of the Void Quadrant was a

terrifying spectacle of discipline and resentment. I stood rigidly in the third rank, the only small, unscarred figure surrounded by the towering, brooding presence of the Marked Ones. Jax, Teron's second-in-command, positioned himself directly behind me, his breath hot on the back of my neck, his hatred palpable.

Teron stood before them, his presence an oppressive wave of Void Signet energy that commanded absolute silence.

"Cadets," Teron stated, his voice flat, emotionless, yet carrying immense weight. "Today's exercise is a joint drill: Void Suppression and Kinetic Counter."

He turned to me. "Cadet Varen, you will lead the practical demonstration. You will demonstrate why a fragile body and a defensive Signet are necessary assets to the most powerful attacking force in the Zenith."

The statement was a direct, public challenge to the fundamental belief system of the Zenith—that only brute strength mattered. It was a calculated risk that angered his own troops. Jax bristled, but remained motionless, bound by the Code of the Marked.

"He risks his command for your visibility, Conduit. The motive is political dominance. Use the opportunity." Zephyr's mental voice was a sharp calculation.

The Void Exercise: Testing the Limits

The Shockwave Testing Ward was the largest enclosed space in the Spires, designed to withstand massive Aetherial discharges. It was here that Teron intended to make our alliance brutally clear.

The exercise was simple, terrifying, and brilliantly strategic: Teron and Morgal would execute a full-power Void Crush—an immense kinetic attack designed to simulate the collapse of a fortress wall. I, with Zephyr, would be positioned directly in the path of the attack. My task: survive and maintain the Still Point at the epicenter of his destruction.

Teron and Morgal ascended to the viewing platform. Morgal, the massive Void Aetherial, was a terrifying anchor of pure darkness. I stood fifty yards away on the cracked granite floor, the silver stylus anchor clasped tightly in my hand.

"Cadet Varen," Teron's amplified voice commanded from the platform. "The Void Signet will compress the air around you with crushing force. It seeks to suppress all kinetic energy. Your Kinetic Signet must counter this by creating a perfect, zero-resistance sphere—a vacuum within a vacuum. Fail to hold the Still Point for three full seconds, and the force will shatter you."

I knew this was the ultimate test—and the ultimate lie. Teron wasn't trying to crush me; he was demonstrating the capability of our combined Signets to the Council, daring my mother to intervene.

"The force is coming, Conduit. It is pure density. Find the zero, or be scattered." Zephyr cried out mentally.

Teron raised his hand. His face was a mask of cold resolve, but I felt the tremor of suppressed intensity through our mental link. He was pouring every ounce of his massive power into this maneuver.

"Void Crush. Now!"

Morgal unleashed the Signet. The world seemed to stop breathing. A massive, invisible wave of crushing Void Energy slammed forward. The pressure was immense—a physical weight that flattened the air, sucking the sound out of the vast hall. My bones groaned under the sudden, agonizing compression.

I fell instantly to one knee, fighting the gravitational crush. My mind screamed with the desire to escape, but I forced the panic down, finding the Still Point through sheer will and the memory of Teron's warm, protective presence.

Focus on the boundary! I am the zero!

I channeled my Kinetic Resonance through the stylus. A sphere of Kinetic Stillness—a shell of perfect zero resistance—flickered into existence around me. The Void energy slammed into the shell, but instead of resisting, the two Signets neutralized each other. The Void's crushing force was channeled and consumed by the Kinetic Signet's capacity for perfect stillness.

I stood up within the sphere, whole and breathing, while the world outside the sphere was crushed in absolute silence.

I held the Still Point for one second. Two seconds. Three.

Then, at Teron's mental command, the Void Signet abruptly ceased. The pressure vanished. The sudden return of sound and air was almost as dizzying as the crush itself.

I stood trembling, profoundly exhausted, but unbroken.

The Hall was silent. The demonstration was a catastrophic success. I, the frail Scribe's daughter, had just neutralized the full kinetic force of the Zenith's most powerful Void Aetherial.

The General's Fury and The Public Lie

The political fallout was immediate. General Varen was observing from a secondary, concealed viewing box. She marched onto the testing floor, her face white with suppressed rage.

"What in the hell was that, Wingleader Draken?" the General demanded, her voice cutting through the silence. "That was not conditioning; that was a tactical demonstration of Void-Kinetic Counter-Signature. You have utilized a dangerous, unprecedented synergy!"

Teron Draken descended from the platform, approaching the General with a cold, formal military bearing. I took my place silently beside him, our bodies close, our Signets humming in defiant sync.

"General," Teron replied, his voice calm, respectful, yet laced with defiance. "Cadet Varen is a necessary countermeasure to our weaknesses. The Void Quadrant, due to its immense mass, is susceptible to unpredictable kinetic shifts. Cadet Varen's ability to create a zero-resistance field is the perfect defense. We trained her to withstand an internal Signet collapse. We have stabilized the asset."

He had created the Public Lie: our synergy was not personal treason, but strategic necessity for the Void Quadrant's survival.

"The two Signets are incompatible!" the General protested.

"Respectfully, General," I interjected, speaking with cold precision, channeling the confidence of my Aetherial. "Our Signets are absolute opposites. The Void creates maximum density; the Kinetic creates maximum neutrality. Together, they create optimum stability. This synergy must be utilized to defend the Spires."

Teron placed a large, possessive hand on my shoulder, a clear signal of ownership. "The Void Quadrant will absorb her training, General. She is essential to our unit's survival."

The General was trapped. She could not argue against the pure, undeniable military logic of the demonstration. To deny the synergy was to admit the Void Quadrant had a massive, exploitable weakness. She had no choice but to concede.

"Very well, Wingleader. Cadet Varen remains under your command," the General relented, her eyes blazing with cold hatred for her daughter and her enemy. "But every move she makes will be monitored. Do not compromise the Zenith."

As the General spun on her heel and departed, the Hall erupted in muted discussion. The Marked Ones—Teron's troops—no longer looked at me with contempt, but with grudging respect. I was their countermeasure, my Scion of Static, and a necessary weapon.

The Planning: Dreadnought Nexus

Later that night, Teron and I met in a rarely used, high-altitude hangar—our only moment of peace. We stood beneath the massive, silent shape of Morgal, the Void Aetherial's immense presence acting as a natural sound dampener.

I pulled the silver stylus and the hidden data chip. "The performance was flawless, Teron. But we have bought ourselves, at most, a week before the General attempts another assassination. The Void-Kinetic counter-signature is too dangerous for her to tolerate."

"Agreed," Teron said, his voice dropping to a low growl. He pulled me close, the formal distance dissolving instantly, his arms wrapping around my waist, pulling me flush against his chest. "I need to know the full schedule of the collapse. Tell me about the Dreadnought Nexus."

I leaned my head back against his shoulder, finding the perfect anchor in his massive core. I projected the data through the bond, using the precise, clinical language of the Scribe reports.

Nexus location: Beneath the central training ward. Failure estimate: Three weeks, due to localized Aetherium overload. Depressurization Plan: Requires Signet synchronization at the nexus point.

Teron absorbed the data, his body tensing with the weight of the enormous, world-ending truth. "It's a suicide mission, Lyssa. The Nexus will emit raw Miasma energy. It will incinerate any living thing that gets close."

"Not if we deploy the Kinetic Shield at the moment of depressurization," I countered, pulling away slightly to meet his gaze. My eyes were burning with desperate conviction. "The Miasma is raw kinetic chaos. My Signet is the absolute neutralization of that chaos. We anchor the Miasma with your Void Signet—you stop the motion of the bedrock. I create a perfect Kinetic Vacuum around the Nexus, neutralizing the explosive energy, allowing the depressurization to proceed safely."

Our eyes locked. The plan was audacious, insane, and based on the flawless synergy we had just demonstrated. It required absolute trust.

"The sheer force of that stabilization would shatter the

life out of you, Varen," Teron said, his hand moving to gently trace the fragile line of my jaw. "The residual feedback would be catastrophic."

"Not if you absorb the residual heat into your Void core," I argued, my voice barely a whisper. "You are the anchor, Teron. You stabilize the bedrock, and you stabilize me. We absorb the chaos together."

The physical and emotional intensity of the moment was overwhelming. Our plan was not a military strategy; it was an act of desperate, forbidden intimacy—a joint, mutual sacrifice.

Teron kissed me then, fiercely, with crushing possession, his hands tangling in my hair. It was a kiss of fear, commitment, and pure, raw need. The Void and Kinetic Signets surged, neutralizing the tension in the space around them, creating a perfect, dangerous sanctuary.

"If we do this, Scion," Teron muttered against my mouth, his voice dark with a promise that went beyond vengeance. "There is no going back. We expose the General, we save the Zenith, and we are both executed as traitors. Our purpose will be fulfilled."

"Then let us fulfill it, Wingleader," I responded, my heart pounding against his chest. "We are the Scion of Static and the Son of the Void. We are the necessary chaos."

We spent the remaining hours planning the specific flight vectors, the timing, and the extraction path. We would strike the Dreadnought Nexus during the final full-squad flight exercise—the last chance before the General's patience snapped entirely. The entire existence of the Zenith Spires now hung on the flawless synchronization of our forbidden bond.

CHAPTER 16

THE FINAL VOW AND THE TRAITOR'S BLADE

The air in the Void Barracks was thick with imminent violence. My survival was a raw nerve in the side of the Marked Ones. Teron Draken's public protection had bought me life, but it had not earned me loyalty. After the public display of the Void-Kinetic Counter-Signature, the resentment had festered, coalescing into a final, deadly plan: eliminate the Scion of Lies before I compromised their Wingleader.

The ambush was meticulously coordinated by Jax, Teron's second-in-command, and Roric, the demoted Blazer, now acting as an informant for General Varen.

The Ambush at the Annex Bridge

The General's final, lethal tactical move was subtle: she scheduled a routine, mandatory maintenance check of the North Bridge—the site of my narrow escape—and ordered me, as the most 'skilled in structural kinetic analysis,' to participate alone.

Teron was scheduled for an all-day tactical flight drill with Morgal, a maneuver designed to keep him far from the Spires.

I knew the trap was absolute.

I walked onto the narrow bridge, the silver stylus anchor clasped tight in my fist, Zephyr's mental presence a cold, quiet alarm in my mind. The wind was ferocious, whipping across the stone.

The ambush was sprung halfway across. Jax, followed by three heavy-set Void Cadets, emerged from the Annex side. They were clad in maintenance gear, concealing their Signet activation. Roric, flanked by two of his loyal Blazers, blocked the main spire side. I was trapped between pure density and crude aggression.

"Nowhere to run, Scion," Jax stated, his voice devoid of emotion, his eyes burning with years of suppressed hatred. "The General's daughter has caused enough instability. The Code of the Marked demands stability. Your life is forfeit for the greater mission."

Treason against the Zenith, I thought, my mind instantly shifting into the Still Point preparation. *And treason against Teron's command.*

Roric grinned, his Magma energy making the air shimmer with oppressive heat. "The Void Wingleader is busy, Scion. No one is coming for you. Let's see how your fancy physics holds up against real force."

Roric and his Blazers unleashed their Magma Signets—a coordinated blast of pure, high-velocity heat and kinetic energy designed to incinerate or hurl me into the Miasma.

Jax and the Void Cadets, simultaneously, activated their Void Signets, creating a field of crushing, paralyzing density around me, intended to immobilize me, preventing the Kinetic Resonance from deploying its necessary movement.

I was caught in a lethal pincer attack: Magma Chaos slamming into a Void Anchor.

The Void-Kinetic Unleashed

The combined force was catastrophic. I was slammed to my knees, the crushing weight of the Void pinning me, while the scalding heat of the Magma attempted to boil me alive. The simultaneous, contradictory forces threatened to rip my body and mind apart.

"Unacceptable pressure! Fracture imminent, Conduit! We cannot stabilize both forces!" Zephyr's frantic mental cry was a sharp spike of pain.

Not alone! I screamed mentally. *Teron!*

In that moment of absolute, desperate need, Teron Draken's presence—miles away on a flight drill—flared. He felt the catastrophic surge of Signet energy on the North Bridge through our secret mental link. He knew I was seconds from collapse.

Teron broke formation. He channeled a devastating counter-force, pushing Morgal's Void Signet to its absolute limit, not for attack, but for long-distance communication and stabilization.

I felt the surge—a massive wave of Void Energy that eclipsed the local, inferior Void pressure from Jax's squad. It was a projection of pure, possessive power, aimed entirely at my defense.

"Stabilize, Scion! Anchor the Void! Use my force!" Teron's mental command was a low, powerful roar that shook

my core, overriding all panic.

I seized the stability. I channeled the excess Void energy from Teron's remote projection into the silver stylus, anchoring the incredible force. I then directed my Kinetic Resonance to neutralize the Magma Chaos.

I created a thin, localized Kinetic Vacuum around my body. The Magma heat, unable to find a stable kinetic medium for transfer, collapsed inward, dissolving harmlessly into steam. The Void pressure, anchored by Teron, became a stabilizing field, rather than a crushing weight.

I stood up, pale and shaking, entirely untouched. The sheer power of my synchronized defense was a terrifying spectacle.

Jax and the Void Cadets recoiled, their faces stunned by the sudden, massive projection of Void power that had just defended the General's daughter. They realized: Teron Draken's protection was absolute, even from miles away.

The Traitor's Blade

Roric, fueled by pure, unadulterated hatred, abandoned his Signet and resorted to brute force. He drew a wicked, razor-sharp Traitor's Blade—an antique weapon traditionally used for rebel executions—and lunged across the bridge, aiming for my throat.

I didn't use my Signet this time; I used my Signet's logic. I knew the precise vector, the acceleration, and the trajectory of the strike. I didn't dodge.

As Roric's blade reached the killing vector, I executed the

maneuver Teron had taught me: I used the Kinetic Resonance to create a momentary, highly focused field of zero-resistance on the edge of Roric's blade.

The physics were instantaneous and violent: the immense energy of Roric's forward motion, suddenly encountering zero resistance, sheared the steel. The Traitor's Blade shattered into a thousand fragments of cold, useless metal, the force of the momentum harmlessly absorbed by the air.

Roric, left with a useless hilt and his body violently overextended, could only stare in paralyzed defeat.

I stepped forward, my voice a cold whisper of absolute authority. "Your momentum is worthless, Roric. Your treason against the Zenith Code—attempting to murder a fellow Rider—is complete. You fail."

Jax, watching the impossible destruction of the blade and the silent, terrifying projection of Teron's power, made his decision. His loyalty was to his Wingleader, not to a failed plot.

"Void Cadets!" Jax roared, stepping forward. "Roric has committed treason against the Zenith Code! Restrain the Blazer and his cohorts!"

The Void Cadets, relieved to be given an honorable enemy, immediately surrounded Roric and the two Blazers. Roric fought, screaming curses at me and the General, but he was quickly overwhelmed by the crushing density of the combined Void Signets.

I had won. The conspiracy against me was shattered, and Roric, the General's pawn, was restrained for military justice.

The Final Vow: Betrayal and Acceptance

Minutes later, the official detail arrived. Roric and his squad were taken into custody. I stood on the bridge, the silence broken only by the wind. I waited.

I didn't have to wait long.

Teron Draken landed Morgal on the bridge—a massive, silent statement of command. The Void Aetherial's scales scraped against the granite, radiating suppressed fury. Teron leaped down, striding toward me. He was breathing heavily, his face etched with strain from pushing his Signet to its limit.

He didn't speak a word of command or military protocol. He simply seized me, pulling me into a fierce, desperate embrace, crushing me against his strong, warm body.

"You risked everything, Teron," I whispered against his tunic, clinging to his stabilizing heat.

"I risked nothing compared to the mission, Lyssa," he countered, his voice rough with raw emotion. "I felt the pressure, the heat, the terror. Never leave the stylus, Scion. Never abandon the Still Point."

He pulled back, his eyes searching mine, no longer cold, but burning with a profound, terrifying devotion.

"Jax reported everything. You neutralized their plot and arrested Roric. Your value is now undeniable to the Void Quadrant. They will protect you until the mission is complete." Teron paused, his expression hardening. "This is our last night of quiet. The Nexus is failing rapidly. We execute Project Nightingale tomorrow. There is no more training. There is only treason."

I nodded, placing my hand over the silver stylus, my Kinetic Anchor. "I know the cost. Exposure of the lie will save the Zenith, but it will expose the treason, Teron. They will execute us both."

Teron looked out over the vast, black chasm of the Miasma. "We accept the price. I swore an oath to expose the truth that killed my father. You swore an oath to survive. We fulfill both."

He pulled me close again, and our kiss was a shared, solemn vow. It was long, deep, and final—a desperate collision of two souls accepting their fate as martyrs for a higher truth. The Void and Kinetic energies merged in a perfect, temporary singularity, creating a moment of absolute, total peace in the center of their pending destruction.

"If the Spires fall," Teron muttered against my mouth, his voice thick with unshakeable resolve. "We will fall together, Lyssa. But we will fall as the people who broke the General's lie."

We separated. The choice was made. Tomorrow, we would execute Project Nightingale, expose General Varen, and face the executioner's blade together. Our love was forged in necessity, sealed by treason, and destined for a glorious, final collapse.

CHAPTER 17

THE DREADNOUGHT NEXUS

The mission was scheduled for the final major flight exercise before the annual winter lockdown—the perfect window to hide a treasonous maneuver in the chaos of hundreds of Riders in the air. The mood in the Void Barracks was unusually tense. The cadets knew this was not a routine drill; they sensed the gravity of their Wingleader's suppressed intensity.

I, clad in my new Void Quadrant leathers, felt the silver stylus press cold against my skin. I had achieved the Still Point for hours, my mind a fortress of perfect, cold silence, holding the kinetic chaos at bay. All that remained was the final, devastating commitment.

I met Teron Draken on the main flight deck. He was already mounted on Morgal, the colossal Void Aetherial, whose scales shimmered like polished obsidian. Teron looked devastatingly resolved, his face stripped of all emotion except a grim, singular purpose.

"The coordinates are locked, Scion," Teron stated, his voice professional, loud enough for the nearby Wingleaders to hear. "Follow my lead. Maintain absolute synchronization. Your failure risks the entire Void formation."

I nodded, mounting Zephyr. The crystalline Wind Aetherial launched silently, effortlessly, its perfect kinetic motion gliding into position beside Morgal. The two Aetherials—one the embodiment of crushing density, the other of frictionless flow—flew side-by-side, an impossible pairing.

"The synergy is profound, Conduit. We ride the edge of the Void's current. Do not falter." Zephyr's mental voice was a low, powerful thrill of professional commitment.

The Treacherous Flight

Our journey was a study in forbidden intimacy. Teron and I flew in the core of the Void formation, surrounded by the loyal, suspicious Marked Ones. But our true communication was conducted in a secret mental channel, a terrifying, passionate dialogue between the Void and the Kinetic.

"The General's command Aetherial is not in the air. A calculated absence. She is waiting for us to expose ourselves, Lyssa," Teron projected his tactical assessment.

"She is planning to intercept us personally after we fail the maneuver," I replied, the data flowing through the bond. *"We must maintain the appearance of the exercise until we breach the Nexus. Fly high, Teron. Force them to spread the formation."*

Teron executed the command instantly, pushing Morgal into a steep, high-altitude climb. The Void formation stretched out across the sky, their massive Aetherials black anchors against the blue.

As we flew, I projected the Project Nightingale data into Teron's mind—the exact architectural schematics of the Dreadnought Nexus and the precise, complex energy signatures required for the depressurization sequence. It was a complete sharing of the final, lethal truth that would seal our fate.

Interception: The General's Trap

We were twenty minutes into the flight, moving toward the lower, unstable Second Spire where the Nexus was located, when the air currents suddenly shifted.

A colossal, blazing figure—a Ruby Magma Aetherial—flashed into existence above us, blocking our path. It was Titan, the personal Aetherial of General Lilith Varen.

The General herself was mounted on Titan, clad in full military armor, her face a mask of cold fury. She had predicted our move and waited for us to commit to the descent.

"Wingleader Draken! Cadet Varen!" the General's voice boomed across the sky, amplified by Titan's massive, resonant Signet. "You have deviated from the flight plan! Return to the formation immediately, or face charges of treason!"

The surrounding Void formation faltered, their Signets flickering with surprise and shock at the General's sudden appearance.

Teron did not hesitate. "Jax! Hold the line! We proceed!"

He urged Morgal forward, ignoring the General's command.

The General retaliated instantly. Titan, the Magma Aetherial, unleashed a devastating wave of Kinetic Blast—a pure, compressed wall of superheated air designed to smash the Void formation apart and send Teron and me tumbling into the Miasma.

"Void Riders, brace!" Teron roared, deploying Morgal's Void Signet to absorb the initial kinetic shockwave. The massive Aetherial groaned under the force, but the formation held.

I knew this was my moment. The Magma blast was raw, chaotic kinetic force—the perfect energy for my Signet to neutralize.

Protect the anchor, Zephyr!

I channeled my Kinetic Resonance, projecting a massive, defensive Kinetic Shield around Morgal and Zephyr. The Magma blast slammed into the shield, and the two opposing forces—Magma's heat and Kinetic's stillness—neutralized each other with a blinding flash of energy that left us untouched.

"They are too powerful together, General!" one of the flanking Wingleaders shouted.

The General's eyes, fixed on me, narrowed with lethal resolution. She drew a brilliant, shimmering blade—her legendary Vindicator Sword.

"This is treason, Draken! Varen! You will not compromise the Zenith!"

The Final Descent: The Dreadnought Nexus

Teron knew we couldn't waste time fighting. The General's objective was to delay us until the Nexus reached critical mass, collapsing the Spire with me inside.

"Full descent, Morgal! Now!" Teron commanded.

Morgal executed a terrifying, vertical dive, dropping instantly toward the unstable Second Spire. Zephyr followed, weaving around the Magma Rider's attempts to cut us off, me expertly stabilizing our motion against the terrifying vertical plunge.

The descent was blindingly fast. We crashed through the cloud layer, emerging above the cracked, ancient stone of the Second Spire. Below us was the target: the Dreadnought Nexus—a massive, circular crystalline plate, now visibly weeping plumes of thick, raw Miasma energy. The structural decay was exponentially worse than the reports had predicted.

"Catastrophic failure imminent! The energy is unstable! We must deploy immediately!" Zephyr's mental cry was a desperate alarm.

We landed hard on the cracked granite of the Spire. The ground trembled violently.

Teron dismounted immediately, running toward the Nexus. I leaped off Zephyr's back, sprinting to meet him.

"The time is critical, Lyssa! We deploy the stabilization sequence now!" Teron yelled, pulling the Vulnerability Injector—a complex, obsidian device—from his saddlebag.

We reached the edge of the crystalline Nexus. The Miasma surged upward, a toxic, raw kinetic fog that promised agonizing death.

"Void Anchor, Teron! Full power! Stop the bedrock!"

Teron slammed his hand onto the stone beside the Nexus, activating Morgal's Signet. The massive Void Aetherial, hovering above us, unleashed a devastating wave of Void

Density, crushing the bedrock beneath the spire. The structure stabilized momentarily, but the pressure was agonizing.

"Kinetic Shield! Contain the release!" Teron screamed, his body taut with the effort of holding the void.

I forced my mind to absolute, perfect silence. I pressed my silver stylus to the Nexus plate, pouring my entire consciousness into the Kinetic Resonance. I didn't fight the Miasma; I neutralized its chaos.

A perfect, shimmering sphere of Kinetic Stillness erupted from the stylus, enveloping the entire Nexus. The poisonous, explosive Miasma release was contained, held in absolute, zero-resistance stillness.

"Now, the depressurization!" I gasped, my body on the verge of splintering under the pressure.

Teron plunged the Injector into the crystalline plate. The device began to siphon the excess, unstable Aetherium from the bedrock—the first step of Project Nightingale.

The instant the siphon began, the Kinetic Shield failed. The force of the raw Miasma release, suddenly finding a path, slammed into me.

Sacrifice and Betrayal

The pain was agonizing, blinding, shattering. I felt the uncontrolled kinetic energy rip through me, aiming straight for my fragile core. My bones screamed, my muscles seized—I was collapsing, fracturing, seconds from complete disintegration.

"System failure! The Conduit is collapsing! Severing the bond!" Zephyr's frantic mental voice was a final, desperate alarm.

But before the bond could be severed, Teron acted.

He released the Void Anchor and lunged forward, catching my collapsing body. He pulled me against him, pressing my head to his chest, placing my silver stylus directly against his Void-scarred shoulder.

"Absorb it, Morgal! Take the fracture!" Teron screamed.

He activated his Void Signet again, this time not for suppression, but for absorption. He channeled the full, catastrophic kinetic energy backlash from my collapsing Signet into his own massive body and Morgal's core. The sheer force was immense, but the Void's purpose was density—it could contain the excess force where my body could not.

I felt the pain dissolve, replaced by a searing, stabilizing heat. I was saved, anchored by the massive power of the Void.

A deafening sound—a massive, rhythmic CLANG— erupted from the Nexus. The Depressurization was complete. The Zenith Spires were stabilized.

Teron collapsed, pulling me down onto the cold stone beside him. He was breathing heavily, his body trembling with the massive kinetic force he had just absorbed.

"It is done, Lyssa," Teron whispered, his voice hoarse, raw with exhaustion and triumph. "The Spires are safe. The lie is exposed."

The triumph was fleeting. The General landed Titan fifty feet away, her face a mask of furious, devastating defeat. She stared at the stabilized Nexus and then at me and her enemy, lying together on the cracked stone.

"You have committed the ultimate treason," the General stated, her voice dangerously calm. "You have compromised the Wards and allied with the enemy."

I pushed myself up, supported by Teron. I knew the end had come.

"We saved the Zenith from your lie, General," I replied, my voice weak but steady. "His father's execution was unnecessary. The Wards were compromised by structural failure, not external attack. The truth is exposed."

The General raised the Vindicator Sword, its blade shimmering with Magma fire. "The truth is what the Zenith dictates. And the Zenith dictates loyalty."

She turned to Teron Draken. "The price of treason is death. You will be executed, Wingleader."

She then turned the sword on me, her expression fracturing into a cold, terrifying grief. "And you, Lyssa. You chose treason over blood. The price of betraying the Varen name is also death. But first, you will witness the destruction of your allies."

Before the General could move, a wave of Void Riders descended, landing between the General and the two traitors. Jax, Teron's second-in-command, dismounted from his Aetherial.

"General Varen," Jax stated, his voice ringing with loyalty to the rebellion's true purpose. "The Spires are stabilized. Lord Karsus Draken's name is cleared. Wingleader Draken saved the Zenith. We will protect the Wingleader and the Scion."

The General's forces were immediately surrounded. The Void Cadets, the Marked Ones, had finally chosen their truth.

The standoff was absolute: the General and her Magma forces against the newly redeemed Void Quadrant.

The Inescapable Consequence

The battle did not last. The General knew she was outnumbered and politically exposed. The stabilization of the Nexus was undeniable proof of her lie.

The final consequence came not from fire, but from cold, military protocol.

"Treason is treason, General," Captain Korvin's voice cut through the air. He had flown in, observing the entire scene. "Wingleader Draken is under arrest for insubordination and the use of unauthorized Signet countermeasures. Cadet Varen is under arrest for unauthorized access and violation of the Zenith Code. The Wards are safe, but the discipline must be upheld."

Teron looked at me, his face grim, but his eyes holding a profound, peaceful acceptance. Our victory was complete, but our fate was sealed.

Teron Draken and I were led away, separated and bound, marched under heavy guard. We had saved the Zenith, exposed the lie that fueled my mother's tyranny, and sealed our forbidden bond with an act of ultimate sacrifice. As we were marched into the detention block, our eyes met one last time. The Void and Kinetic Signets surged, a final, fierce mental message of love and absolute commitment passing between us.

Our lives were over, but our cycle of vengeance and love had just begun.

CHAPTER 18

THE VAULT OF SILENCE

I was not taken to a military prison. I was taken to a Vault— a specialized disciplinary block beneath the oldest, most stable foundation of the Zenith Spires. The walls were not granite, but composite layers of obsidian and Null-crystal, designed specifically to dampen Aetherial Signet energy.

The cell was a small, circular cylinder, devoid of furniture save for a hard, stone slab for a bed. The only light was a perpetual, dim glow from a shielded lamp, casting no shadows. It was a space designed for complete sensory deprivation, but its true horror was its primary function: absolute silence.

The Null-crystal walls immediately absorbed all ambient kinetic energy. The wind, the tremors of the Spires, the frantic pulse of my own heart—all sounds vanished. I was entombed in a profound, heavy, absolute stillness that was the ultimate, perverse counter to my Kinetic Resonance.

"The silence is oppressive, Conduit. The flow is dead. We are stagnant. I cannot perceive the exterior." Zephyr's voice, normally sharp and calculating, was a faint, struggling whisper in my mind.

The pain of separation from the Aetherium was immediate. I felt disconnected, weak, and terrified. My Signet, which required motion and external kinetic flow to function, was starved. I was reduced to the frail body I had started with, trapped in the prison built by my mother's technological genius.

The Agony of Separation

The worst agony, however, was the loss of the Void-Kinetic Link.

I tried desperately to reach out to Teron Draken. I focused my entire being, channeling my weakened Kinetic Resonance through the silver stylus anchor. I pushed the tremor of my anxiety outward, searching for the massive, familiar, stabilizing pressure of the Void Signet.

Nothing.

The Null-crystal absorbed the signal instantly. There was no Void, no warmth, no anchor. Only the terrifying, dead silence.

I realized the devastating truth: Teron was likely imprisoned in an identical cell, and his Void Signet, which required immense external pressure to effectively channel its density, was equally stifled. We had relied on the synergy of our opposite Signets to survive and communicate. Now, separated by stone and Null-crystal, we were isolated islands, unable to send or receive even the faintest mental pulse.

I sank onto the stone floor, curling my body around the stylus. My mind, suddenly stripped of the constant rush of kinetic data and the stabilizing presence of Teron's emotional anchor, plunged into chaos. The fear returned, sharp and overwhelming.

He must be alive. He must be plotting. I gripped the stylus, channeling my chaotic thoughts into a desperate mantra.

The minutes stretched into an eternity of silence. I had saved the Zenith, exposed the lie, and earned a single, solitary fate: abandonment.

The General's Interrogation

After a day of agonizing isolation, the reinforced door hissed open. General Lilith Varen entered, flanked by two heavily armored, non-bonded Guards. The General wore her ceremonial white armor, emphasizing her position of absolute power.

She didn't look triumphant; she looked utterly, coldly heartbroken.

"Look at you, Lyssa," the General stated, her voice echoing unnaturally in the crystal vault. "Broken, alone, reduced to the sickly Scribe you always were. You traded your life, your legacy, and your mother's unconditional love for a moment of juvenile triumph with a rebel's son."

I forced myself to stand, facing my mother, channeling the memory of Teron's strength. "I traded a lie for a truth, General. I saved the Zenith from your arrogance. The Nexus is stable. The structural failure is exposed."

"The Nexus is stable because I ordered the stabilization sequence the moment I saw your intended vector," the General countered, lying smoothly. "The narrative is that I saved the Zenith from you. The tribunal has accepted the military report: you and Draken were attempting to collapse the spire to cover your father's political sabotage."

The General walked closer, her eyes blazing with cold fire. "You chose the rebel's Signet. You chose the traitor's sword. You chose to destroy your family's name for a boy who swore vengeance on your blood. Tell me, Lyssa, was his forbidden kiss worth the executioner's blade?"

The General had anticipated my emotional weakness. She had weaponized the forbidden intimacy.

I held my ground. "I chose the truth that Lord Draken died for. And I will not betray the only person who helped me survive your traps."

"Foolish, pathetic loyalty." The General sighed, a sound of profound disappointment. "But your defiance means nothing now. The execution is scheduled for the next full moon—a swift, public incineration to reassert the loyalty of the Riders. You will be purged."

The General then played her final card—a crushing psychological blow. She leaned in, her voice dropping to a low, intimate command. "I will give you one last chance to save yourself, Lyssa. Tell me, what is the full kinetic frequency of Draken's Void Signet? Give me the necessary counter-signature, and I will pardon you and make him the sole martyr. You will live."

I realized the General's true fear: the Void-Kinetic Counter-Signature. The General knew this synergy was the only force capable of challenging her power. She wanted the intelligence to neutralize Teron's immense Signet permanently.

I smiled, a cold, painful twitch of my lips. "I don't know the full frequency, General. Because the power of the Void, like the power of my Signet, is not quantifiable. It's absolute. And it is forever bound to the man you intend to kill."

The General stared at me, rage and defeat battling in her eyes. She had failed to break me.

"You have chosen your end, Lyssa," the General stated, turning away sharply. "Enjoy the silence. It will be the last peace you ever know."

The door hissed shut, plunging me back into the oppressive, suffocating silence.

The Cracks in the Silence

Days passed. I lost all track of time. My world was the cold stone, the dim light, and the struggle to maintain my sanity against the absolute stillness. Zephyr was weak, his voice a barely perceptible tremor.

I resorted to the only defense I had left: my Signet's logic. I knew that even Null-crystal had a resonant frequency. I began to use my Kinetic Resonance to find the weakness in the material.

I pressed the silver stylus against the wall, channeling my weak, starved Signet. I didn't try to shatter the crystal; I tried to find its harmonic frequency—the perfect note that would allow a tremor to pass through.

I focused, fighting the mental suppression, pushing my will outward, trying to make the silent crystal sing.

Nothing. I was too weak.

I collapsed again, tears of frustration and exhaustion tracing paths through the dust on my cheeks. I was going to fail. I was going to die alone, separated from the man I loved, our vengeance unfinished.

Then, just as despair threatened to consume me, I felt it.

A minuscule, rhythmic tremor—a faint, tapping vibration—came from the bedrock far beneath the cell. It was too small to be sensed by a normal human, but my highly refined Kinetic Resonance registered it instantly.

It was not the massive, heavy pulse of the Void. It was the subtle, high-frequency signal of Structural Resonance.

"Intrusion! Non-Aetherial, structural signal! Low power, extremely subtle!" Zephyr's mental cry was a jolt of alarm and triumph.

I gasped, scrambling back to the wall, pressing my ear to the cold stone. I used my Signet to amplify the tiny tremor.

The signal was faint, complex, and utterly familiar. *It was Eysa.*

Eysa, using her newly discovered Structural Resonance Signet, was reaching out, not through the air, but through the physical architecture of the Spires itself.

The tapping was a complex rhythm, based on an old Scribe cipher Eysa and I had created as children. It took me several minutes of agonizing focus to decipher the message, fighting the Null-crystal suppression.

The message was slow, rhythmic, and perfectly clear:

W... E... C... A... N... B... R... E... A... K... Y... O... U... O... U... T... T... H... E... M... A... R... K... E... D... A... R... E... W... I... T... H... U... S... F... U... L... L... M... O... O... N... M... I... D... N... I... G... H... T... T... E... R... O... N... I... S... A... L... I... V... E...

The message ended abruptly. The faint tremor vanished,

replaced by the crushing silence of the Vault.

I collapsed against the wall, my body shaking, not with fear, but with profound, dizzying hope. Eysa had found me. Eysa was alive and active. The Marked Ones had chosen the truth over the General's lie.

And Teron was alive.

The execution was scheduled for the next full moon—only three days away. The time was impossible. The risk was absolute. But I, the frail Scribe's daughter who was supposed to be reduced to ash, had just received my final set of coordinates. The rebellion, born of a kiss and sealed by treason, was not over. It was about to explode.

CHAPTER 19

THE CODE OF THE SCARS

The execution was set for the full moon in less than forty-eight hours. The knowledge was a cold, hard comfort in the absolute silence of the Vault of Null-crystal. I had received Eysa's signal, but the communication was a single, fragile thread of hope woven into a massive tapestry of despair.

The message—*We can break you out. The Marked are with us. Full moon midnight. Teron is alive.*—was incomplete. Eysa had signed off with the word: *Scars.*

Scars. It was a word of profound meaning to the Marked Ones, referring to the jagged, dark brands that symbolized the General's betrayal. It was also the code for the physical location of the rebellion's first act.

I had to decipher the final piece of the plan without any external input, relying only on the faint, unstable memory of Eysa's Structural Resonance and the constant, internal logic of my Kinetic Signet.

Preparing for Motion

My preparation was a silent, agonizing physical and

mental battle. My Kinetic Resonance was starved in the Null-crystal vault, but I fought the suppression by exploiting the material itself. I realized that the Null-crystal, while dampening ambient motion, still possessed a massive, rigid structure. I could use this density as a target.

I pressed my palm to the cold wall, channeling my weak Signet outward, not to shatter the crystal, but to find its perfect stillness. I had to stabilize my power, ready for the moment of explosive movement Eysa's rescue would require.

"The crystal is resisting, Conduit. It absorbs our energy. It seeks to reduce us to pure potential, inert." Zephyr's mental voice was barely a whisper.

"Then we will use the potential," I thought back, my focus absolute. I used my mind to push against the crystal's stillness, forcing my Signet to activate through sheer, sustained internal pressure. It was the reverse of my normal training: instead of neutralizing external chaos, I was generating kinetic flow within a field of absolute stillness.

I began a brutal physical regimen: pushing against the stone, holding the pose, and using my Signet to neutralize the friction between my skin and the stone for fractions of a second. I used the pain and the effort to anchor my resolve. Every successful neutralization of friction, no matter how small, was a tiny triumph, proving that the General's prison could not completely contain the Scion of Static.

The hours bled into a single, aching vigil. I focused relentlessly on the final piece of the cipher: *Scars.*

It couldn't be a random location. It had to be a place of maximum symbolic and tactical value, a location defined by the memory of the execution. The Marked One Scars were carved onto the skin in the image of the first execution site: The Black Summit, overlooking the Miasma.

The Black Summit. I realized with a profound chill. It wasn't just a place. It was the highest, most exposed point of the Zenith Spires, rarely guarded, and the most dangerous location for a breach.

If they break us out there, they risk exposure from every single external guard. The plan was suicidal, but perfectly aligned with the desperate, symbolic vengeance of the Marked Ones. The execution was scheduled to be televised at the main spire, but the extraction would happen at the Black Summit.

The Final Solitude

The last night was long and cold. I had the plan, but I was agonizing over the final, missing piece: Teron. Eysa's message had confirmed he was alive, but was he in on the plan? Or would I be breaking out alone, only to find him still trapped?

Then, I received the faint, rhythmic shockwaves from the bedrock—his Signet response. The impact was dull, but the message was clear: He understood. He was ready.

I spent my final hours of solitude preparing my body and mind for the explosion. I was going to be broken out of a Signet-suppression vault by a Structural Resonance Scribe, rescued by a desperate band of rebels, and flown away by the Void Wingleader I loved. The irony was devastating.

I stood in the center of the silent vault, pressing the stylus to my heart. I was frail, but I was now a weapon.

I am the Scion of Static. I will achieve the Still Point. I will survive this chaos to expose the corruption.

As the dim light faded and the midnight hour approached, I heard the faintest sound I had heard since my imprisonment: a low, resonant hum coming from the walls.

It was Eysa's Structural Resonance, now fully activated, pushing against the Null-crystal with focused, determined energy. She was not fighting the wall; she was finding its breaking point.

The hum intensified, rising in pitch until the silent vault began to thrum with a terrible, contained energy. I closed my eyes, readying my Kinetic Resonance for the moment of catastrophic release.

"The chaos is coming, Conduit. Ride the motion. Do not hesitate." Zephyr's mental voice, no longer a whisper, but a powerful, clear command, resonated with absolute finality.

I accepted the chaos. My heart, which had trembled in fear on the Parapet, now beat with the fierce, cold rhythm of absolute commitment. I was ready to be broken out, to flee, to fight, and ultimately, to fulfill the vow I had sealed with my enemy.

The execution was imminent. The rebellion had begun.

CHAPTER 20

THE BLACK SUMMIT

The full moon rose above the Zenith Spires, casting the crystalline peaks in an eerie, silver light. Below, in the Vault of Null-crystal, the silent hum of Eysa's Structural Resonance reached a deafening pitch.

I was ready. I stood in the center of the cell, the silver stylus anchor clasped tight. My body was rigid, channeling my Kinetic Resonance against the absolute stillness of the Null-crystal. The walls were my enemy, but now, they were also my signal.

The high-pitched hum of Eysa's Signet intensified, finding the harmonic frequency of the Null-crystal walls—not the crushing, low frequency of the granite, but the precise, fragile note of the containment material.

Suddenly, the hum reached a critical peak. With a single, sharp CRACK that resonated violently in the silent vault, the heavily reinforced door buckled inward. The frame twisted, its integrity shattered by the targeted structural vibration.

The sound was instantly replaced by motion. I felt the ambient kinetic energy rush back into the vault, a deafening wave of freedom and chaos.

The Breach and the Reunion

Eysa stood in the doorway, her face pale with strain, her hands shaking from the immense power she had just channeled. Behind her stood Jax, Teron's second-in-command, and two other heavily armed Marked Ones.

"Go, Scion! Jax has the coordinates!" Eysa yelled, her voice hoarse. "I've hit the prison's structural supports—the lock system will fail in five minutes!"

I didn't waste a second on gratitude. I burst out of the vault, my Kinetic Resonance surging back to full power. The world instantly snapped into clear, terrifying motion—I could feel the footsteps of the distant guards, the shifting wind, the tremor of the entire Spires.

"The Void cells are next! Jax, lead the way!" I commanded, seizing control of the moment. I used my Signet to neutralize the friction beneath my boots, sprinting with silent, terrifying speed toward Teron's cell.

We reached the adjacent Void Vault. Eysa had hit the door with the same precision, but the thicker Null-crystal had only cracked.

"Jax, Signet activation!" Eysa screamed, pointing to the cracking fault line. "Hit the weak point!"

Jax and the two Marked Ones slammed their hands onto the cracked crystal, unleashing their Void Signets—a massive, focused wave of crushing density.

I added my Kinetic Resonance. I didn't fight the Void; I focused on the fracture point, creating a microsphere of zero-resistance beneath the cracking crystal. The Void's density slammed into the frictionless void, amplifying the destructive force.

The combined Signets worked with devastating efficiency. The door imploded, scattering Null-crystal dust.

Teron Draken stood inside the shattered vault, his body rigid, his eyes burning with controlled fury. He was free, and his Void Signet surged instantly, filling the air with heavy, stabilizing power.

His eyes locked onto mine. The reunion was not marked by tenderness, but by a powerful, desperate, shared purpose.

"The delay is costly, Scion! Move!" Teron's mental command slammed into my mind, backed by the raw power of Morgal.

Teron seized my arm, the contact electrifying. We were a single, unified force of raw power and absolute precision.

The Race to the Summit

The Spires were now screaming with alarm. The General's reaction was predictable: Magma Riders were scrambling to intercept. Jax led the retreat, navigating the labyrinthine, cold corridors toward the Black Summit.

"They are closing the flight wards! We have minutes!" Jax yelled.

The ascent was brutal. We encountered the first interception team—six fully armored Zenith Guards—in a narrow stairwell.

"Kinetic Shield! Void Crush!" Teron roared, his command seamless.

Teron and I fought back-to-back. The Guards fired kinetic nets designed to bind Aetherial conduits.

I activated my Kinetic Shield, neutralizing the velocity of the incoming nets, causing them to fall harmlessly at our feet. Teron, seizing the momentary immobilization, unleashed his Void Signet. The air compressed around the Guards, their armor groaning under the immense, crushing density. The Guards collapsed instantly, paralyzed by the weight of the Void.

We proceeded up the spire, leaving a trail of collapsed and neutralized Guards in our wake. Our synergy was flawless: my precision neutralizing the threat, Teron's power eliminating the obstacle.

We burst onto the Black Summit. The high-altitude plateau was freezing, exposed, and swept by a violent, chaotic wind.

Morgal and Zephyr were waiting. Eysa had used her Structural Resonance to tap into the Spires' external communication grid, sending a masked signal to the Aetherials, disguised as a structural integrity report.

Morgal, colossal and black, stood as a silent anchor, suppressing the wind with its localized Void energy. Zephyr, crystalline and small, moved with impossible speed, clearing the landing zone.

"Jax! Cover the path!" Teron commanded, vaulting onto Morgal's saddle. "We neutralize the primary threat!"

The Final Interception

Just as I mounted Zephyr, the main threat arrived. General

Lilith Varen, riding Titan, her massive Ruby Magma Aetherial, landed with a ground-shaking thud on the Summit. She was flanked by four elite Magma Riders—a devastating firewall of fire and raw kinetic force.

"You will not leave these Spires, Traitors!" the General screamed, her voice a weapon of pure, cold rage. "You have corrupted the Marked and disgraced the Varen name! Your execution begins now!"

Titan, the Magma Aetherial, unleashed a massive blast of superheated air and kinetic force aimed directly at Zephyr, intending to shatter the smaller, crystalline creature.

"Kinetic Defense, Varen! Full output!" Teron roared.

I met the blast head-on. I channeled my Kinetic Resonance through my stylus, creating an enormous Kinetic Vacuum that enveloped Zephyr. The Magma blast, a wave of crushing chaos, hit the vacuum and vanished.

The General stared in disbelief. Her deadliest weapon had been neutralized by the perfect defense of my Signet.

"Teron! Their flank! The Magma Riders!" I shouted, my Signet strained to its limit.

Teron and Morgal moved instantly. Morgal launched into the air, its powerful wings generating massive turbulence, while Teron unleashed a targeted Void Crush at the Magma Riders' flank. The crushing density slammed into them, throwing them off-balance, disrupting their formation.

Jax and the Marked Ones charged into the chaos, engaging the disorganized Magma Riders in brutal hand-to-hand combat on the freezing granite.

The Escape Vector

"We have less than a minute before the Spires Guards arrive!" Teron shouted, urging Morgal closer to the exposed edge of the summit. "Lyssa, we need to breach the primary defense ward! Use the Nexus data!"

The final layer of defense was the Summit Ward, a localized field designed to prevent unauthorized Aetherial flight. I had the schematics from Project Nightingale.

Target the frequency flux point, Zephyr! We need to create a kinetic tear!

I focused my Kinetic Resonance on the exact, complex frequency flux point of the Summit Ward. I didn't try to power through; I focused on neutralizing the kinetic resistance of the ward itself.

I unleashed a subtle, high-frequency kinetic pulse. The Ward did not crash; it simply opened, dissolving its resistance in a localized, crystalline tear—a temporary, silent exit vector.

"Now, Teron!"

Teron launched Morgal instantly. Zephyr followed, gliding through the silent tear in the Ward.

As we plunged out over the dizzying void, I looked back. General Varen was standing on the Black Summit, her massive Magma Aetherial roaring in impotent fury. The General didn't look defeated; she looked consumed by a cold, murderous resolve.

Plunging into the Miasma

Teron and I plunged into the Miasma—the raw, toxic

kinetic fog that leaked from the spires' foundation. It was chaotic, poisonous, and deadly.

"Void Anchor! Stop the kinetic pull!" Teron commanded.

Morgal immediately deployed a massive Void field, stabilizing the air around us, creating a tunnel of calm density through the toxic, churning Miasma.

I, channeling my Kinetic Resonance, simultaneously enveloped Zephyr in a Kinetic Shield, neutralizing the residual kinetic chaos and preventing the Miasma from poisoning us.

We flew through the toxic clouds, a perfect, synchronized unit of Density and Stillness, our Signets protecting our bodies and our secret.

As we flew away from the Zenith Spires, I reached out through the mental link, sending one final, raw surge of feeling to Teron: *We are free. The treason is complete.*

Teron's mental response was a fierce wave of absolute, unyielding love, commitment, and victory. *"We are free, Scion. But the war has just begun."*

We flew out of the Miasma, emerging into the cold, clear night, leaving the towering, traitorous Zenith Spires behind us. Our life as traitors and outcasts had officially begun, and the world was now a dangerous, wide-open space.

CHAPTER 21

EXILE AND THE UNSPOKEN VOW

The flight from the Black Summit was a terrifying, violent descent into the unknown. Morgal, the colossal Void Aetherial, and Zephyr, the crystalline Wind Aetherial, tore through the night sky, side-by-side, plunging into the dense, toxic clouds of the Miasma.

The escape was a physical agony for both of us. I was trembling from the cumulative force of the Void Crush I'd sustained, and Teron was straining under the enormous residual kinetic energy he'd been forced to absorb during the depressurization of the Dreadnought Nexus.

The Miasma enveloped us, a churning, chaotic cloud of unstable Aetherium that tore at the stability of our Signets. Teron maintained the massive Void Anchor—a dense, suppressing field that carved a clear, stable tunnel through the toxic fog. I, holding the silver stylus anchor until my fingers were numb, layered the Kinetic Shield over our tunnel, neutralizing the smaller, explosive pockets of chaos within the raw magic.

"The containment is costly, Conduit. The Void core is

absorbing our instability. Our synergy is a profound risk. " Zephyr's mental voice was strained, a rare indicator of the Aetherial's exertion.

"The cost is irrelevant, Scion. We are whole. We are free, " Teron projected a wave of grim reassurance through the Signet Link.

The Shared Trauma

After twenty minutes of sustained, desperate flight, we breached the last layer of Miasma and emerged into the clear, cold air of the lower valley—the unclaimed territory beyond the Zenith's influence. Teron guided Morgal to a concealed landing zone deep within a dense, unmapped forest.

Morgal landed with a heavy, earth-shaking thud. Zephyr, elegant and silent, landed beside him.

Teron immediately dismounted, collapsing onto one knee, his body spasming from the Signet exertion. I jumped off Zephyr, my legs wobbly. I rushed to Teron, ignoring the exhaustion and pain in my own body.

"Teron!" I whispered, kneeling beside him. "The kinetic backlash—it's too severe. You pushed the Void too far."

He looked up at me, his glacial gray eyes clear, but etched with profound fatigue. The sight of his vulnerability—the loss of his absolute, iron control—was more shattering than any threat we had faced in the Spires.

"I am stabilized," he rasped, forcing himself to stand. "I will not collapse. The Void must endure."

I reached out and placed my hand on his chest, right over his heart, feeling the immense, rhythmic drumbeat and the residual warmth of the Signet energy. I wasn't treating the wound; I was reaffirming the bond. "You saved me from the fracture, Teron. I won't let your self-sacrifice destroy you now."

I closed my eyes, channeling my Kinetic Resonance. Instead of neutralizing his energy, I performed an act of profound trust: I used my Signet to harmonize his kinetic flow—gently smoothing the chaotic, painful vibrations left in his muscles by the Void's immense exertion.

Teron gasped, a low, guttural sound. He seized my wrist, his grip tight, not in anger, but in shock. "What are you doing? That is unauthorized Signet use!"

"I am healing you," I whispered. "My Signet stabilizes motion. Your body is motion. I am reducing the chaos you absorbed."

He stood silent for a long moment, allowing the soothing, controlled precision of my Signet to flow through him. The pain receded, replaced by a profound, terrifying calm.

"Never do that without my express command," Teron finally stated, his voice now lower, thicker with unwanted emotion. "That is the ultimate vulnerability, Scion. To allow a Kinetic Conduit inside your flow..."

"I risked it," I countered simply, pulling my hand away.

"Because we are no longer military assets, Wingleader. We are traitors. And our survival depends on this level of absolute, mutual compromise."

The Unspoken Truth and the Fire

We sat together beside a small, meager fire Teron built, eating cold rations. The silence was different here—not the oppressive stillness of the Spires, but the vast, overwhelming silence of the outside world.

"We have bought them time," Teron said, staring into the flames. "The stabilization will hold the Zenith for years. But the General is already hunting us. She will use the full force of her Signet and the Spires' resources."

"And Roric?"

"Roric will be executed for treason against my command," Teron clarified, a grim satisfaction in his voice. "The General won't protect him after he compromised her trap. Jax will take his place, leading the Marked Ones in my absence. They will be our eyes and ears in the Zenith—our inner circle of vengeance."

I looked at him, seeing the full, agonizing burden of leadership he carried. "You risked your life for the truth. And you sacrificed your career for me. Why, Teron? Why did you risk everything for the daughter of the woman who killed your father?"

Teron looked up, his eyes blazing in the firelight. The raw, emotional shield he usually wore was momentarily lowered.

"My father taught me that vengeance is pointless if it perpetuates the lie," he confessed, his voice a low, heavy confession. "He died to expose the truth of the Wards. You were the only person who believed that truth enough to fight for it. When you stood there, ready to collapse but still fighting the Void, I realized you weren't the General's daughter. You were the Scion of Truth. And I needed that truth more than I needed to hate the Varen name."

He reached out and traced the line of my jaw, his touch surprisingly gentle. "The moment I felt your Kinetic Resonance counter my own Signet, I knew we were intrinsically linked. You are the only person in the world who can stand at the epicenter of my power and survive, Lyssa. You are my counter-force. My absolute, necessary balance."

He pulled me into his arms, our kiss a slow, profound seal of our new reality. It wasn't the violent, desperate collision of our prison kiss; it was a deep, shared moment of painful, mutual acceptance.

The Aetherial Warning

As we embraced, a profound, urgent mental intrusion slammed into both our consciousnesses—a simultaneous warning from our bonded Aetherials.

"Riders! Look to the horizon! The Zenith is blind to the

true threat!" Morgal's voice was a deep, resonant alarm, mixing with Zephyr's sharp, crystalline frequency.

Teron and I separated instantly, our faces grim. We looked up, following our Aetherials' mental guidance.

Morgal and Zephyr projected a shared mental vision to us: a massive, dark shape moving rapidly toward Navarre from the outer, unmapped regions beyond the Miasma. It wasn't a Magma Aetherial, nor was it a simple gryphon. It was something far older, far larger, and infinitely more malevolent—a creature of pure, raw, destructive chaos.

"The General's forces are fighting ghosts! The Miasma leak was a warning, not the attack! This is the true enemy—the Void Weaver! It seeks to consume the Aetherium and collapse the entire continent!"

The vision shattered our perception of reality. The General's lie was not just a political maneuver; it had blinded the entire kingdom to the actual, world-ending danger bearing down on them. Lord Karsus's rebellion had been correct about the structural failure, but even he hadn't known about the true scale of the external threat.

"The Void Weaver," Teron whispered, his face etched with grim understanding. "An ancient evil, spoken of only in the most obscure Scribe texts."

I understood immediately. "The General's tyranny created the perfect defense against an internal enemy, Teron. But she stripped the Zenith of the necessary forces—the loyal Marked

Ones, the strategic Signets—needed to fight a true external war. She made us vulnerable."

The reality of our exile shifted instantly. We were no longer simply traitors seeking vengeance. We were the only two Riders who knew the truth of the external threat and possessed the perfect, necessary counter-synergy—Void Density and Kinetic Stillness—to stop it.

"We have to warn the Spires," I urged, reaching for my Aetherial.

"No," Teron stated, his eyes hardening with renewed, cold resolve. "The General will only execute us. We are useless in prison. We fight this war from the outside. We gather the other outcasts and rebels—the true loyalists. We create an army that fights for the truth."

He seized my hand, pulling me to my feet. The fear of death was replaced by a shared, massive purpose.

"Our vengeance is secondary, Lyssa. Our treason is now necessary. We are fugitives, outcasts, and traitors. But we are also the only hope against the Void Weaver."

Teron swung himself onto Morgal's saddle, pulling me up behind him, settling me against his strong, warm chest. Zephyr rose into the air, taking his place as the vanguard.

"We fly South," Teron commanded, his mental voice ringing with new, clear authority. "To the rebel territories. The General taught us ruthlessness. Now we teach her the price of the truth."

We flew away from the Zenith Spires, plunging into the dark, uncharted lands of exile. The massive, steady presence of the Void surrounded me, and the sharp, precise power of the Kinetic flowed through me. Traitors and lovers, we were the perfect balance, united against a world that was blind to its impending destruction.

CHAPTER 22

THE FIRST NIGHT AND THE FUGITIVE'S KISS

The flight path took us deep into the Unclaimed Territories—the vast, treacherous canyons and forests bordering the Miasma, lands the Zenith rarely dared to police. We flew low, skimming the tops of the massive, ancient pines, trusting the superior perception of our Aetherials to detect threats.

I clung to Teron Draken's waist, my body tucked securely against his immense, stabilizing frame. The physical proximity was no longer a tactical maneuver; it was a desperate necessity. The cold, unmapped night air was bitter, and the relentless, exhausting flight demanded our Signets work constantly to suppress the friction and turbulence.

"The General's pursuit is slow, Conduit. She assumes failure. She assumes we will collapse due to chaos." Zephyr's mental voice was a low, calculating hum of vigilance.

"We will deny her the chaos," Teron projected, his mental voice a steady, powerful anchor. *"We fly until dawn. We need distance and concealment."*

The Scion of Static and the Burden of Void

The strain of maintaining our counter-Signet synergy was immense. Morgal, the Void Aetherial, exerted a constant, tiring Void Density to stabilize the air around us, ensuring we weren't tossed by unpredictable wind currents. I used my Kinetic Resonance to reduce the friction in the air ahead of us, allowing our Aetherials to glide with unnatural speed and efficiency, conserving their energy.

But my body was screaming from the exertion. I was using my fragile frame as a conduit for continuous kinetic neutralization, a task I had trained for only under highly controlled conditions.

"Teron," I finally managed, my voice strained, barely audible over the wind. "I can't maintain the kinetic stabilization. The residual energy is draining my anchor."

Teron immediately responded, slowing Morgal to a steady hover and projecting a wave of strong, immediate concern through the link. *"We stop now. Landing zone visible below— heavy cover. Prepare for descent."*

Morgal and Zephyr executed a coordinated landing in a tight, sheltered grove surrounded by massive, ancient redwood-like trees. The forest floor was dark, soft earth and pine needles. The air, far from the Zenith's influence, was thick with the scent of pine and damp soil.

Teron slid off Morgal, his powerful body moving with a rigid, contained grace that betrayed the immense fatigue of his

Signet. He reached up and gently helped me dismount, his hands supporting my weight.

"You pushed too far, Scion," Teron stated, his voice now low and guttural, the physical strain evident. "Your Signet is precision, not endurance. You need rest."

I leaned against him for a moment, letting the heavy, stabilizing heat of his presence wash over me. "And you, Wingleader. Your Signet is absolute endurance, but the emotional drain of commanding a Void field while in treason must be catastrophic."

Teron ignored the emotional assessment, his gaze sharp and calculating. "We need cover. Morgal and Zephyr will cloak the immediate perimeter. No fire. No light. Only silence."

The two Aetherials immediately moved to the trees, using their opposing powers to create the perfect fugitive camp. Morgal manipulated the density of the air around the grove, creating a thick, heavy screen that absorbed sound and light. Zephyr used his Kinetic Resonance to gently neutralize the wind flow around the perimeter, ensuring our scent wouldn't carry. We were in a cocoon of absolute, weaponized concealment.

The Fugitive's Camp

Teron immediately set about securing our meager supplies. We had only our Signet anchors, two days of rations stolen from the Void mess hall, and the clothes on our backs.

He found a sheltered rock outcropping and spread a thick, waterproof cloak he had carried. "Rest," he commanded, gesturing to the cloak.

I moved to the spot, but paused, watching him. He was standing with his back to me, meticulously checking the pressure on his flight gear, his muscles moving beneath the taut leather with a weary grace.

"Teron," I said quietly. "We are no longer Wingleader and Cadet. We are equals, bound by treason. Your command is necessary for the external world, but here, in the silence, we are just Lyssa and Teron."

He stopped, his shoulders rigid. He slowly turned, his glacial eyes searching my face. The mask of iron control slipped slightly, revealing the exhaustion and the cold, terrifying weight of the truth.

"There is no 'just Teron,' Lyssa," he replied, his voice rough. "There is only the Son of the Executed. Every decision I make must be based on the vengeance that cost my father his life. And every touch I give you must be measured against the fact that you are the daughter of the woman who ordered that execution."

He pulled his tunic away from his shoulder, revealing the dark, jagged Marked One scar—a brand of treason and pain. It was a raw, visual symbol of the political chasm between us.

I walked toward him, my hands trembling. I reached out and gently placed my fingers on the cold, raised skin of the scar.

"I know this scar," I whispered. "My mother gave it to you. But the man beneath it is the only person who holds my future. Let the anger be, Teron. Let the truth be the only thing that matters."

He leaned into my touch, a small, involuntary movement that shattered his carefully constructed barrier. He seized my hands, his grip tight, pulling me close.

"The truth is that you are an addiction, Lyssa," Teron ground out, his voice thick with suppressed emotion. "You are the single greatest risk to my mission, and the only person who can stabilize the chaos in my mind. You are the stillness that counters my void."

He kissed me then, not with the violence of the prison, but with the slow, deliberate intensity of absolute acceptance. It was a kiss that sealed our exile, tasting of pine, fear, and the unshakeable weight of our future. It was a kiss of mutual surrender to a necessary, forbidden passion.

The Fugitive's Kiss and the Shared Void

Teron pulled away, his breathing ragged. He pulled me down onto the cloak, holding me close, our bodies a single, heat-generating mass against the cold night.

"We must rest," he muttered against my hair, his arms wrapped around my waist, providing the physical anchor I needed to replenish my Signet.

I closed my eyes, feeling his immense, powerful heart beating against my back. I channeled my Kinetic Resonance not for action, but for restoration—gently neutralizing the residual kinetic noise within my own body, allowing my mind to sink into a deep, protected sleep.

Just as I drifted, a faint, disturbing thought broke through the Signet Link, not from Zephyr, but from Morgal, who was still stabilizing the perimeter.

"Rider, the Miasma is active. Too active. It is spreading outward, consuming the forest line."

Morgal projected a sharp, visual sensation: the toxic, dark-red plume of Miasma was not receding; it was slowly, deliberately advancing on the Unclaimed Territories, burning the ancient trees and poisoning the ground.

Teron immediately felt the raw data. He tensed, his body surging with renewed Void energy. "The Void Weaver," he whispered, his voice dark with realization. "The General's lie about the Wards didn't just blind the Zenith—it let the true enemy breach the perimeter!"

He gripped me tightly. "We can't rest, Scion. The Miasma is a living border. We have to move."

My eyes snapped open. I felt the terrifying, encroaching chaos in my Kinetic Resonance. Our journey wasn't a desperate flight from the General; it was a deadly race against a world-ending ecological enemy.

"The Void Weaver is moving faster than we anticipated,

Teron," I confirmed, my voice now sharp with renewed focus. "If it's already breaching the border, the Spires are next. We need to reach the Outer Fiefs—the General's original line of defense—before the Miasma consumes them. We need a faster, safer passage."

Teron pushed me away slightly, his eyes burning with renewed purpose. "There is only one route that offers a tactical advantage this far south: the Sky-Canyon Path. It's the most dangerous flight in the world, unpatrolled because the kinetic shifts are catastrophic. It would shred any normal Aetherial."

"But not us," I stated, seizing my stylus and strapping it to my forearm. "My Kinetic Shield can neutralize the chaotic kinetic flow. Your Void Anchor can stop the falls. It's the perfect route for our synergy. Void Density and Kinetic Stillness are the only way through."

Teron looked at me, his face grim, a silent acknowledgment of our shared fate and our necessary sacrifice. "The Sky-Canyon it is, Scion. We fly at maximum speed. We don't sleep until we reach the rebel allies."

He mounted Morgal, pulling me up behind him, settling me close against his chest. The danger was immense, but the warmth of his body and the silent strength of our shared Signet link made the fear irrelevant. We were fugitives, lovers, and the only force capable of fighting the oblivion closing in on the world.

CHAPTER 23

THE SKY-CANYON PATH AND THE SIGNET FUSION

The Sky-Canyon Path was a treacherous scar across the earth, a deep, narrow rift where the tectonic plates of the continent met. It was utterly unpatrolled by the Zenith, not because of regulation, but because the compressed air currents flowing through the chasm created a constant, chaotic, and lethal kinetic storm. Any Aetherial flying through it would be shredded by the raw, unpredictable force of the wind.

This was the fastest, deadliest path to the rebel territories of the Southern Fiefs.

I was mounted behind Teron Draken on Morgal, staring down into the abyss. The canyon was dark, the air inside a churning maelstrom of gray and white fog that boiled with sheer kinetic energy.

"The sensors are useless here, Scion," Teron stated, his voice tight with controlled intensity. "The chaos is absolute. We will be relying solely on our Signet synchronization. This is not training, Lyssa. This is fusion. We link our cores, or the chaos rips us apart."

"The kinetic noise is immense, Conduit! It seeks to compromise the integrity of the bond!" Zephyr's warning was a sharp, high-pitched alarm in my mind.

I nodded, gripping Teron's tunic. I closed my eyes, channeling my Kinetic Resonance through the silver stylus. "I am ready, Teron. I will stabilize the external chaos. You stabilize us."

The Descent into Chaos

Teron urged Morgal into the chasm. The descent was violent and immediate. The air pressure dropped, and the kinetic forces hit us with the physical weight of liquid granite. I felt the familiar rush of the Void Anchor—Teron activating Morgal's Signet to create a massive, crushing sphere of density around us, stabilizing us against the wind's lateral violence.

But the sheer, chaotic motion inside the Canyon was unlike anything I had experienced. The wind currents were unpredictable, slamming into our Void field from multiple, constantly shifting vectors—up, down, and sideways simultaneously.

I screamed, the pain of the uncontrolled kinetic force tearing at the fragile structure of my Signet. My Kinetic Shield was not fast enough to neutralize the multi-directional chaos.

"I can't stabilize the whole field!" I yelled, battling the dizzying spin. "The vectors are too erratic! It's overloading the Signet!"

Teron immediately adjusted his strategy. He pulled me closer, his massive arms wrapping around my waist, our bodies pressed flush against the saddle. He didn't speak with his mouth; he commanded through the bond, the Void Signet flooding my core.

"Kinetic Core Merge! Stop fighting the Void, Lyssa! Channel the Kinetic through my anchor!"

It was the ultimate act of trust. I had to release my independent defense and route my entire Kinetic Resonance through Teron's body, utilizing his dense, stable Void Signet as my external conduit.

I surrendered, releasing the localized shield. I poured my entire consciousness, my power, and my desperation into the silver stylus, pressing it hard against Teron's chest. My Kinetic Resonance flowed out of me and into his core.

The effect was instantaneous and profound: Signet Fusion.

Teron's Void Anchor—the dense, gravitational field—was now layered with my Kinetic Stillness. We were no longer fighting the chaos; we were neutralizing the *very idea* of it. The Void held the gravity, and the Kinetic eliminated the unpredictable motion within that gravity.

We moved through the chaotic torrent with an impossible, breathtaking stillness—a stable point of absolute zero within a raging kinetic storm.

The Agony of Shared Consciousness

The physical synchronization brought with it a profound, terrifying mental merge. I wasn't just using Teron's Signet; I was experiencing his mind, his pain, and his memories through the flow of energy.

As we flew deeper, the kinetic strain on Teron's Void Signet became immense. He was anchoring our entire team against a natural disaster, and the effort was tearing at his control.

I felt the deep, bone-aching fatigue of the Void Signet's relentless exertion. I felt the fierce, rigid discipline of his will—the absolute dedication to vengeance that had defined his life.

But beneath the anger, I saw a flood of raw, buried emotion: The memory of his father's execution on the Black Summit. The raw grief, the helpless rage, and the isolation of his entire childhood flowed into my mind, a devastating wave of trauma.

Teron fought the exposure, his mental voice sharp with pain. *"Retreat, Scion! Do not breach the privacy! Focus on the kinetic flow!"*

"I can't retreat!" I projected fiercely, my own shame and guilt rising to meet his memory. *"We are fused! I feel your truth, Teron!"*

I responded to his pain by channeling a wave of pure, stabilizing Kinetic Stillness directly into his chaotic memory-space. I didn't try to erase the grief; I simply neutralized the violent kinetic tremor of the trauma, allowing his mind a momentary, precious respite from the rage.

Teron groaned, the physical pain and the emotional relief overwhelming him. He relinquished the struggle, allowing the Kinetic Stillness to flow through the turmoil of his mind.

In that moment of shared vulnerability, I felt the full, absolute measure of his love for me—a fierce, possessive need that was terrifyingly intertwined with his vengeance. He needed me to live, not just for the mission, but to keep his soul from collapsing into the Void of his own anger.

The Final Kinetic Wall

The Signet fusion held us through the core of the Canyon. We flew for what felt like hours, two perfect, stable points of light cutting through the chaos.

We reached the final obstacle: a sheer, vertical climb out of the canyon, where the compressed air created a final, massive, oscillating Kinetic Wall—a wave of chaotic motion that threatened to shake us into oblivion.

"The force is too great, Conduit! It will shatter the fusion!" Zephyr warned.

"No time for evasion!" Teron roared, pushing Morgal into the climb. "We hit it head-on! Void Crush!"

Teron slammed his full, remaining Void Signet into the kinetic wall, attempting to neutralize the entire chaotic structure with sheer density.

The forces collided with a soundless, devastating impact. Teron groaned, the veins on his neck bulging—he was pushing his Aetherial beyond its limit.

The Void held the density, but the chaotic Kinetic Wall still possessed a massive, destabilizing tremor that slammed into the fusion point—the interface between our two Signets. I felt the destructive vibrations instantly.

"Not density, Teron! Find the zero point!" I commanded, surging my Kinetic Resonance to its absolute limit.

I targeted the kinetic interface between the Void and the Wall, creating a tiny, perfect kinetic vacuum. I didn't fight the chaos; I swallowed the vibration.

The Void held the shape, and the Kinetic neutralized the motion. We burst through the Kinetic Wall, emerging from the Canyon in a blinding flash of perfect synchronization.

The Price of Fusion

We flew out of the chasm and into the clear, quiet night, landing hard on the first stable ridge we found. Morgal collapsed onto the ridge, exhausted. Zephyr shimmered violently, his crystalline structure stressed to the limit.

Teron and I separated, collapsing onto the cold, quiet stone.

"We survived," I whispered, my voice rough, hoarse.

Teron simply pulled me to him, crushing me against his chest, burying his face in my hair. It was a fierce, raw, desperate embrace—no longer an anchor, but a shared survival mechanism.

"The fusion was complete, Scion," Teron muttered against my neck, his voice thick with emotion. "We are no longer two Riders, Lyssa. We are a single, combined force. Our minds, our Signets, our vengeance. All of it is one."

He looked at me, his eyes blazing with the profound truth we had just shared. "You felt my Signet's weakness. I felt your soul's absolute, fearless commitment to the truth. There are no more secrets, Lyssa."

He leaned down and kissed me, a kiss of ownership and absolute commitment. It was a physical and emotional seal of our fusion—a terrifying, irreversible step.

I pulled away slightly, the icy clarity of our shared mind leaving me profoundly destabilized. "You felt the moment my mother killed your father, Teron. I felt the trauma. This isn't just a bond; it's an irreversible scar on both our souls. You are now the guardian of my mind, and I, the silent witness to your deepest pain. How do we ever go back to command and cadet after this?"

Teron didn't answer with words. He answered with the cold, absolute density of his Void Signet, pressing into my core: *"We don't go back, Scion. We only go forward."*

"We are traitors to the Zenith," Teron stated, his voice ringing with renewed, absolute resolve. "But we are the perfect weapon. We are the only thing that can stop the Void Weaver."

I nodded, accepting the terrifying truth. Our lives were no longer my own. We were two broken people, fused into a single weapon, driven by vengeance, exiled by our own truth, and bound by a love born of necessity and shared survival.

The Sky-Canyon Path had tested us, and we had succeeded. Now, we were ready to face the outside world and build the army that would save the Zenith from the General's blindness and the coming destruction.

CHAPTER 24

THE REBEL FIEF AND THE SOUTHERN ALLIES

The journey to the Southern Fiefs was long, cold, and silent. We flew for twelve grueling hours, navigating the rough, unmapped terrain beneath the radar of the Zenith's far-reaching patrols. Morgal and Zephyr maintained a constant, exhausting Void-Kinetic Fusion, ensuring our stability, but the effort drained our Aetherials to the core.

I, still nestled against Teron Draken's solid back, used the time to recover my internal balance. The Sky-Canyon Path had fused our Signets, but it had also laid bare the immense, terrifying emotional dependency that now fueled our survival. We spoke only through the Signet Link, our thoughts concise, professional, and punctuated by desperate, shared assurances of commitment.

"The risk of the Void Weaver is immense, Lyssa. We cannot delay," Teron projected his urgency.

"We need proof that speaks louder than our betrayal, Teron. They won't trust the daughter of the General," I cautioned, projecting the sharp, cold reality of our political position.

Arrival at the Outskirts

We landed hours after dawn in a hidden, heavily forested canyon, the air thick with the smell of woodsmoke and damp moss. The Southern Fief was not a city; it was a sprawling, well-guarded community of outcasts, dissidents, and former Zenith personnel who had chosen exile over the General's tyranny.

The moment we landed, we were surrounded.

Dozens of armed guards, their faces grim and wary, emerged from the tree line. These were not the well-fed, uniform Guards of the Zenith; these were hardened, desperate fighters, clad in mismatched leather and armor, carrying a mix of antiquated weapons and crude Aetherial-infused tech.

Leading the group was a woman of immense authority—tall, middle-aged, with close-cropped gray hair and eyes that held the hard resolve of decades of resistance. This was Anya Karsen, the primary strategic leader of the Southern Rebel Faction. She carried a heavy, ancient Structural Signet Hammer, a weapon I immediately recognized as requiring precision, not brute force.

Anya Karsen did not look impressed. She looked dangerous.

"Identify yourselves," Karsen commanded, her voice low and uncompromising. "You carry the mark of the Zenith, and the Void Aetherial with you is immense. We have no patience for spies."

Teron dismounted, stepping forward with his hands

visible, radiating a contained, powerful calm. I stayed close to Zephyr, my silver stylus in hand.

"I am Teron Draken, Wingleader of the Marked Ones," Teron stated, pulling his tunic aside to reveal the brutal, black scars on his shoulder. "And this is Cadet Lyssa Varen. We are both traitors to the Zenith, seeking alliance against the General and the Void Weaver."

Karsen laughed, a short, harsh sound of contempt. "Teron Draken, the Son of the Executed, is a traitor. I believe that. But Lyssa Varen, the General's daughter, is a spy until proven otherwise. I saw the General's broadcast: she claimed you both attempted to collapse the Spires. Tell me why I shouldn't execute you now for the crime of attempted mass murder."

The Trial by Truth

Teron stepped closer, his Void Signet flaring with controlled intensity, meeting the challenge of Karsen's gaze. "The General lied. We saved the Spires. We exposed her greatest secret: the Miasma is not an external enemy; it is the structural failure of the Zenith bedrock."

He pulled the encrypted chip from my stylus and handed it to Karsen. "This contains Project Nightingale—the General's own reports on the Nexus failure. Read the data, Karsen. It is the truth Lord Karsus died for."

Karsen examined the chip, her expression hardening. "Data is easily falsified, Draken. You expect me to risk everything based on a chip from the General's daughter?"

I knew this was my crucible. I stepped forward, ignoring Teron's silent warning to stay back. I projected my Signet outward, but not as a threat.

"I can prove the structural failure without the chip, Karsen," I stated, my voice sharp with conviction. I looked at Karsen's Structural Signet Hammer. "Your hammer relies on Structural Resonance—the ability to find a material's weak point. I possess Kinetic Resonance—the ability to find its most *stable* point."

I then targeted the massive redwood-like tree stump nearest Karsen. I channeled my Signet, not to move the stump, but to map its kinetic structure.

"This stump," I said, my eyes closed in deep focus. "It appears solid. But my Signet detects a profound internal tremor running through the north-western grain. A strong wind, or a slight shift in the soil, will cause the entire structure to collapse along that line. The Zenith Spires are equally brittle."

Anya Karsen stared at the stump, then back at me. She raised her Structural Signet Hammer, its massive head humming with controlled energy. Karsen didn't strike the stump with brute force; she tapped the top of the wood with the hammer's tip, injecting a tiny pulse of Structural Resonance.

The effect was instantaneous and shocking. The entire stump began to vibrate violently, not along the surface, but along the precise, unseen internal line I had predicted. With a loud, splintering groan, the massive stump collapsed neatly along the predicted internal fissure.

The surrounding guards murmured in stunned disbelief.

Karsen lowered her hammer, her face a mask of shocked respect. "You didn't guess. You used your Signet to read the material's fatal flaw. That level of precision is unprecedented."

"The Zenith is failing, Karsen," I pressed, my Signet still vibrating with the effort. "And the problem is exponentially worse. My Aetherial, Zephyr, and Teron's Morgal shared a vision: a massive, external threat, the Void Weaver, is advancing on our continent, exploiting the chaos caused by the Miasma leakage. The General's cover-up has blinded us all."

Karsen's eyes widened at the mention of the Void Weaver, a name whispered in the deepest fear of the exiled. She looked at Teron, seeing not the rebel, but the strategic mind.

"The Void Weaver is a Signet of Total Consumption. If it breaches the outer defenses, the entire continent collapses," Karsen conceded, her voice grim. "If what you say is true, the General is trading our survival for her reputation."

The New Alliance and the Price of Treason

Anya Karsen gave a short, sharp nod, lowering her hammer. "You are not prisoners, Draken. You are a strategic asset. Your Signet synergy—Void and Kinetic—is the only defense capable of neutralizing the Void Weaver's chaos. We accept your claim."

She turned to her guards. "Secure the perimeter. The Wingleader and the Scion are now under my protection. Prepare quarters. They need immediate Signet recovery."

The tension dissolved instantly, replaced by the grim determination of a unified military goal.

Karsen led us to a concealed bunker—the rebel faction's command center. The air inside was warm and thick with the scent of old leather and oil.

"We have information," Karsen stated, pulling up a crude map of the Southern Fiefs. "The General, in her panic, has accelerated the search for a permanent Counter-Signet Weapon to use against you, Draken. She fears your combined power more than the Miasma itself."

"A weapon?" Teron asked, his eyes narrowing.

"A prototype, rumored to be housed at the Iron Keep—an old, abandoned Zenith outpost on the Southern Coast. It is said to neutralize the Void Signet instantly. If she succeeds, she can assassinate you both without resistance, proving her narrative correct."

The realization was stark: we had escaped the executioner's blade only to face a superior technological weapon aimed directly at our combined Void-Kinetic fusion.

Teron looked at me, his face set with cold resolve. "The General will not give us the time to rest, Scion. We must neutralize this Counter-Signet Weapon before we can even begin to fight the Void Weaver."

I nodded, feeling the immense weight of the mission. I was a fugitive, but I was no longer alone. I was the countermeasure, the asset, and the Scion of Static who now held the fate of the entire continent in my hands.

The Fugitive's Rest

Karsen provided us with a small, private cabin—a raw, quiet space carved into the bedrock. Teron and I were left alone, the adrenaline slowly receding, replaced by deep, bone-aching exhaustion.

Teron immediately secured the door, then turned to me, his massive body moving with heavy fatigue. He didn't speak. He simply crossed the space and pulled me into his arms, crushing me against his chest.

This time, the embrace was not a tactical maneuver or a shared vow; it was a desperate, raw plea for emotional and physical refuge.

"We are safe, Lyssa," Teron whispered against my hair, his Signet weak but present, stabilizing us both. "You convinced them. You are their only hope."

"And you are mine," I murmured, pressing my face against his neck, inhaling the cold, clean scent of his skin and his Signet.

We sank onto the rough-hewn bunk together. I used my Kinetic Resonance to gently soothe the deep muscular strain in his legs and back—the physical cost of maintaining the Void Anchor through the Sky-Canyon. Teron simply held me, his vast warmth and density providing the only stillness I needed.

"The Iron Keep is too far for Zephyr and Morgal to fly without significant rest," I calculated, my mind already racing through the new tactical data. "We need a new Signet—a specialized, fast travel Aetherial that can cut the distance safely."

Teron looked down at me, a rare, soft acknowledgment in his glacial eyes. "We need a Lightning Aetherial, Scion. The fastest, most unpredictable flight in the world. And they bond only with the most reckless, chaotic Riders."

I knew the implication: we would need an impossible ally—a rogue Rider from a different Quadrant, one who embraced the chaos I was so desperately trying to neutralize.

The rebellion had found its strategic asset. Now, it needed its chaos agent.

CHAPTER 25

THE CHAOS RIDER AND THE IRON KEEP PLAN

The hidden bunker of the Southern Fief was no sanctuary; it was a war room. Teron Draken and I stood before Anya Karsen, the rebel leader, facing a massive, rough-hewn table upon which a crude but accurate map of the Southern Coast was laid. Our mission: neutralize the Counter-Signet Weapon housed at the Iron Keep.

"The Iron Keep is an abandoned Zenith outpost, built into the cliffs overlooking the sea," Karsen stated, her hand resting on the projected image. "The General's forces moved the weapon there for maximum security and Null-crystal containment. We estimate they are six days from finalizing the Signet dampening codes."

"Six days is too long to fly," Teron countered, his massive hands resting on the map. "Morgal and Zephyr need a minimum of seventy-two hours of full rest after the Sky-Canyon. A frontal assault is suicide. We need speed. Absolute, unpredictable speed."

"Precisely," Karsen confirmed, meeting Teron's cold gaze.

"The Iron Keep is protected by multiple layers of Torrent Signet wards—thick, unpredictable currents of air and water designed to smash any conventional Aetherial approach. If we approach by sea, we drown. If we approach by air, we are stalled."

I stepped forward, my mind already racing through the kinetic possibilities. "We don't need to fly through the currents, Karsen. We need to bypass them. We need a Signet that doesn't rely on flight, but on instantaneous translation of energy."

Karsen offered a grim, knowing smile. "You mean, a Lightning Rider. The fastest, most chaotic Signet in the world. And I happen to know the only one reckless enough to fly into a Magma-guarded trap."

The Chaos Rider: Lyra Zyth

Karsen led us out of the bunker and into a separate, deep cavern used for Aetherial concealment. The air here was sharp, charged with ozone and residual electrical energy.

Sitting on a makeshift perch was a slender, wiry woman with a wild mess of dark, static-charged hair and eyes that constantly twitched with contained energy. This was Lyra Zyth, a former Zenith prodigy who had rebelled after her family was wrongly accused of treason. She was restless, reckless, and deeply unpredictable.

Her Aetherial, Jolt, was coiled beside her—a breathtaking creature made entirely of crystallized electrical energy and raw thunder. Jolt was smaller than Zephyr, but vibrated with a terrifying, contained power that constantly crackled with residual electricity.

"Lyra," Karsen introduced, "These are the traitors I told you about: Teron Draken and Lyssa Varen. They need you to fly them into the most heavily fortified Zenith outpost in the Southern Fiefs."

Lyra Zyth didn't stand. She simply tilted her head, her eyes assessing me with piercing intensity. "The Void Wingleader and the General's Scion. You're either incredibly brave or incredibly stupid. I'm inclined toward the latter."

"We need your Lightning Signet for infiltration," Teron stated, cutting straight to the tactical point. "We need to utilize the instantaneous translation of energy—the electrical short-cut—to bypass the Torrent Wards on the Southern Coast. No other Signet is fast enough."

Lyra laughed, a high, sharp sound of pure contempt. "My Signet isn't a taxi, Draken. It's chaos. And I don't fly for people who wear the scent of the Zenith. Why should I risk my life and Jolt's energy to save the General's own backyard?"

I knew logic wouldn't work. Lyra was driven by pure, unpredictable emotion and resentment.

"Because the Void Weaver is coming," I countered, stepping forward, radiating the cold truth of my Kinetic Resonance. "The Miasma is breaching the perimeter, and the General is building a weapon to neutralize the only force capable of stopping the Void Weaver—Teron's Signet."

Lyra's face hardened. "The Void Weaver is a ghost story, Scion. A political tactic."

"It is not," I insisted. I placed my silver stylus on the ground and channelled my Signet. I didn't attack Lyra; I projected the pure, chaotic, terrifying kinetic tremor of the Void Weaver's approach, amplified by Zephyr's desperate warning. "I felt the chaotic energy of its advance. Teron felt the consuming silence of its Void. Our fused Signet detects the truth of the external threat. We need your chaos to defeat the General's static control."

Lyra paused, her eyes wide. She looked from my pale, intensely focused face to Teron's grim, honest resolution. She believed the fear.

"Fine," Lyra conceded, pushing herself off the perch. "I will fly you. But the price is absolute, Draken. I fly for chaos, and I fly for vengeance against the General. I don't follow military commands. I follow my own Signet. You interfere with my chaos, and I throw you both into the sea."

The Infiltration Plan: Void, Kinetic, Lightning

The plan was complex, requiring a suicidal level of synchronization between the three wildly divergent Signets.

Karsen laid out the tactical strategy on the map:

1. Phase I: The Approach. Lyra and Jolt would fly us in a massive, high-altitude loop over the coast, using their

speed to confuse the Zenith radar systems. Teron and I would ride Morgal, maintaining Signet silence until the final drop.

2. Phase II: The Infiltration Jump. Lyra would use her Lightning Signet—the instantaneous translation of energy—to drop Teron and me onto the Iron Keep's roof, bypassing the perimeter walls. This required me to use my Kinetic Shield to stabilize the immediate landing spot against the immense electrical discharge.

3. Phase III: The Neutralization. Inside the Keep, Teron would use the Void Signet to suppress the Signet energy of the Counter-Signet Weapon, and I would use my Kinetic Resonance to find its structural frequency—its breaking point.

"The greatest risk is the Lightning Signet," Karsen warned. "It is pure, unstable power. It needs perfect, absolute neutralization at the moment of discharge, or it will shatter your fragile kinetic shield, killing you both instantly. Lyra is chaos. Varen, you must be the perfect still point within that storm."

I looked at Lyra, seeing the wild, unpredictable energy of the Lightning Rider—the complete opposite of my own nature.

"We trust the Signets," I said, my voice steady. "The Void holds the gravity. The Kinetic holds the stillness. The Lightning provides the motion."

The Clash of Personalities

The next thirty-six hours were spent in brutal, synchronized practice jumps—Lyra generating short, localized electrical fields, and me desperately trying to match the instantaneous chaos with an equally instantaneous Kinetic Shield.

The clash between Lyra and me was immediate and electric.

"You're too slow, Scion!" Lyra yelled during one failed attempt. "You think too much! Lightning doesn't wait for your little geometric calculations! It hits the path of least resistance *now*!"

"Your chaos is dangerous, Lyra!" I retorted, my body aching from the kinetic backlash of the failed shield. "If you discharge too early, my Signet will not be able to contain the velocity! You risk burning the Void Wingleader!"

Teron stood between us, a massive, silent anchor of contained fury. He didn't take sides; he maintained the rigid demand for perfection. "The Signets must synchronize. The Void is the final defense. We fail, we all die. Focus, both of you."

During a brief, tense break, Lyra pulled me aside. "I know your mother, Scion. She hunted my family for months. She taught me that loyalty is an illusion. Tell me why I should believe that the Draken vengeance won't end the minute he gets what he wants."

I met her gaze, no longer pleading, but commanding with the cold truth of our shared survival. "Because our betrayal wasn't for vengeance, Lyra. It was for the Void Weaver—a threat that will consume the entire continent, Zenith and Fiefs alike. Teron Draken needs me to survive that threat. And I need him to survive my mother. Our survival is a necessity, not a choice. Our bond is built on a shared, unavoidable truth."

Lyra considered this, a rare moment of stillness in her chaotic eyes. "Necessary survival," she mused. "That, I understand. Fine. We fly tonight. But I choose the trajectory, Scion. You just try to keep up."

The Final Synchronization

As night fell, the three of us prepared for the perilous flight. Teron and I stood in the cavern, performing our final, necessary act of Signet fusion.

Teron pulled me against him, his massive arms wrapping around me. He activated his Void Signet, its crushing density stabilizing my mind.

"We are one force, Scion," Teron muttered, his mouth close to my ear, his breath warm and dangerous. "Channel your stillness into me. I will contain the chaos of the Lightning. Lyra's Signet will be your conduit. My body will be your shield. Trust the fusion, Lyssa."

I pushed my entire Kinetic Resonance into him, surrendering the last vestige of my independence to the necessity of his power. The fear dissolved, replaced by a cold, absolute resolve.

I looked at Lyra, who was mounted on Jolt, her eyes already glowing with nascent electrical power.

"Ready for chaos, Scion?" Lyra called out, a wild, challenging grin on her face.

"Ready for stillness," I countered, vaulting onto Morgal's back.

The three Aetherials launched into the night sky, Jolt a silent, blazing missile of electrical energy, Morgal and Zephyr a synchronized, defensive anchor right behind him. The journey to the Iron Keep would be the ultimate test of our combined treason and our chaotic, necessary alliance.

CHAPTER 26

IRON KEEP INFILTRATION AND THE SIGNET DESTROYER

The three Aetherials sliced through the night sky toward the Southern Coast. Jolt, the Lightning Aetherial, flew like a silent, contained bolt of pure energy, carrying Lyra Zyth with terrifying speed. Behind them, Morgal and Zephyr maintained a heavy, stable, Void-Kinetic Fusion, protecting Teron Draken and me from the turbulent friction of the high-velocity flight.

The destination, the Iron Keep, rose before us—a squat, obsidian fortress built into the jagged, wind-battered cliffs. It was a picture of brutal, silent efficiency, guarded by the chaotic, swirling Torrent Wards that made the final approach suicidal for any conventional Aetherial.

Final Prep: The Acceptance of Chaos

I clung to Teron, our bodies a single, fused entity of opposing forces. The constant Lightning Signet energy from Jolt filled the air, a high-frequency whine that threatened to destabilize my core.

"The electrical chaos is immense, Scion. It challenges our stillness," Teron projected through the bond, his mental voice

steady, suppressing his own rising agitation.

"We embrace the chaos, Wingleader," I countered, channeling my Kinetic Resonance to neutralize the electrical static around my own skin. *"Lyra's speed is our only chance. We trust the fusion."*

We communicated the final tactical check with Lyra. *"Lyra, target the apex of the central turret. We need the drop to be vertical, minimizing exposure to the Torrent Wards."*

"I don't do vertical, Draken. I do instantaneous," Lyra snapped back mentally, her voice laced with manic excitement. *"You get one second of synchronization. If the Kinetic Shield fails, Jolt consumes the residual discharge. You trust the chaos."*

The risk was absolute. If my Kinetic Resonance failed to stabilize the immense electrical discharge from Lyra's Signet during the drop, the force would not only incinerate me, but the resulting electrical-kinetic explosion would kill Teron instantly.

Phase I: The Lightning Jump

Jolt soared higher, executing a complex, spiraling trajectory that baffled the Zenith's lower radar systems. We approached the Torrent Wards—a blinding wall of swirling, water-based energy currents.

"Now, Scion!" Teron commanded. "Prepare the Void Anchor! I will punch the hole!"

Teron unleashed a sudden, massive, focused blast of Void Signet energy. The crushing density slammed into the Torrent

Ward. It didn't destroy the ward, but it created a micro-second tunnel of absolute stillness through the churning chaos, holding the swirling water currents rigidly in place.

Lyra shot through the tunnel instantly. The sudden burst of speed tore the air around us.

We were above the Keep. Lyra positioned Jolt directly over the central turret.

"Jump!" Lyra shrieked, her voice wild with the thrill of the chaos.

Teron and I jumped from Morgal, plummeting toward the roof.

Lyra activated her Lightning Signet. Jolt unleashed a searing sphere of electrical translation *at our target*. It was not flight; it was the instantaneous conversion of potential energy into kinetic force. I felt a devastating surge of pure, raw electricity—the chaotic energy threatening to dismantle my Signet entirely.

"Stabilize the discharge! Kinetic Shield!" I screamed internally, pouring my entire Signet into the silver stylus.

I channeled the Kinetic Resonance into the precise point of impact—the roof of the central turret—creating a perfect, zero-resistance field directly beneath us. The massive electrical discharge from Lyra's Signet hit the frictionless field and was instantly stabilized, the energy safely dispersed into the granite, preventing an explosive impact.

We landed silently, perfectly still, on the cold, hard granite roof. Lyra and Jolt vanished instantly, pulling back from the electrical discharge. The entire maneuver had taken less than a second.

Teron and I stood alone on the turret roof, the massive effort shaking our bones.

"Signet link confirmed. We survived the jump," Teron muttered, his body trembling from the residual Void strain. "You are the most precise thing I have ever known, Lyssa Varen."

Phase II: The Sentinel and the Counter-Signet Weapon

Teron immediately used his Void Signet to suppress the limited kinetic energy of the door lock beneath us, and we slipped into the Keep. The interior was a maze of cold, reinforced corridors.

The archive data had pinpointed the Counter-Signet Weapon to the Null-Crystal Forge, a sub-level designed for the crafting of Signet-dampening materials.

We moved quickly, me leading the way. My Kinetic Resonance, though fatigued, was perfectly suited for infiltration. I neutralized the friction of our footsteps, making our movements silent, and used the subtle tremors in the air to anticipate the location of the Zenith Guards.

We reached the forge. The room was dominated by a massive, pulsing crystal furnace. In the center, mounted on a pedestal, was the Counter-Signet Weapon: a colossal, humming Null-crystal rod, radiating a massive, chaotic Signet-dampening field.

But the weapon was guarded. Standing before it was a colossal, hulking figure—a massive, armored Rider with a cold, terrifying Structural Signet. This was The Sentinel, the General's personal master of materials and defense.

The Sentinel didn't speak. He lifted a massive, obsidian fist, and slammed it onto the granite floor.

Structural Signet Activation. The entire floor of the Forge began to vibrate at its harmonic frequency—the perfect frequency to shatter the bones of any living creature standing on it.

I screamed, the pain instantaneous and paralyzing. The Sentinel was weaponizing the structure itself.

"Void Anchor, Teron! Full power!" I shrieked, fighting to maintain my focus.

Teron unleashed his Void Signet, focusing the density beneath our feet. He countered the vibration by crushing the structural integrity of the granite beneath us, creating localized, anti-vibrational patches of absolute density. The floor still trembled violently, but the fatal frequency was absorbed.

The Sentinel sneered, recognizing the desperate counter. He charged, pulling a massive, blunt, obsidian war-hammer.

"I will shatter the traitor and his Scion!" the Sentinel roared, swinging the hammer in a crushing arc aimed at Teron's head.

I knew the Void Signet couldn't hold both the structural defense and the kinetic attack simultaneously.

Kinetic Shield!

I charged forward, slamming my silver stylus anchor onto the Sentinel's armor just before the hammer struck. I channeled a massive surge of Kinetic Resonance, creating a localized vacuum of zero momentum around the hammer's head.

The hammer's massive, crushing kinetic energy vanished.

It stopped mid-swing, inert and useless.

The Sentinel stared at the weapon, shocked by the impossible stall. Teron seized the moment.

"Void Crush!" Teron roared, channeling the full weight of Morgal into a localized Void Signet attack directly at the Sentinel's armor. The immense pressure slammed into the Sentinel's chest plate. The armor groaned and imploded, sending the Sentinel stumbling backward in agony.

Phase III: The Final Sacrifice

We had bought ourselves seconds. Teron ran to the pedestal, raising his hand to neutralize the Counter-Signet Weapon with his Void Signet.

But the Sentinel, recovering instantly, pointed to the colossal, humming Null-crystal rod. "Activate the dampeners! Full frequency!"

The Counter-Signet Weapon roared to life. A massive, chaotic wave of Signet-dampening energy slammed into the room.

Teron and I were hit simultaneously. The effect was immediate and catastrophic: our connection snapped.

I collapsed, the life draining out of me. My Kinetic Resonance dissolved instantly; the world plunged into dizzying, painful chaos. Zephyr's mental voice vanished. I was reduced to the frail, weak Scribe I was before the bond.

Teron fell to his knees, his Void Signet utterly suppressed. He was just a massive, strong man, stripped of his immense power. The Sentinel was triumphant.

"No Signet can save you now, Traitor! The Zenith endures!" the Sentinel shouted, retrieving a laser pistol and aiming it at Teron.

I knew the Signet suppression was our death sentence. We had to destroy the rod.

"Not the Signet, Teron! The structure!" I screamed, my mind clear despite the pain. *I remembered Eysa's lesson. Find the fatal flaw.*

I crawled toward the Sentinel, using the last remnants of my physical strength. I grabbed a heavy, discarded Null-crystal testing rod. I slammed the rod against the pedestal, pouring my desperate will, not my Signet, but my *focus*, into the crystal. I mentally searched for the structural frequency of the Counter-Signet Weapon—the weapon's fatal flaw.

The Sentinel fired. The laser blast slammed into Teron's shoulder. Teron roared in pain, but his sheer physical size absorbed the shot.

I found the frequency. The Counter-Signet Weapon was massive, but it was built on a single, high, crystalline frequency.

I screamed, slamming the testing rod against that precise point with every ounce of my remaining strength, channeling my desperate will into the impact, amplifying the fatal frequency *manually*.

The Counter-Signet Rod began to vibrate violently. The chaotic Signet-dampening field intensified, but the structural integrity failed. The massive Null-crystal rod EXPLODED in a silent, contained burst of crystalline fragments and discharged energy.

The Signet-dampening field vanished.

The Void-Kinetic Fusion slammed back into Teron and me. The life surged back into us, painful but glorious.

Teron immediately unleashed his full, devastating Void Signet—a massive, crushing wave of gravity aimed at the Sentinel. The Sentinel, caught in the returning Signet power, was crushed to the floor, paralyzed and defeated.

The Final Retreat

"We have to go!" Teron roared, pulling me to my feet. We had destroyed the weapon, but the alarm was blaring. Zenith Guards were scrambling toward the Forge.

We burst out of the sub-level and onto the roof. Lyra and Jolt were waiting, the chaos Rider having successfully evaded all Zenith patrols.

"Jolt! Full discharge!" Teron commanded.

Lyra activated her Lightning Signet. Jolt enveloped us, not in a sphere, but in a blinding bolt of raw electrical energy.

The instantaneous translation of energy—the electrical short-cut—slammed us across the coast. We vanished from the Iron Keep in a massive flash of blue light and ozone, leaving the massive, defeated Sentinel behind us.

We emerged minutes later, landing hard in the protective canopy of the Southern Fiefs. We were bruised, burned, and utterly exhausted, but the weapon was destroyed.

Teron turned to me, his face raw with pain, and pulled me into a desperate embrace. "The cost was absolute, Scion," he muttered, tracing the burn on his shoulder. "But the General is now blind. We won this battle." I nestled against him, my body aching but whole. I had faced the Zenith's ultimate weapon and survived. We were traitors, but our fusion was absolute, our love forged in the fires of treason and necessary survival.

CHAPTER 27

THE RISE OF THE REBEL ARMY AND THE EXTERNAL WAR

The successful raid on the Iron Keep had achieved its primary objective: the Counter-Signet Weapon was neutralized, and General Varen was temporarily blind to our defensive capabilities. But the immediate triumph was short-lived, replaced by the crushing weight of our new reality. We were fugitives, and our lives were no longer measured in days, but in the rapid advance of the Void Weaver.

The Unspoken Coronation

The Southern Fief war room—the same concealed bunker where we had negotiated our alliance—became the center of the nascent rebellion. Anya Karsen, the initial rebel leader, immediately deferred command to Teron Draken. Karsen, a strategist of resource management, recognized that the war now required the raw, military authority and powerful Signet command that only Teron possessed.

Teron stood before a council of skeptical Fief commanders and the few trusted Marked Ones who had followed Jax into exile. He was clad in rough, unadorned rebel leather, but his presence, backed by the immense, silent mass of Morgal just outside the bunker, was absolute.

"We have proved the General's lie," Teron stated, his voice ringing with hard authority. "The Dreadnought Nexus is stable, proving her treason. But our war is no longer against the Zenith. Our war is against the Void Weaver."

He then ceded the floor to me. It was a strategic move: the disgraced General's daughter, the Scribe, would present the technical truth. I stood beside Teron, radiating a cold, precise confidence. I was the factual anchor to his overwhelming power.

I presented the analysis, projecting the Project Nightingale data onto a large, crystal display—the schematics of the failing Spires and the catastrophic Miasma leak.

"The Miasma is not a defense; it is a symptom," I explained, my voice steady. "It is the structural bleeding of unstable Aetherium. The General's cover-up blinded the Zenith, leaving the outer defenses weak. This weakness has been exploited by the Void Weaver."

I then presented the terrifying, Aetherial-projected vision we had received during our escape.

"The Void Weaver is a consciousness that manipulates raw, chaotic energy," I continued. "It uses the existing structural chaos of the Miasma to expand its influence, consuming all Aetherium—all magic—in its path. Its advance is not measured in flight, but in the rapid, molecular collapse of all life and material it touches."

The room plunged into shocked silence. The Fief Commanders, focused on political resistance, had not grasped the apocalyptic scale of the threat.

Teron seized the moment. "The Zenith is a fortress with a blind command. We are the only defense left. Our Void-Kinetic fusion is the only force capable of neutralizing the Void Weaver's chaotic collapse. We are no longer traitors. We are the necessary army."

The Recruitment Challenge: Scars and Fiefs

Teron's next challenge was unifying the disparate rebel groups. He needed the firepower of the Marked Ones—the Zenith-trained riders—and the structural knowledge and resourcefulness of the Southern Fief commanders.

Jax, Teron's second-in-command, stood up, his gaze sweeping over the Fief commanders. "We, the Marked Ones, follow the Son of the Executed. We fight for the truth that killed our fathers. But the Fiefs must commit all their resources. No more hiding."

A stout Fief commander named Garin countered immediately. "We trust Karsen, and we believe the General is a tyrant. But we do not trust the Zenith's power. Your Void Aetherial is immense, Draken, but it is too slow. The Void Weaver moves like a plague. We need speed and unpredictability."

I immediately countered the tactical objection. "Garin is correct. The Void Weaver is too fast for Morgal. We need a specialized force that can strike its kinetic core and disrupt its advance. We need more than just Void and Kinetic."

Teron looked at me, the shared solution already clear in the bond. "We need to recruit a Chaos Signet—a force that the Zenith deemed too unstable to control."

"We need the Lightning Riders," Karsen concluded grimly. "They are the most powerful, most volatile, and most unpredictable Signet. They were the first to flee the General's tyranny, taking their Signets into exile. They fly outside the Zenith's flight maps."

The task was clear: Teron would command the army; I would recruit the Chaos.

The Strategic Divide

The final, devastating strategy session concluded with the council establishing two primary objectives.

"The first," Anya Karsen stated, "is fortification. Jax, you and the Marked Ones will stay with me. We will use our resources to build the Void Barrier Teron designed. We will hold the Southern Fief against the Miasma."

"And the second objective?" Teron asked, his voice a low rumble.

"Recruitment," I said, stepping forward. "The Void Weaver is too fast. We need the Lightning Riders. Lyra Zyth and I will fly to the Eastern Wastes. I will be the... anchor."

The word felt wrong. I was the anchor of *stillness*, but Teron was the anchor of my *strength*. The thought of separating sent a spike of kinetic panic through my core.

Teron felt it instantly. He stepped forward, his massive form eclipsing the map. "No."

The room went silent.

"Wingleader," Karsen began, "the plan is sound. We need—"

"The plan is flawed," Teron cut her off, his Void Signet flaring with cold authority. He looked at Lyra, who was buzzing with chaotic energy in the corner. "Lyra Zyth is a chaotic element. The Lightning Fief is a nest of pure, unstable kinetic energy. You do not send *stillness* to recruit *chaos* without an anchor to hold the two."

He turned his gaze to me, and the message was clear, possessive, and absolute.

"I am the anchor," he stated. "The Void-Kinetic fusion is the *only* thing that can stabilize Lyra's Signet. It is the *only* force that can neutralize the Kinetic Firewall in the Wastes. We do not separate. We are a single weapon."

His decision was final. The tactical logic was undeniable. The rebellion's greatest weapon—our fusion—could not be split.

Lyra Zyth just grinned, her eyes flashing. "Finally. A plan with some real energy. Fine. You two provide the stability, I'll provide the speed. Let's go hunt some lightning."

The new plan was set. Anya Karsen and Jax would fortify the Southern Fief, creating a stronghold for the coming war. Teron, Lyra, and I would fly to the Eastern Wastes.

As dawn broke, the three of us prepared for the perilous flight. Teron and I stood in the cavern, performing our final, necessary act of Signet fusion. He pulled me against him, his massive arms wrapping around me, the Void Signet stabilizing my mind.

"We are one force, Scion," Teron muttered, his mouth close to my ear. "We will contain the chaos. We will not fail."

I nodded, pouring my Kinetic Resonance into him, surrendering to the necessity of his power. I looked at Lyra, who was mounted on Jolt, her face a mask of wild, challenging excitement.

"Ready for chaos, Scion?" Lyra called out.

"Ready for the fight, Chaos Rider," I replied, mounting Zephyr.

The three Aetherials launched into the night sky—Jolt a silent, blazing missile of electrical energy, Morgal and Zephyr a synchronized, defensive anchor right behind. The journey to the Iron Keep was a memory; the hunt for the Lightning Fief was our new reality. We flew together, a single, fused weapon aimed at the heart of the coming storm.

CHAPTER 28

THE EASTERN WASTES AND THE LIGHTNING HUNT

The flight into the Uncharted Eastern Wastes was not a strategic maneuver; it was a violent, chaotic torment. I, mounted on Zephyr, was now part of a volatile, three-Signet formation.

Teron flew Morgal beside me, his Void Signet a heavy, stabilizing anchor against the turbulent air. But flying point was Lyra Zyth on Jolt, a creature that was less an Aetherial and more a bolt of raw, unpredictable energy. Jolt's body constantly discharged residual electrical static, and the energy was pure, high-frequency chaos—the absolute antithesis of my need for perfect stillness.

"The motion is volatile, Conduit!" Zephyr's mental voice was sharp with distress, his crystalline form vibrating. "The Lightning Signet compromises our internal stabilization!"

"Channel the chaos, Scion! Stop fighting my energy!" Lyra projected mentally, her voice laced with manic excitement.

I fought to maintain my composure. My Kinetic Resonance was in a constant, exhausting battle with the electrical overload. The only reason I wasn't seizing up was Teron. He had extended his Void Field to envelop all three of us, a massive, draining effort to contain Lyra's chaos and create a stable pocket for my stillness. The separation I had dreaded in the Fief was gone, replaced by a new, exhausting, and intimate fusion.

"Maintain the link, Lyssa," Teron's mental voice cut through the static, a low, powerful anchor in my mind. "I will absorb the electrical backlash. You focus on neutralizing the friction. Lyra, maintain velocity."

The flight was a continuous, three-way argument between Chaos, Control, and Command.

"We need a structured, high-altitude search pattern!" I projected, forcing my thoughts to be concise. "Your trajectory is random, Lyra! It wastes energy!"

"The Wastes are random, Scion! You can't map chaos; you ride it!" Lyra countered, executing a sudden, terrifying drop.

"Enough!" Teron's Void Signet flared, momentarily crushing the ambient energy. "Lyra is correct. A straight flight is a target for Zenith patrols. But Lyssa is also correct. Your random flight path is inefficient." He projected his decision to both of us. "Lyra, you maintain the chaotic trajectory. Lyssa, you will be our sensor. Focus your Resonance past the static. Find the anomaly. I will hold the fusion."

His command settled the conflict. Lyra's chaos was given

purpose, and my precision was given a target.

We flew for days, our only sustenance the intense energy exchange between our Aetherials. During a brief, tense stop in a jagged, metallic canyon, Lyra confronted me while Teron stood guard, his hand on his obsidian dagger.

"Why do you fight the current so hard, Scion?" Lyra demanded. "The Void Wingleader understands power—he uses density to crush. But you use nothing. You try to make the world stand still. That's not strength; that's fear of motion."

"It's not fear; it's precision," I snapped back. "The Void Weaver is pure, consuming kinetic chaos. If we fight chaos with chaos, the world collapses. We must neutralize the motion with perfect stillness. I am the only one who can stabilize your energy for a tactical strike."

Teron spoke, his voice low and final. "And I am the only one who can anchor you both. The argument is over. Lyssa, you have a target."

I closed my eyes, focusing my Kinetic Resonance. I pushed my senses past the electrical static, past the natural wind, searching for a pattern that defied the natural chaos.

"The motion is random, Lyra... except for the eastern peaks. There is a precise, high-frequency kinetic wave that vanishes abruptly. It's too smooth. It's a disguised barrier."

Lyra looked at the desolate peaks, a landscape shrouded in violent electrical storms. "That's impossible. No Aetherial can fly into those peaks. The kinetic turbulence is catastrophic."

"The turbulence is intentional," I countered, my mind racing. "It is a Kinetic Ward—a defensive wall built to appear as natural chaos. It's a layer of maximum, synchronized resistance. We need to create a zero-resistance path through it."

Lyra's eyes began to glow. "A kinetic firewall? I fly into firewalls, Scion. How do we open it?"

Teron stepped forward, his gaze fixed on the peaks. "This is a three-Signet maneuver. The firewall is maintained by constant, patterned energy. We need to disrupt its frequency."

He looked at Lyra. "You fire a lightning bolt at the core of the turbulence."

Then he looked at me. "I will use the Void to punch a momentary hole, creating a vacuum. Lyssa, you will use your Kinetic Resonance to stabilize the discharge at the point of impact, turning the chaotic energy into the key. You will neutralize the firewall's resistance."

The ultimate precision. The ascent to the kinetic firewall was treacherous. We positioned ourselves directly before the shimmering, invisible barrier of pure, high-velocity wind.

"Ready, Scion? Wingleader?" Lyra's voice was a low thrum of power. "If your stillness fails, we are vaporized."

"Hold the Void Anchor, Teron!" I commanded.

Teron and Morgal unleashed a focused pulse of Void density, creating a momentary, crushing vacuum in the kinetic wall.

"Now, Lyra!"

Lyra unleashed her Lightning Signet. Jolt fired a massive, blinding bolt of electrical energy directly into the vacuum.

The collision was catastrophic. The kinetic energy of the wall slammed into the electrical energy of the bolt, all centered in Teron's Void.

"Stillness!" Teron roared.

I seized the moment of chaotic collapse. I channeled my Kinetic Resonance into the core of the explosion, creating a perfect, spherical vacuum of zero-resistance.

The firewall did not collapse; it opened—a tunnel of still, clear air leading straight into the heart of the mountains.

The three of us plunged into the opening, emerging into a vast, hidden, electrically charged valley—the Lightning Fief.

The air here was a constant, crackling static. Hundreds of Lightning Riders and their Aetherials were gathered here. They immediately surrounded us, their eyes narrowed in suspicion. They recognized Lyra, but Zephyr, Morgal, and the two of us were a terrifying, unknown intrusion.

The leader of the Fiefs, a scarred, powerful man named Torvin, dismounted from his massive, thunder-scaled Aetherial, Volt.

"Lyra Zyth," Torvin stated, his voice ringing with latent

electrical power. "You bring the scent of the Zenith and a Void Wingleader into our sanctuary. And the General's daughter— the Kinetic Conduit. Justify your treason."

Lyra stepped forward. "I bring the truth, Torvin. The General is blind, and the Void Weaver is coming. This fusion"—she gestured to Teron and me—"is the only thing that can stabilize our power to fight it."

Torvin's gaze dismissed Lyra and settled on me. "The General's daughter. You have her blood. You are a lie."

"I am the Scion of Static," I said, my voice quiet but cutting. I dismounted from Zephyr. "I did not come to petition, Torvin. I came to offer you a choice. We have neutralized the General's weapon and proved her lies. Now, you join us, or you face the Void Weaver alone."

The confrontation was set: my stillness, Lyra's chaos, and Teron's density, all aimed at the raw, volatile power of the Lightning Fief.

CHAPTER 29

THE NEGOTIATION AND THE TRUE ENEMY

The air in the Lightning Fief was electric, charged with the palpable hostility of hundreds of exiled Lightning Riders. Lyra, Teron, and I stood before Torvin, the Fief leader.

Lyra, never one for patience, spoke first. "We don't have time for this, Torvin. The General is blind, and the Void Weaver is coming."

Torvin, a massive man scarred by raw electrical burns, scoffed. "Your Zenith politics mean nothing here, Zyth. We fled your General's tyranny for safety, not a suicide pact. The Void Weaver is a tale told to keep cadets in line." His eyes flicked to me. "My people fight fire with fire—not with stillness."

Teron Draken stepped forward, his Void Signet flaring just enough to make the air heavy, commanding respect. "The Void Weaver is not a tale. It is a consciousness that consumes Aetherium. Your 'fire' will only feed it."

As Teron spoke, the ambient electrical crackle in the air intensified, a low, unsettling roar coming from the western peaks. Volt, Torvin's Aetherial, suddenly tensed, its thunder-scaled body snapping with latent power.

"Intrusion! High-frequency chaos! The Void Weaver is testing the perimeter!" Volt's warning was a jarring, terrifying mental projection shared instantly by Jolt, Zephyr, and Morgal.

The atmosphere in the valley plunged into chaos. A massive, black plume of Miasma, thicker and more dense than any I had seen, poured over the western peaks. It was an unnatural, silent wave of consumption.

"That is not natural Miasma," I shouted, my voice cutting through the panic. "That is the Void Weaver's advance! It seeks to neutralize our Aetherium!"

Torvin watched, his eyes wide with shock. The Miasma moved with a deliberate, hungry intelligence, consuming the electrical static from the metallic peaks.

Teron immediately moved into command. "This is your proof, Torvin! Lyra, with me! We neutralize the head of the plume! Lyssa, you are the anchor! Stabilize our fusion!"

Lyra was already mounted on Jolt, her face alight with adrenaline. "Chaos ready, Wingleader!"

The deployment was a single, synchronized act of desperation. Teron vaulted onto Morgal, and I onto Zephyr. The trio of Aetherials—Zephyr (Stillness), Morgal (Density), and Jolt (Chaos)—launched toward the approaching plume.

Lyra and Jolt flew the point, generating an immense,

blinding Lightning Signet field, striking the perimeter of the Miasma. The electrical energy slammed into the consuming chaos.

The plume retaliated instantly. The Void Weaver channeled the electrical energy back at the Riders, amplifying the kinetic chaos, threatening to tear Jolt and Lyra apart with their own power.

"Teron, hold the density! Create a channel!" I commanded.

Teron and Morgal unleashed a focused Void Field, anchoring the chaotic Miasma, creating a stable "tunnel" of density amidst the plume's chaos.

"Kinetic Shield! Full containment!" I projected to Lyra. I channeled my Kinetic Resonance, enveloping Jolt and Lyra in a protective shell of perfect stillness *within* Teron's Void tunnel.

The Miasma plume surged forward, attempting to consume the stabilizing field.

"Lyra, hit the core! A focused blast! Teron and I will hold the fusion!" I screamed, pouring the excess kinetic force from the Miasma into my silver stylus, which grew dangerously hot.

Lyra unleashed Jolt's Signet. A massive, concentrated bolt of lightning, stabilized and focused by my kinetic field and Teron's Void channel, shot directly into the heart of the plume. The Miasma, pure chaotic energy, encountered the stabilized blast and stalled, its advance arrested.

The three Signets held the terrifying balance: Lightning providing the disruptive energy; Void providing the anchor; and Kinetic neutralizing the chaotic motion.

The plume held for ten seconds, then silently, reluctantly, receded, pulling back from the overwhelming counter-synergy. The immediate threat was repelled.

We returned to the Lightning Fief. The valley was silent. Torvin and the Lightning Riders stared at us, their faces etched with shock and dawning realization. They hadn't seen a Signet battle; they had seen an impossible counter-force that neutralized the very definition of chaos.

Torvin finally spoke, his voice reverent. "No single Signet could have survived that. The Void Weaver is real."

He walked over to Teron, bowing his head in military submission. "Wingleader Draken, I was wrong." He then turned to me. "And Scion of Static... your stillness is the only defense. The Lightning Fief commits to the cause. We are your army."

The transfer of power was seamless. We had secured the first, most crucial ally for our war. The victory was absolute. I looked at Teron, and our shared glance through the Signet link was one of grim, tired triumph. We had the chaos army. Now, we had to get them to the war.

CHAPTER 30

THE CHAOS BARRIER AND THE VOID WEAVER'S GAZE

The dawn broke cold and clear over the Unclaimed Territories, but the eastern sky was already corrupted— a vast, churning black cloud of Miasma that pulsed with a destructive, chaotic energy. This was the front line of the war against the Void Weaver.

I flew point with Lyra Zyth, our two Aetherials—Zephyr (Kinetic) and Jolt (Lightning)—executing a deadly, synchronized pattern. Behind us, the Lightning Fief Vanguard, a formation of dozens of electric Aetherials, followed, a massive, crackling shield of raw power.

I maintained a fragile, constant Kinetic Shield around Jolt and Lyra, neutralizing the electrical chaos just enough to allow communication and focus. The effort was immense, requiring me to ride the very edge of the Still Point.

"The consumption is accelerating, Conduit! The Miasma absorbs the ambient Aetherium!" Zephyr's mental voice was sharp with urgency.

"We have to hit the perimeter before it breaches the outer ridges! Lyra, maximum velocity!" I projected through the bond.

"Chaos engaged, Scion!" Lyra shrieked back, her excitement a tangible, high-frequency current that slammed into my mind. Jolt transformed into a blur of raw electrical energy, accelerating our flight to a terrifying, unsustainable speed.

The General's Last Trap

The first threat was not the Void Weaver, but the General.

Mid-flight, a silent, disciplined patrol of Magma Riders and Torrent Riders emerged from the lower clouds, led by General Varen's right-hand commander, Colonel Verrin. They were flying a calculated interception pattern.

"Traitors! Surrender your Signets!" Verrin bellowed, his voice amplified by his Magma Aetherial. "The General commands your immediate arrest!"

Lyra laughed—a sharp, manic sound. "The Zenith still fights ghosts! Teron was right! They're blind!"

Teron's military strategy was clear: Do not engage the General's forces directly. They are a distraction.

"Lyra, tactical bypass! Target the Torrent Ward on their right flank—the kinetic resistance is unstable! We create a tear!" I commanded, channeling the Kinetic Resonance to map the structural weakness in the air.

Lyra, with stunning obedience to the strategy, executed a complex, lightning-fast maneuver. Jolt unleashed a focused bolt of electrical energy at the precise coordinate I provided. I simultaneously neutralized the kinetic resistance at the impact point. The Torrent Ward protecting the patrol collapsed, sending Verrin's formation into momentary, chaotic disarray.

Lyra and I tore through the opening, the rest of the Vanguard streaming after us, leaving the General's forces confused and compromised. We had achieved the strategic bypass.

Building the Chaos Barrier

We flew past the collapsed Zenith patrol and reached the front line of the Miasma. The black plume was enormous, boiling with a soundless, terrifying energy that seemed to consume the light itself.

"This is the perimeter, Lyra! We build the Chaos Barrier here! Full Signet sustained discharge!" I commanded, pulling Zephyr into a wide, sweeping arc.

The plan was audacious: Lyra and the Lightning Riders would deploy a massive, sustained Electrical Signet Shield along the entire Miasma line. My task was the impossible: I had to use my Kinetic Resonance to stabilize the entire Chaos Barrier, preventing the high-frequency electrical energy from simply dissipating or collapsing onto itself.

The Lightning Riders unleashed their full power. The sky exploded in a massive, shimmering web of pure electrical energy. Hundreds of thousands of amps of power surged into the Miasma, creating a defensive shield of pure, unstable chaos.

Zephyr and I flew into the heart of the resulting electrical storm. I poured my entire Kinetic Resonance into the vast electrical field, channeling the silver stylus anchor until it burned my skin. I didn't fight the chaos; I imposed stillness upon it, neutralizing the internal vibrations of the electrical field, making the Chaos Barrier cohesive, stable, and terrifyingly potent.

"The strain is too immense, Conduit! The Void Weaver is sensing our stillness! It is retaliating!" Zephyr's cry was a panicked mental screech.

The Void Weaver's Gaze

I had anticipated a physical counter-attack, perhaps a blast of raw Miasma energy. I had not anticipated the mental assault.

As the Chaos Barrier solidified, a massive, crushing mental presence slammed into my mind. It was cold, ancient, and utterly consuming—the consciousness of the Void Weaver.

The Weaver did not speak; it communicated through pure psychological trauma. It flooded my mind with the memory of absolute abandonment—the terrifying feeling of sinking into the Miasma during the Crossing, amplified by the total silence of my prison cell. It was trying to shatter the Still Point by weaponizing my greatest fear.

I screamed, the mental pressure nearly paralyzing me. I fought back, channeling my Kinetic Resonance to suppress the Weaver's intrusive thoughts, but the Signet was already strained to its limit stabilizing the Chaos Barrier.

"Teron! I need the anchor!" I screamed through the bond, a desperate, raw pulse of kinetic panic.

From somewhere behind me in the formation, Teron Draken felt the shockwave. *"The Void Weaver is attacking the mind! Full Signet deployment!"*

Teron's massive Void Signet surged outward. He aimed his entire consciousness at me, projecting the counter-force: absolute, unwavering commitment and stabilizing density.

I felt the familiar, heavy wave of the Void Anchor slam into my mind, shielding me from the Weaver's psychological attack. The crushing emotional density of Teron's love and loyalty neutralized the crushing emptiness of the Weaver's abandonment trauma.

"Hold the stillness, Scion! I am your anchor!" Teron's mental voice, thick with fierce protective possession, cut through the chaos.

I gasped, recovering instantly. I focused on the core truth: *The fusion is absolute.* The Chaos Barrier held, shimmering fiercely against the Miasma. The Void Weaver was successfully contained.

The Betrayal: The Serpent's Kiss

The danger was not over. The Void Weaver, blocked by the Chaos Barrier, executed a tactical retreat, its Miasma plume receding slightly. The Lightning Riders roared in triumph.

But victory was premature.

As the Lightning Riders began to lower the Chaos Barrier, a devastating, silent attack slammed into the heart of the Vanguard.

A small, high-frequency kinetic spike—sharp, precise, and designed to shatter the Kinetic Signet's structural stability— struck Zephyr mid-flight. The attack was not from the General's arsenal, nor was it from the Void Weaver. It was an internal, tactical strike.

Zephyr screamed—a profound, agonizing mental shriek that ripped through my consciousness. The sudden kinetic shockwave overwhelmed my Signet. The Chaos Barrier instantly collapsed, and the entire Vanguard formation plunged into catastrophic, chaotic disarray.

I, physically seizing up from the electrical and kinetic backlash, lost my grip on Zephyr. I tumbled through the sky, the wind rushing past my ears, plummeting toward the earth.

Lyra Zyth, the Chaos Rider, watched the collapse not with surprise, but with a horrifying, cold satisfaction. She didn't move to save me. *"I fly for myself, Scion. The General pays better when the odds are stacked,"* Lyra's cruel, final thought echoed in the dying bond, a confession of pure, pragmatic treason.

And then, Colonel Verrin, the General's commander, executed the final betrayal. He flew in from the clouds, seizing Lyra and Jolt.

"Good work, Zyth!" Verrin shouted, his voice tight with triumph. "The General's Counter-Signet was too crude. Your Chaos Signet was the perfect, surgical weapon to break the Kinetic-Void fusion!"

Lyra—the trusted rebel ally—was actually the General's most effective spy, working with Verrin to dismantle the rebellion from the inside. She had provided the speed and the chaos needed to set the ultimate trap.

I plummeted toward the earth, the wind screaming past my ears, the realization of the ultimate betrayal shattering my mind.

"Lyra! You betrayed us!" I screamed internally, the Signet collapsing entirely.

The Anchor of the Void

I was falling, helpless, unconscious. My Kinetic Resonance was shattered.

But the Void Anchor held.

Teron Draken, flying in the formation, saw my fall. He felt the catastrophic collapse of my Signet—the mental shockwave of the betrayal and the terrifying physical vector of my fall.

He unleashed Morgal's full power, pushing the Aetherial to an impossible speed. He plunged into the sky, riding the chaotic collapse of the Chaos Barrier he had just witnessed.

Teron reached my falling body just moments before impact. He seized me, holding my fragile body close. Morgal enveloped us both in a massive, protective sphere of Void Density, cushioning the crushing final deceleration.

We landed hard, bruised, but safe. Teron held me, unconscious and broken, in his arms. The Chaos Barrier was shattered. The General's forces had captured a handful of the exposed Lightning Riders, but the majority, realizing Lyra's sole defection, were scattered and enraged. The Void Weaver was still out there.

Teron looked up at the retreating form of Lyra and Colonel Verrin. He knew the rebellion had lost an ally, but Lyra's tactical failure had proved to the remaining Lightning Riders that their power required the Kinetic Stabilizer. His face was a mask of cold, devastating fury. He had lost his weapon, his army, and his trust. But he had me.

I felt him hold me close, channeling his immense Void Signet not for war, but for the most personal act of protection. Through the haze of my collapsing consciousness, I felt his final thought.

"I have you, Scion. You will not break. We will not fail."

The war had not ended. It had just become absolute. The General was closer than ever, and the true threat was looming.

CHAPTER 31

THE RECOVERY AND THE ULTIMATE THREAT

My first sensation was silence, followed by a crushing, familiar weight. I was not falling.

I was still. I was in a hidden crevice, cradled in Teron Draken's arms as he sat with his back against the cold stone. The grove he had landed in was a place of deep, immediate silence. I was not physically broken by the fall—his Void Anchor had seen to that—but the rapid, double shockwave of the Signet fracture and Lyra's betrayal had pushed my fragile body past its breaking point.

He held me gently, his movements heavy with fatigue and a crushing wave of guilt. My skin felt deathly pale, and I could feel the faint, stinging scorch marks from the electrical static. My silver stylus anchor lay uselessly beside me. Zephyr, weakened almost to invisibility, shimmered faintly over my body, a tiny, distressed crystalline light barely visible in the dark.

"The Conduit is critically fractured, Rider. The Signet core is offline. She has absorbed too much opposing energy. She requires complete, absolute stillness for the core to reset."

Zephyr's mental voice was a faint, strained pulse of desperation.

I felt Teron's massive hands tremble as he checked my pulse. His immense Void Signet was useless for healing; it could only stabilize, only anchor.

He pulled me tighter against his chest, cradling me in the fierce embrace that had become our sanctuary. He had activated his Void Signet, channeling a soft, low wave of absolute density around us. This wasn't for defense; it was for healing. He was using the Void to create the perfect, silent, absolute-zero environment my Signet core needed to safely purge the chaotic energy and rebuild. He *was* the Still Point for me.

He held the vigil for what felt like agonizing hours. I drifted in and out of consciousness, my body wracked by tremors. In the depths of the Signet Link, I could feel him bearing the burden of my recovery, pushing his own exhaustion aside, forcing his immense power into sustained, protective stillness.

When I finally woke, it was with a sharp, shuddering gasp. I looked up at Teron, my eyes immediately seeking his.

"The Miasma," I whispered, my voice rough, barely audible. "The Void Weaver—"

"Is stalled," Teron confirmed, his voice thick with relief. "The Chaos Barrier, despite the collapse, bought us twenty-four hours. We have time, Lyssa. We are safe."

The Reckoning: No More Secrets

I struggled to sit up. I looked at Teron, and the shared knowledge of the betrayal—Lyra's cold, calculated surrender—was a raw wound between us.

"Lyra Zyth," I whispered, my eyes burning with cold fury. "She was the General's weapon. She used her chaos to create the perfect Signet-fracture weapon."

"She was a traitor, paid in the promise of power," Teron conceded, his hands tightening into fists. "But the failure is mine, Lyssa. I let my personal anger blind me to the danger. I should have trusted my first tactical assessment: never rely on chaos you cannot anchor."

"Your anchor saved my life," I countered, placing my hand on the silver stylus. "The General knew our fusion was the only counter. She attacked our reliance on external force. She knew the Void and the Kinetic are only weak when separated, or when a third, unstable force is introduced."

We looked at each other, the ultimate, painful understanding passing between us. We had lost our army, lost our allies, and lost our time. We were reduced to the core truth: We were all we had left.

"We have to go back," I stated, my voice clear, absolute. "We have to use the political chaos created by the failed arrest to expose the General once and for all. We have to defeat the Void Weaver at the source."

The Final, Impossible Plan

Teron knew we could not defeat the General's army and the Void Weaver with brute force. He laid out the final, desperate strategy, using the raw earth as his map.

"The Void Weaver will move toward the Dreadnought Nexus," Teron analyzed, tracing a line in the dirt. "It is the largest source of unstable Aetherium—the perfect fuel for its chaos. The General will attempt to cover the Nexus again, creating a political target for us."

"The plan is two-pronged," I summarized, my strategic mind already snapping back into place. "We use the political truth to split the Zenith's loyalty, and we use the Signet truth to defeat the Weaver."

Prong I: The Political Collapse (The General's End)

"The General has one flaw left: Eysa," Teron stated. "She witnessed the Nexus stabilization and she possesses the Structural Resonance Signet. Eysa knows the structural weakness of the Command Tower—the General's personal fortress."

I nodded. "Eysa will use her Signet to send a coded warning—a Structural Resonance signal that the Command Tower is unstable. She will force the General into a public evacuation."

"When the General leaves her Command Tower," Teron

finished, his voice cold. "We strike. Lyssa, you will infiltrate the abandoned Command Tower. You will access the Master Wards Control terminal. We will use the Project Nightingale data to broadcast the full truth—the General's confession, the Nexus data, the treason—to every communication system in the Zenith."

Prong II: The Signet Solution (The Weaver's End)

"The Void Weaver is pure, chaotic consumption," I said, my voice rising with certainty. "It feeds on motion and instability. It cannot be fought with Magma or Lightning. It must be fought with its opposite: absolute stillness."

I grasped Teron's hands. "We execute the Kinetic Singularity. You use the Void Signet to create a crushing, unyielding Field of Absolute Density around the Void Weaver, trapping it. I use the Kinetic Resonance to create a Singularity of Stillness at the center of your Void field—a perfect, non-moving vacuum that neutralizes all motion, consuming the Weaver's chaos entirely."

The silence in the grove was absolute. This was the most powerful, most destructive, and most dangerous maneuver imaginable. It required both of us to push our Signets far beyond their safe limits, risking total self-annihilation.

"The Kinetic Singularity will require a massive energy dump," Teron pointed out grimly. "It will drain your core entirely. You will be powerless and vulnerable."

"And the Void Field required to trap the Weaver will demand a sustained output that will drain your core to absolute zero," I countered. "The price of the Singularity is mutual, complete sacrifice."

Teron looked at me, his eyes blazing with fierce, absolute acceptance. We were not planning a victory; we were planning a glorious, final martyrdom.

"We have no choice," Teron stated, pulling me close, the embrace heavy with our shared destiny. "We strike the General and the Void Weaver simultaneously. We die as the only force that saved the Zenith."

The Final Vow

We spent the final hours before the flight preparing our Aetherials. Teron reforged our strategy into a concise, three-part plan: Exposure, Isolation, Singularity.

As the time came for us to leave, Teron pulled me onto Morgal's saddle. He held me close, our final moment of profound, intimate stillness before the final chaos.

"If we succeed, Lyssa," Teron whispered, his lips brushing my ear. "The Zenith will be saved. But we will be executed as traitors, our names purged from history."

"Our names are irrelevant, Wingleader," I replied, my voice filled with cold, perfect resolve. "The truth survives. And we fulfilled the ultimate vow: we fought together, we loved together, and we exposed the lie."

Teron kissed me then—a deep, fierce, final kiss that was a bond of absolute love and absolute treason.

We launched into the night sky, two lone Riders, one Void and one Kinetic, flying toward the Zenith Spires—our home, our prison, and our funeral pyre. The General was waiting. The Void Weaver was advancing. The time for the final sacrifice had come.

CHAPTER 32

THE POLITICAL BOMB AND THE FINAL FLIGHT

The mission was a desperate symphony of synchronized treason. Teron Draken and I flew toward the Zenith Spires under the cover of a massive, manufactured electrical storm created by the scattered Lightning Riders—a final tactical gift from our temporary allies. The sky was a churning chaos of lightning and wind, masking our approach.

We flew in a tight, silent formation, Morgal and Zephyr maintaining their perfect Void-Kinetic Fusion against the turbulent air.

"Eysa is ready. She has the coordinates. General Varen is in the Command Tower," Teron projected through the bond, his mental voice cold and absolute.

"We hit the political target first, Wingleader. The truth must be broadcast before the Void Weaver arrives," I confirmed, my focus locked on the crystalline architecture of the Spires.

The Structural Signal

Our landing zone was the heavily guarded Command Plateau, the flat pinnacle where the General's personal fortress stood. We landed Morgal and Zephyr silently in a blind spot, cloaked by Morgal's ambient Void Signet.

I dismounted, my heart pounding with a cold, terrifying clarity. I reached out with my mind, searching for Eysa's Structural Resonance—the faint, rhythmic pulse that was our only signal.

Eysa was stationed in the deepest sub-levels of the Scribe Archives, her body pressed against the cold bedrock that ran beneath the Command Tower. She was channeling her entire Structural Signet into the foundation.

"I have the frequency, Lyssa. I am amplifying the critical structural flaw beneath the General's private office. It will look like a geological shift. " Eysa's mental pulse was weak, strained, and laced with immense pain.

I knew the cost. Eysa was pushing her specialized Signet to create a massive, controlled structural instability—a feat that could permanently fracture her own bone structure.

"Now, Eysa! Full force!" I whispered, looking up at the colossal, imposing Command Tower.

Miles below, Eysa unleashed her Structural Resonance. The entire bedrock beneath the Command Tower began to hum at a deafening, invisible frequency. The crystal and granite foundation groaned in protest.

In the General's private office, the floor cracked violently. Dust rained down from the ceiling. Alarms blared across the entire command level, signaling a Critical Structural Failure.

The General's Forced Retreat

General Lilith Varen, who was holding a tense, coded

meeting with her remaining loyalists, was furious. She knew this was no accident. She stormed out of her office, ordering an immediate Evacuation Protocol.

Teron and I watched from our hidden vantage point as the General and her command staff spilled out onto the plateau, scrambling toward the temporary safe zone—the heavily guarded Sky-Dock. The General was forced to abandon her impenetrable Command Tower.

"Eysa succeeded," Teron muttered, his voice thick with a mix of awe and dread. "She just bought us the political window. The Tower is clear."

I knew Eysa's risk was catastrophic. I sent a final, desperate pulse to my friend. *"Eysa, retreat now! The damage is done!"*

"I am fine, Lyssa. Go. Expose her," Eysa replied, her mental pulse now faint, fading rapidly.

The Traitor's Infiltration

Teron and I sprinted across the plateau. We reached the command tower entrance, which was now sealed by a massive, reinforced blast door.

"Void Anchor!" Teron commanded.

Teron slammed his fist onto the door, channeling Morgal's Void Signet. The immense, crushing density neutralized the door's structural integrity. I followed, using my Kinetic Resonance to exploit the weakened molecular bonds, creating a micro-fracture. The massive door imploded silently, collapsing inward.

We stormed into the abandoned Command Tower. The room was dark, sterile, and still reeked of the General's power. I ran straight for the Master Wards Control terminal—the large, crystalline console that managed all Signet communications and defense protocols across the Zenith.

"Void Suppression, Teron! Neutralize any residual security Signets!" I commanded, slamming my silver stylus into the terminal port.

Teron moved to the center of the room, unleashing a focused Void Signet that suppressed all external energy input, creating a safe, silent bubble around the console.

I went to work. My Scribe knowledge and my Kinetic Resonance were perfectly suited for the task. I used the Kinetic Signet to neutralize the terminal's complex friction-based locks and the embedded Void Suppression logic of the General's security.

I inserted the encrypted chip containing Project Nightingale and the General's Confession communique.

"The broadcast will be immediate," I muttered, typing furiously. "It will overwrite all existing Zenith protocols and communications. General Varen's entire life is about to be exposed."

The Broadcast of Truth

I hit the final command.

The console lit up, the data stream confirmed. "It's sending," I whispered.

The words were barely out of my mouth when a new,

shrieking alarm blared. Red lights flashed across the console, and a heavy *thud* echoed through the tower as kinetic dampeners slammed into place.

'MASTER SECURITY WARD: ACTIVATED'
'EXTERNAL BROADCAST CONTAINED'

"No!" I slammed my fist on the console. "She had a failsafe! The broadcast is being contained. It's not going public!"

"She's cut us off," Teron snarled, his Void Signet flaring as he sensed the new energy wards. "The truth is trapped in this tower."

I looked at the data stream. The main broadcast was failing, but the *source* file was still active. The connection was contained... but not severed.

"She contained the *public* broadcast," I realized, my fingers flying across the console. "But she can't stop a *private* signal. I'm rerouting the data stream."

"To who?"

"To our allies," I said, a grim, cold smile touching my lips. I bypassed the public network and targeted the encoded, secure Signet channels I had memorized—the ones I knew Eysa and Jax monitored.

"I can't reach the public... but I can reroute the signal to the Scribe Archives and the Marked Ones' private comms. Eysa... Jax... *Now!*"

The data stream confirmed. The packet was sent. It was not the massive political bomb we had intended; it was a surgical strike.

The broadcast was not public, absolute, or devastating to the masses. But for General Varen, it was infinitely worse. A select, powerful few now had the unassailable facts:

1. **The Confession:** General Varen's signed communique...
2. **The Evidence:** The full schematics of the Dreadnought Nexus...
3. **The Warning:** The Aetherial vision of the Void Weaver's advance...

The political effect was now a targeted poison. The General's public authority was intact, but her *true* enemies—the ones with power—now had the exact proof they needed to justify a coup. The illusion of her stability was shattered, but only to us.

Confrontation on the Plateau

Teron seized me, pulling me away from the terminal. "It's done! We have to move! The General will know we are here!"

We raced out of the Command Tower and back onto the plateau. The General, standing on the Sky-Dock, was staring at the Tower, her face a mask of incandescent, cold fury. She knew the failsafe had been triggered. She knew the broadcast had been contained... but she also knew *who* we would have sent it to. Her lie wasn't over, but the truth was now a poison dagger in the hands of her enemies.

"You have signed your death warrant, Lyssa!" the General screamed, her voice shaking with rage and devastating personal betrayal. "You have destroyed your lineage! Titan! Incinerate the traitors!"

Titan, the massive Ruby Magma Aetherial, roared and unleashed a full, devastating Magma Fire Blast—a torrent of superheated fire and kinetic force aimed at the two of us.

Teron and I vaulted onto Morgal's saddle. I, already channeling my Signet, directed Teron's Signet.

"Void Anchor, Teron! Crush the fire vector!"

Teron unleashed his Void Signet. The immense, crushing density slammed into the core of the Magma blast. The fire's kinetic force was neutralized, forced into a contained, impotent sphere of heat that harmlessly dissipated in the air.

"We go now! To the Nexus!" Teron commanded. The political bomb was detonated; now we had to face the final, military target.

We launched Morgal and Zephyr into the air, flying toward the Second Spire and the Dreadnought Nexus—the point where the Void Weaver was expected to strike.

The General watched us fly away, her Magma Signet failing under the immense psychological and political stress. I had delivered the political death blow.

But the final confrontation was yet to come. As we flew, a new threat emerged—not the Magma Riders, but the subtle, consuming energy of the Void Weaver, which was now advancing on the Spires, drawn by the chaos and the broadcast truth.

"The truth is chaos, Conduit. The Weaver approaches. Prepare for Singularity!" Zephyr's mental voice was sharp, absolute.

The Zenith Spires were fracturing, politically and structurally. The time for the final, ultimate sacrifice had arrived.

CHAPTER 33

THE KINETIC SINGULARITY AND THE FINAL SACRIFICE

The Dreadnought Nexus—the immense, scarred crystalline plate that covered the fault line of the Second Spire—was glowing with a sickening, chaotic black light. The Void Weaver had arrived.

It was not a beast or a physical creature, but a massive, amorphous consciousness—a swirling vortex of raw, chaotic Miasma energy that covered the entire Nexus. It communicated through an immense, silent wave of absolute, consuming emptiness, sucking the Aetherium—the very life force—from the surrounding stone.

Teron Draken and I flew toward the Nexus on Morgal and Zephyr, two desperate points of light in a sea of encroaching darkness.

"The Weaver is not biological, Conduit. It is the crystallization of absolute entropy. It seeks total consumption. The time for Singularity is now!" Zephyr's mental voice was a high, strained command.

I, mounted on Zephyr, flew in perfect sync with him,

channeling the silver stylus anchor. My mind was a fortress of cold, final resolve. We had accepted our fate: we would die, but we would win.

The Execution: The Void Field

We flew directly into the chaotic energy field of the Weaver. The raw Miasma energy tore at our Aetherials, trying to rip the Void-Kinetic Fusion apart.

Teron executed the first, critical step of the plan. He brought Morgal into a steep, horizontal spiral directly over the Nexus.

"Void Field! Full deployment!" Teron roared.

Morgal unleashed its full, agonizing power. The massive Void Aetherial did not attack; it became a Field of Absolute Density. The crushing, immense gravitational pressure slammed onto the entire Nexus, enveloping the churning vortex of the Void Weaver.

The effect was instantaneous and profound: the chaotic, swirling Miasma was trapped. The Void Weaver was held fast within a suffocating, immovable sphere of ultimate gravity, prevented from expanding or consuming more energy.

Teron collapsed onto Morgal's saddle, his body seizing up from the immense, sustained output. He was pushing his Void Signet to its physical limit.

"Anchor is set, Scion! Now! The Singularity!" Teron's

mental voice was a raw, guttural pulse of exhaustion and pain.

The Kinetic Singularity

I plunged Zephyr into the Void Field. The crushing density was immense, but I was prepared. I separated from Zephyr, dropping onto the surface of the crystalline Nexus, placing my silver stylus directly onto the glowing, cracked plate.

I poured my entire being into the Kinetic Resonance. This was the ultimate, suicidal maneuver. I was generating a force that my fragile body was never meant to sustain: perfect, absolute stillness within a field of absolute, crushing density.

I did not fight the chaos; I consumed it. I created a Singularity of Stillness—a perfect, non-moving vacuum that pulled all existing motion into itself.

The Void Weaver, trapped by the Void Field, was suddenly attacked by its antithesis. The chaos of its being, the massive consumption of motion and life, was pulled violently into my Kinetic Singularity. The energy collision was silent, absolute, and terrifying.

I screamed, the sound tearing out of my lungs. My body convulsed, the silver stylus burning white-hot in my hand. My Kinetic Resonance was draining my core entirely, consuming my physical strength to fuel the stillness. My skin tore, my veins pulsed—I was on the verge of fracturing into a billion pieces.

"The core is failing, Conduit! Release the Singularity!"

Zephyr's cry was a desperate, final warning.

I ignored it. I looked up at Teron, his face masked in pure agony as he held the Void Anchor. Our eyes locked—the final moment of mutual, absolute sacrifice.

The Final Surrender

The Void Weaver, trapped and neutralized, let out an immense, silent psychic scream—a final, ancient burst of chaotic resistance aimed at the two of us.

Teron and I were slammed by the last defense.

But the Weaver failed. The Singularity consumed the final chaos. The great, churning vortex of the Void Weaver shimmered violently, then vanished—consumed by the perfect stillness of the Kinetic Singularity. The threat was neutralized.

I collapsed onto the Nexus plate, my Signet core dark, my body spent. I had achieved the impossible.

But the price was absolute.

Teron, his task fulfilled, released the Void Field. The crushing density vanished. He let out a final, raw gasp of pure exhaustion, his Signet core drained to absolute zero. He slumped over Morgal's saddle, unconscious. Morgal and Zephyr, their power spent, descended slowly, landing gently beside their broken Riders.

The General's Final Move

The Zenith Spires were saved. The Void Weaver was destroyed.

The resolution was swift, brutal, and tragically predictable.

General Lilith Varen, who had been watching the entire spectacle from the Command Plateau, flew in. Her face was a mask of cold, devastating victory. She had watched us, seen our courage, our bond, and the completion of our mission. But she also saw our ultimate vulnerability.

She landed Titan beside the two of us, her personal guard—now her only army—surrounding the scene.

"They saved the Zenith," the General stated, her voice devoid of emotion. "They exposed my lie and they destroyed the final enemy. They fulfilled their purpose."

She looked at me, her fallen daughter, her expression a mix of profound grief and cold, political resolve. "But treason is treason. And the narrative of my command must survive."

The General commanded her remaining loyalists to place the two of us, unconscious traitors, under arrest.

I was roused by the harsh hands of the Zenith Guards. I looked up at my mother, who stood over me, the Vindicator Sword raised.

"You proved yourself worthy, Lyssa," the General whispered, for my ears only. "You were worthy of the Varen name. But you chose the lie of freedom over the truth of survival. The price is paid."

The General did not strike us down immediately. She ordered us transported to the Execution Platform—the highest, most visible point of the Zenith Spires—to face the military tribunal.

"They will die as traitors, covering the final truth," the General declared, her political mask back in place. "The Zenith survives, thanks to my command."

Teron Draken and I, broken, unconscious, but alive, were loaded onto a flight transport. We had won the war, but we had lost the battle for our lives.

CHAPTER 34

THE JUDGEMENT AND THE SCARS' VENGEANCE

The Execution Platform was the highest, most exposed point of the Zenith Spires—a massive, circular granite disc that jutted out over the sheer drop, reserved only for those who committed the gravest treason. It was a stage for the General's unwavering authority.

The platform was surrounded by a massive crowd of students, soldiers, and citizens, all forced to witness the spectacle. Overhead, hundreds of Magma Riders and Torrent Riders patrolled the air, ensuring no possibility of escape. The atmosphere was thick with silence and the oppressive, chilling weight of the General's martial law.

Teron Draken and I stood at the center of the platform, clad in simple, rough linen tunics that offered no dignity or protection. Our Aetherials, Morgal and Zephyr, were nowhere to be seen, locked away in Signet-dampened cages. The two of us were bound by massive Null-crystal shackles that suppressed our core Signet energy, reducing us to our raw, human vulnerability.

The General's Final Lie

General Lilith Varen stood on an elevated dais, flanked by

her highest-ranking commanders. Her face was a mask of cold, devastating victory. She had survived the broadcast of Project Nightingale by immediately executing a public campaign of psychological warfare: Teron and I were not martyrs; we were master saboteurs who had used a falsified report to destabilize the Spires for the rebel cause.

The General initiated the Military Tribunal, her voice amplified to ring across the entire Execution Platform.

"Citizens of Navarre, you witness the final consequence of treason," the General announced, her voice laced with feigned grief and unyielding authority. "These two individuals, driven by personal ambition and the chaotic bloodline of the executed Lord Karsus Draken, attempted to collapse the Zenith Spires from within. They used advanced, unsanctioned Signet fusion to attack the Dreadnought Nexus, a vital component of our Wards."

I looked at the General, not as a tyrant, but as my mother. I saw a profound, devastating fissure in her composure—a flash of pure, maternal grief that broke the cold armor. The choice was finally absolute, and the General's private agony was briefly visible to the world.

I locked eyes with the General, trying to push a final, desperate burst of Kinetic Truth through the Null-crystal bonds, but the shackles held fast.

The General continued, her narrative weaving its final, crushing tapestry of lies. "They claim their actions were to save us from the Void Weaver—a rebel fabrication. But the truth is simple: they were tools of chaos. They succeeded in destabilizing the Wards, but my command neutralized them before they could achieve total collapse."

The verdict was announced with chilling finality: Execution by incineration at the hands of the Magma Riders.

The Hour of Synchronization

As the final command was given, the sky darkened. Four massive Ruby Magma Aetherials descended, hovering directly over the platform, their scales glowing with superheated energy, their Riders aiming the inevitable blast.

Teron and I stood shoulder-to-shoulder, our hands chained together, unable to touch, unable to fuse our Signets. We accepted our fate, our final message—our love and our truth—already broadcast to the world.

Just as the Magma Riders prepared to unleash the blast, the execution platform was rocked by a massive, grinding tremor.

It was not a structural failure; it was a Structural Resonance signal.

Eysa had struck.

From the deepest bedrock beneath the Spires, Eysa unleashed her full Structural Signet—not on the platform, but on the Command Tower miles away, amplifying the flaw I had felt. The towering structure began to groan violently, a sound of catastrophic metal fatigue.

The General's remaining command staff immediately panicked. "General! The Command Tower is failing! Critical structural integrity breach!"

The General, though furious, had to maintain the narrative of control. "Ignore the tremor! The execution proceeds!"

But the distraction was complete. The synchronized plan moved into its second phase: Chaos and Breach.

A massive burst of Lightning Signet energy slammed into the air above the Execution Platform—a signal of absolute chaos. The remaining Lightning Riders—allies of the rebellion—had arrived, flying high to distract the Magma Patrols.

The sky exploded into a wild, chaotic dogfight between the high-speed Lightning Riders and the heavy, disciplined Magma Riders.

The Scars' Vengeance

The final wave of the coordinated attack came from the ground.

With the Zenith's defenses distracted, a squad of heavily armed Marked Ones, led by Jax, burst onto the Execution Platform from a hidden maintenance tunnel. They were not fighting to save the Spires; they were fighting to avenge their fathers.

Jax screamed, his Void Signet blazing with fierce loyalty. "The General's law is broken! Roric committed treason against the Zenith Code by attempting murder! We fight for the Wingleader who fought the Void Weaver!"

The platform plunged into brutal, chaotic combat. Jax and the Marked Ones engaged the General's Guards, their Signets clashing in a deadly, desperate dance of loyalties.

The General realized her tactical error. She had

underestimated the devotion to the truth. She turned, drawing her Vindicator Sword—her personal Signet weapon—to join the fray.

I knew we had to get free. Eysa had given us the chaos; Jax had given us the cover.

Teron, seeing his chance, slammed his chained fist onto the Null-crystal shackles. The suppressive material resisted his raw strength, but not his Signet knowledge.

"Kinetic Focus, Lyssa! Target the binding crystals!" Teron roared, channeling his weak, suppressed Void Signet into the shackle joint.

I focused my last remaining Kinetic Resonance—a weak, flickering energy—into the single point of density Teron created. I used my Signet to neutralize the molecular friction of the lock joint. The chains rattled violently, and with a snap of crystal, our hands were free.

The Final Confrontation

Teron immediately seized the General's attention. He unleashed a full, powerful blast of his newly freed Void Signet at the massive, empty Null-crystal cages that held Morgal and Zephyr. This was the clear, undeniable act of command Jax and the Marked Ones had been waiting for: the Void Wingleader was back. The dense pressure caused the locks to implode.

The two Aetherials, instantly freed from the dampening field, roared—one a sound of crushing gravity, the other a high, crystalline chime of victory. Morgal and Zephyr were back in the fight.

Teron and I grabbed our Signet anchors—the Void Wingleader seizing his heavy obsidian dagger, the Scion of Static retrieving my silver stylus—and joined the fray, fighting back-to-back.

Jax and the Marked Ones had secured the perimeter. The path to the edge of the platform was clear.

Morgal and Zephyr landed, towering over the platform.

The General abandoned the fight. She stood before me, her eyes burning with pure, cold hatred.

"You have won the battle, Lyssa," the General stated, her voice tight with suppressed fury. "You destroyed my command, you destroyed my reputation... but you chose him. You chose the Scars over your own blood."

"But you have nowhere to run. You are traitors. You will die alone."

I looked at my mother, feeling the immense, tragic political burden that drove her. "I chose the truth, General. I choose the world over your legacy."

"Then face the consequence!" the General shrieked, unleashing a final, massive blast of Magma Fire aimed at the two of us.

Teron moved instantly, pulling me behind him. Morgal and Zephyr enveloped us in the protective sphere of their Void-Kinetic Fusion—a simultaneous blast of absolute density and perfect stillness. The Magma fire hit the sphere and dissipated harmlessly into steam.

"Go! Get out of here! I will buy you time!" Jax screamed, throwing himself into the path of the oncoming Zenith reinforcements.

Teron pulled me onto Morgal's saddle. He looked down at the platform, making a decision that was both political and profoundly personal.

He raised his obsidian dagger. "General Varen," Teron announced, his voice ringing with absolute, unyielding victory. "The political lie ends now. Your command is broken. The truth endures."

Teron gave the signal. Morgal and Zephyr unleashed their full, combined Signet power—not an attack, but a massive, sustained blast of Void-Kinetic energy directed at the base of the Execution Platform.

The massive, circular granite platform did not shatter; it was neutralized. The immense force lifted the entire platform, separating it from the main spire, holding it suspended in the air by the perfect, sustained kinetic balance of the Void-Kinetic fusion.

The General and the remaining loyalists were trapped, floating hundreds of feet above the ground, unable to fight, unable to flee, utterly neutralized by the brilliance of the Scion of Static and the raw power of the Son of the Executed.

"You will live with the truth, General," Teron commanded, his final message ringing across the sky. "You will watch us save the world you risked for a lie."

The Irreversible Exile

Teron urged Morgal away, soaring over the paralyzed Zenith Spires. We flew low, our Aetherials exhausted, our bodies aching, but our hearts soaring with the painful triumph of victory.

We flew back to the Black Summit, where the remaining Lightning Riders were waiting, their chaotic faces etched with grim respect.

"The platform is neutralized," their leader shouted, a rare, genuine grin splitting his face. "The General is trapped! You actually did it!"

"The war is not over," Teron countered, pulling me into a tight embrace. "We are traitors. We are fugitives. The General will unleash the full fury of the Zenith upon us. We must disappear."

We gathered the wounded Marked Ones onto the Aetherials, leaving the political chaos we had wrought behind them.

I looked back one last time at the Zenith Spires—my home, my prison, and the center of the political lie I had shattered. I reached out with my mind, finding the faint, steady pulse of Eysa's Structural Resonance—the courageous ally who had paid the ultimate price for the initial breach.

We are safe, Eysa. We are free. Thank you.

As we ascended, I glanced down at the maintenance tunnel one last time. I didn't see Eysa, but I felt the faint, structural tremor of her Signet—a shuddering resonance of bone against crystal. I knew the truth: Eysa's perfect, surgical breach had likely cost her the permanent stability of her own core. The quiet Scribe had become a devastating weapon for the truth, and she was now paying the price in silence and fracture. I tightened my grip on Teron. We were alive only because our friend had sacrificed her future for our cause.

We plunged into the night sky, flying toward the Uncharted Eastern Wastes, the massive Void Weaver still looming on the horizon.

Teron held me close, his massive body providing the only comfort. He kissed me—a long, deep, final kiss that was the seal of our new, absolute reality.

"Welcome to absolute exile, Scion," Teron muttered, his voice thick with raw emotion. "We are heroes to the people we left behind, and traitors to the world we must now save."

I leaned my head against his shoulder, closing my eyes. I was exhausted, wounded, and irreversibly bound to the man who was my enemy, my anchor, and my destiny.

"The war starts now, Wingleader," I replied, my voice firm, resolute. "We are the Scion of Static and the Son of the Executed. We will be the army that saves the world."

EPILOGUE

THE PRICE OF STILLNESS

The wind that ripped through the Uncharted Eastern Wastes was a cold, constant judgment. It was far different from the controlled currents of the Spires—it was free, untamed, and carried the scent of the expanding, poisonous Miasma.

I lay on the rough, silent earth, pressed against the massive, unmoving flank of Morgal. I was fully conscious, but I was profoundly powerless. My Kinetic Resonance remained fractured, a dull, aching emptiness in my core. This was the cost of the Singularity—the final, absolute expenditure of my physical strength and my Signet's capacity. The Zenith's silence, which I had fought in prison, was now the silence of my own depleted soul.

Teron Draken held me, his immense body a blanket of familiar, stabilizing heat. He was awake, his Void Signet already beginning the agonizing process of recovery, slowly drawing ambient energy to replenish the core he had emptied saving the Zenith. He had saved the world, but he was reduced to a vigilant, earthbound anchor.

We were heroes to the people we had saved—the Marked Ones and the Fiefs—but we were now publicly branded traitors by the General. I had exposed the truth of my mother's lie, but the price was absolute: exile, fatigue, and the near-total loss of the power that defined me.

Teron leaned down, his voice rough with exhaustion. "The General's propaganda is already in the air, Scion. We are public enemies. Our escape is a military failure she cannot afford to admit."

I closed my eyes. "Then we give her a target, Wingleader. We find the Ancient Signet. We rebuild the army."

I reached for the silver stylus that lay beside us. It was cold, inert, stripped of its kinetic power.

"We need speed, Teron. We need power that cannot be suppressed by the General's technology. We need a force that neither the Zenith nor the Void Weaver has ever anticipated."

Teron nodded, his eyes fixed on the distant, dark horizon where the Void Weaver still loomed. "We start walking, Lyssa. We start searching. The General made us traitors, but she failed to make us martyrs."

The weight of the world, once borne by the collapsing Spires, now rested entirely on us—two broken Riders, one Void and one Kinetic, bound by a desperate love and the cold, absolute necessity of survival. The war was no longer about revenge. It was about finding the strength to stand against the inevitable end.

THEIR VICTORY WAS ABSOLUTE. THEIR EXILE IS THE PRICE.

Lyssa Varen and Teron Draken won the battle for the Spires, but the devastating Kinetic Singularity cost them nearly everything. Branded traitors and hunted by the full military might of General Varen, they are forced to flee the world they just saved.

Now, the Scion of Static is without her stillness, haunted by the total loss of her Signet. And the Son of the Executed is reduced to an earthbound anchor, his immense power depleted. They must traverse the treacherous, uncharted Shattered Peaks on foot, all while a colossal, consuming enemy, the Void Weaver, closes in.

To survive, they must search for the rumored Ancient Signet—a primal, elemental force that is the true opposite of the Weaver's entropy. But finding the ancient power means risking the deadly new weapons the General has deployed, specialized Magma Aetherials sent to track and neutralize their unique Signet signatures.

Only by facing their deepest vulnerabilities can they rebuild their bond and find the strength to save Navarre from the inevitable end.

SNEAK PEEK:

THE EXILE OF DENSITY (BOOK TWO)

The journey into the Shattered Peaks was a physical torment. Morgal and Zephyr could only manage short, painful flights, and the rest was covered on foot, hauling meager supplies across hostile terrain.

"The Ancient Signet must be here, Wingleader," Lyssa rasped, leaning heavily on Teron's arm. Her Kinetic Resonance was still a dull throb—a phantom limb of power that refused to return.

"The legends say the Ancient Signet was the first defense used against the chaos before the Zenith was founded," Teron stated, scanning the jagged, rock-strewn valleys. "It is pure, elemental force. The opposite of the Weaver's entropy."

They reached the crest of a peak, overlooking a valley shrouded in perpetual, unnatural fog. Teron paused, his Void Signet flickering back to life, sensing a foreign pressure.

"Zenith patrol," he muttered, pulling Lyssa behind a rock formation. "Three Magma Aetherials. They're flying a customized grid. They're not searching randomly, Lyssa. They're hunting us."

A colossal, blazing Magma Aetherial descended toward

the valley floor, carrying two Riders in the General's white armor. They were hunting not just traitors, but their specific Signet signatures.

Lyssa watched, her heart hammering. The General had unveiled a terrifying new tactic—a specialized force dedicated solely to tracking and neutralizing the Void-Kinetic Fusion.

"The General has adapted quickly," Lyssa whispered, reaching for her inert stylus. "She knows our Signets are her biggest threat. But without our fusion, we can't fight them. And without that Ancient Signet, we can't hide."

Teron drew his obsidian dagger, his face grim. "We hide, Scion. But we can't run forever. We find the ancient power, or the General uses her new weapons to finish the execution the tribunal could not."

The shadow of the General's pursuit was long, but the presence of the Void Weaver was longer still. The exile had begun.

ABOUT THE AUTHOR

ELOWEN KAGE

Elowen Kage is a master of high-stakes fantasy romance, known for crafting intricate worlds where intellect is as dangerous as any weapon. Elowen lives in the borderlands between light and shadow, and believes that the deepest connections are forged not in peace, but in absolute, necessary chaos. Elowen's passion for brutal military academies and characters who defy their physical limitations is reflected in *The Scion of Static*, the explosive first book in *The Chained Horizon* series. Elowen is currently at work on the highly anticipated sequel, *The Exile of Density*, where the cost of truth threatens to unravel the bond forged in treason.

AUTHOR'S NOTE AND ACKNOWLEDGMENTS

To my incredible readers—thank you for diving into the treacherous heights of the Zenith Spires and embracing the chaos that is the heart of this story. *The Scion of Static* is a tribute to everyone who has ever been underestimated, proving that precision and stillness are weapons far greater than brute force. This novel was conceived from a simple question: What if your greatest perceived weakness was the only necessary strength to save the world?

Thank you to The Marked Ones—the readers who fight for the truth and demand justice, even when the consequences are terrifying. You are the structural anchor of this rebellion.

I hope the final sacrifice and the undeniable truth of Lyssa and Teron's bond left you breathless. They are alive, but their struggle has just begun. The General is hunting them with new, powerful weapons, and the Void Weaver is closing in.

I look forward to welcoming you back to the next stage of the war. **The Exile of Density** is coming soon. The fight for truth requires a new kind of power, and an even greater sacrifice.

I hope you loved *The Scion of Static* and if you did, I would ve very grateful if you could write a review. I'd love to hear what you think, and it makes such a difference helping new readers to discover one of my books for the first time.

Also, I love hearing from readers! You can get in touch with me through my publisher, MK Storyworks on all social media platforms: @mkstoryworks

Sign up for my newsletter to hear about new releases, giveaways, and promotions at www.mkstoryworks.com

For more information about my books, you can contact me through my publisher, MK Storyworks!

—Elowen Kage

ABOUT THE PUBLISHER

MK Storyworks is a truly global book publisher, dedicated to the timeless mission of connecting compelling authors with enthusiastic readers across the world.

We pride ourselves on curating a diverse and dynamic list that spans the full spectrum of literary interests. Whether you are looking for an immersive escape into a bestselling fiction novel, seeking wisdom and knowledge from groundbreaking non-fiction titles, perfecting a dish with our acclaimed cookbooks, or introducing the magic of reading to the next generation with our enchanting children's books, MK Storyworks delivers stories that inform, entertain, and inspire.

Our commitment to quality, creativity, and global reach ensures that every book we publish finds its place in the hands and hearts of readers, no matter where they are.

Connect with MK Storyworks

Stay up-to-date with our latest releases, author news, and behind-the-scenes glimpses by connecting with us online:

Website: www.mkstoryworks.com